Purlieu

Purlieu

Michaela Daphne

THE HIDDEN GROVE SERIES: BOOK 1

PURLIEU

Be The Good Publishing

Edited by Ocean Reeve Publishing
www.oceanreeve.com

ISBN 978 0 6482241 3 6 Paperback

First Edition.

DEDICATION

To my beloved husband, Shawn, your unconditional love heals me more every day. Thank you for being my biggest fan and for supporting me not just in your words but in your actions too. I would still be drafting this novel if it weren't for your unwavering encouragement.

Kathrina, you have been steadfast throughout my journey of healing in writing this story. I couldn't have asked for a better friend. I'm just sorry I had to cut your favourite character. Long love Mister!

Mum and Dad, thank you for loving me enough to try to save me. For the trip to Hawaii, for the interventions, to breaking up with him for me. Who knows where I would be today if you hadn't.

Yvonne, you have taught me of a different kind of love.

Fr Morgan, I pass back the baton of words we have shared, "There is a season and a time for everything under the sun."

Cheryl, your interest in my writing and my faith were huge morale boosters when I severely needed them.

Nyree, Tye, Sarah, Bryce, Aneta, and all those others that I hold dear, thank you for accepting me in my absences of mind as I pondered the written worlds that follow in these pages. To be loved by a writer is a tricky business.

ACKNOWLEDGMENTS

To all those who supported my Publishizer campaign,
your generosity, support, love, and patience have me
forever grateful. This book is a now a physical object
because of you.

Thank you Addisalem Tsegaye, Adeline Tong,
Adrian Dyer, Alice Magner, Anthony Dyer,
Belinda McCulloch, Beth Davies, Brian & Myléne Hillam,
Bridie Hoey, Bryan Pang, Bryce Hillam, Cara Suplido-Tan,
Cathy Ledwich, Cheryl Lek, Claire Jenkins, Claire Forbes,
Constance Pang, Cristina Iocco, Damien Pang,
Darcie Touton, David de Weger, David Hood,
Debra Sealy, Ebony Franzmann, Erica Ng, Evelyn Paine,
Fr Morgan Batt, Gabriel Patrick, Genevieve Taylor,
Grace Iuliano, Grace Pamo Lawrence, Hayley Lanzon,
Hillaria Juliana, Ingrid Bartkowiak, Irene Boshier,
Ivan Koh, Jacinta Hoffard, Janine Harman,
Jennifer Costin, Jesi Davis, Joseph Grogan, Josh Thorley,
Joshua Walsh, Karen Sealy, Kathrina Paine, Larry Pang,
Lee Constantine, Lizzie Schuh, Luke & Emma Plant,
Martin Waugh, Mary Grace, Mary Dougherty, Matt Ross,
Matthew Riley, Megan MacMahon, Megan Williams,
Melissa Haworth, Michael Curtin, Nicky Ashley,
Nyree Hillam, Patricia Athousis, Percy Pamo Lawrence,
Regina Balaba, Sarah Hillam, Teresa McGrath, Tye Hillam,
Yvonne Pang, and Yvonne Chen.

1

F OR THE TENTH time that day I shook the image of those empty green eyes from my mind. I stared instead at the blazing red of the December poinciana trees that lined the edge of the bushland. A backdrop of eucalyptus trees intensified the display of blossom.

Art journal tucked under my arm, I made my way from the car park and past the Mianjin town museum towards the twin buildings of the art gallery. The dinosaur skeletons cluttered the entrance hall of the museum to my left. The sharp teeth and long-boned wings of the Pterodactyls reminded me of the time I'd visited as a child, unafraid of the large creatures hanging above, safe as I swung between my parents' arms. But that was a long time ago.

The sweltering heat was tempered only by the shadow of the towering concrete mass before me. It was a long journey to take each day, but far better than staying in that house that felt too large and yet suffocating all at the same time.

The hissing gallery air conditioning welcomed me home once more. Here was the one place my mind could wander far enough to forget the gaping hole in my heart.

The walls stretched out before me, wide and glaring, accentuating the paintings that dotted the surface. Though the gallery was the same as yesterday, I eagerly crept closer, my footsteps echoing on the tiled floors past the matching white leather lounge. There, on the arm of the couch, were smudged charcoal fingerprints. I smiled—clearly I was not the only one who found inspiration and solace here.

A lone security guard eyed me from the corner of the room. Ignoring his watchful eye, I stepped up to the painting before me. I'd gazed upon it more times than I could count but always found something new to captivate me. From the way the woman's eyes seemed to follow mine, to the posture with which she held herself, to the layers of intricate shades of pink across her lips, to the sweeping mysterious mountains in the background. The painting called me back time and again.

It was those mysterious mountains that held me today. I could tell they were not Australian mountains. From the perfectly round stones covered in moss in the foreground to the pointing sandstone cliff jutting out behind at odd angles, they resembled an ancient highlander's purlieu. My heart constricted and my hand reached out, wanting to touch the soft, moist moss, to smell its nutrient-rich dirt, to hear the sounds of foreign birdcalls. How I wished to travel to such faraway places, see such remarkable sights, to paint their enchanting terrains. And to get far away from here.

The security guard cleared his throat and I withdrew my hand. I took out my art journal, flipped to an empty page, past portraits of strangers and replicas of countryside paintings, and set to work. The ancient highlander's purlieu was my starting point and I mimicked the odd angles of the mountains. As I began to fill in the detail, I added my own touches—the motion of wind, the glisten of dewfall, the vibrant red of the trees changing season. If only I had graduated from school already, if only I had saved up enough money, I could travel and see such places with my own eyes instead of making a fantasy world to explore in my mind and on the page. Sure, I was about to start my final year at Mianjin Arts Academy, but I'd been waiting and saving up for years now. The end of grade twelve couldn't come fast enough.

I peeped back to the corner of the room where the security guard had now turned his back. My hand slipped silently into my pocket and brought back a small square of chocolate to suck on. Its sweet, smooth surface slowly disintegrated in my mouth. It was the momentary comfort that I needed, for my mind had started to slip back to those eyes that haunted me from the mortuary gurney.

The gallery began to fill with echoing footsteps and hushed tones. People were crowding around me, poking their nosy beaks into what I was drawing, standing just a little too close, wanting the painting of the woman all to themselves. By now, my back was aching from hunching over my art journal, so I gave up my place. Thinking of the white leather lounge in the centre of the room, I turned to make my way through the crowd when I ran into a wall. No, not a wall—a person. My journal flew from my hands as we crashed to the ground, my pencil clattering against the tiles.

I flushed red as people stared and old women tutted at how we'd disturbed the peace. I picked up my pencil and reached for my art journal, spread open on an enchanting charcoal mountain range, and realised it was not mine. The mountain range had an ethereal quality to it that I couldn't quite put my finger on.

I looked up to find the journal's artist thumbing his way through my own journal. His shaggy brown hair hung down, shielding his face. He raked it back with his fingers and looked at me, unabashed. He smelled of cinnamon.

"You are very talented," he said.

His eyes glistened like the dewy moss of my sketches as he reached out to pull me to my feet. My bony hands felt small in his large, rough ones. He looked at my paint-spattered hands.

"You prefer acrylic, then?" he asked.

I nodded. I'd stopped scrubbing at the dried paint on my skin, knowing that the next day would bring new splotches. He didn't see my response; instead, his gaze lingered on my right hand, my weak hand. I whipped it away quickly and shoved it into my pocket. It was none of his business.

I brushed my wild auburn hair out of my face in embarrassment and we exchanged journals. My heart was beating too fast. I began to walk away.

"I am William of Purlieu."

"Of Purlieu?" I asked. Was he kidding?

"Yes. William of Purlieu," he repeated.

I smiled. "Evelyn O'Shea," I said.

He held out his hand to shake but I just stared at it, pointedly, until he drew it back apologetically.

"I hope I did not hurt you."

I couldn't tell if he meant our collision or his blatant staring at my weak hand. It was bad enough that I had to see the mangled ripple across my palm every day, let alone relearn how to paint using my other hand. Like everyone at school, he'd made it far worse by staring, but now he looked at me with such genuine concern. His shining eyes drew me in. My stomach knotted with guilt for turning down his handshake.

It wasn't his fault my hand was curious to look at—and how was he to know that it was still mostly functional? I'd only lost fine-motor skills in the accident.

I shook my head. The crowd had continued on around us, as though nothing had happened. I reached into my other pocket and drew out the bag of chocolate squares.

"Want one?"

He took a square and held it up to the light. His eyes glinted. My stomach turned over.

I motioned for him to put it in his mouth.

"Mmm, food. Is good," I teased him, rubbing my

stomach and mimicking the voice of a Neanderthal.

His eyes lit up as he smiled. "A very accurate impression," he said.

It was a strange thing to say and a strange way to say it. He placed the chocolate in his mouth and started to chew it.

"You're doing it wrong—you're meant to suck on it."

I was hopeless at flirting; that was Tiffany's domain. He took my advice and his cheeks creased into dimples. His smile broadened as though he'd never tasted anything like it before. Such a strange man. And a man he was—bristles had formed across his chin. He had to be older than eighteen, but probably not older than twenty-five.

"I've never seen you around here before," I said.

"I could say the same for you."

"I'm here, like, every day."

"No."

I folded my arms in defiance, tucking my weak hand underneath, out of sight. "What do you mean, no?" I asked.

"I think I would remember a face like yours."

Despite myself, I felt my face flush red again. Cursed Irish skin. I had to change the subject or get out of there fast.

"Where do you get your ideas from?" I asked, nodding at his journal. The magical mountain scape was like nothing I'd seen before. He flipped his journal open again.

"Oh, this?"

I realised now why it seemed so ethereal—the black charcoal strokes made the waterfall appear to be running backwards. I would never have thought of using such a technique.

He scratched at the stubble across his chin. "It came to me, one night in a dream," he said.

I envied him, not for his vivid night-time imagination, but for the fact that he had dreams at night rather than nightmares. The empty eyes gazing up at me from the mortuary gurney flashed through my mind once more. It was enough that I had to relive it night after night, let alone during waking hours too.

"Did I say something to upset you?"

I shook my head, shaking the thoughts away.

"I have travelled far and wide and seen many great and terrible things," he said.

"You don't sound like a local."

"My tongue is influenced by the many people I have met." I envied him even more now. How I ached to travel.

"Is that Shakespeare?" I asked. He laughed, shaking his head.

"English was never my strong subject," I said.

"I take it art is where you thrive?" I nodded.

"It is one of my great loves also," he said.

I was running out of things to say. "Well, it was nice to meet you. Goodbye."

Again, I made to walk away.

"May I see you again, Evelyn O'Shea?"

My stomach constricted. I slowly turned back to face him.

"But I don't know you."

"Ah, but we could come to know each other better, don't you think?"

"But my father..."

"Here, at the gallery. The same time tomorrow?"

Why would a man like him want to spend time with a girl like me? I watched his striking green eyes a moment longer. They were so captivating. *He* was so captivating. I nodded once.

His beaming smile broadened and he rubbed his hands together.

"Wonderful!"

Just wait until I tell Tiffany.

Clothes littered my bedroom floor while Tiffany watched

on video chat. The floorboards under the carpet creaked as I looked at myself from different angles in the cheval mirror. Tiffany's girlish voice filled the room.

"Don't wear that—it makes your boobs look even smaller than they are."

"Can I borrow your boobs for the day, then?" I asked. Maybe her tanned skin too, while I was at it. I ripped off the silk camisole and flopped on my bed.

Why was I so nervous? It wasn't even a real date.

"I still can't believe you're doing this. Your dad is gonna kill you when he finds out."

"He won't find out," I said.

"He has to eventually."

"William is a total gentleman. If and when my father does find out, he'll realise how much he likes him and forget that I went out alone with a complete stranger."

Saying it aloud like that sent a flurry of doubt across my mind. Was this a bad idea?

"You only met him yesterday, and you spoke for, like, two seconds. He's not your boyfriend yet, how do you know what he's really like?"

"Yeah, well, he may not even show."

My stomach constricted. I couldn't figure out what would be worse—if he showed or if he didn't.

"I really wish you'd let me come round to do your make up, just to hide some of your freckles."

"That would require hiding my entire face, arms, and a third of my legs, Tiffany."

We sighed simultaneously. She sounded tired of the conversation. There was a long silence, during which I clenched my fists in frustration. I'd done the pre-date drama plenty of times for her.

"After he kisses you, I expect full details. I've never kissed a guy with facial hair before."

"I've never kissed a guy before—how am I supposed to compare? And he's not going to kiss me. We only just met."

"Yeah, but he's older."

"Yeah, but we only just met."

If he did kiss me, would I want him to? I imagined his big, soft lips crushing against mine. My heart skipped a beat.

"You're not helping, Tiffany. You've been on a ton of dates. What should I wear?"

"Oh, it's a date now, is it?"

"Tiffany!"

"Okay, okay. The summer dress. It's very girl-next-door."

I dragged myself out of bed and into the dress.

"And your hair up off your shoulders. Guys like necks."

I put my art journal into my backpack.

"What are you doing?"

"Packing my bag."

"What are you bringing that for? It's a date."

"We're hanging out at the art gallery. He has a journal too. It's how we met, remember?"

Tiffany sighed and rolled her eyes. I knew she thought I was a big fat nerd. Sometimes I wondered if she wanted to be friends with me anymore. From a rickety seesaw in Kindergarten to Mianjin Arts Academy, we'd been inseparable. Even though we were so different from one another now, we knew things about each other that no one else did. Like how I didn't shed a tear the day of the funeral. Like how her father was making a new family without her and her mum. It was hard to turn your back on so much history, but I was starting to think she was toying with the idea.

"How was pancakes with your dad this morning?" I asked.

"He cancelled again."

I nodded. I didn't know what else to say. I had the opposite problem to her—my father was too involved.

"Well, I'd better get going," I said. I swept my hair up

into a ponytail and grabbed my bag and car keys.

"Don't do anything I wouldn't do," Tiffany said.

"That's not the greatest advice."

She cackled like a kookaburra. I couldn't help but smile. She had the most ridiculous laugh I'd ever heard.

"I know, I know. Message me if he turns out to be a creep and you need an excuse to leave."

"Thanks, Tiff."

I made my way downstairs as quietly as I could, but sure enough, there was my father waiting in the living room that led off the entrance hall. His presence filled the space between the walls, his greying eyebrows crinkled in austerity.

"You're not going to the art gallery again, are you?"

My body tensed up. I wished he wouldn't pounce on me with that stern voice every time I came and went from the house.

"So what if I am?"

"You've been there every day since the Christmas holidays started."

"I want to be an artist. I'd have thought it was good that I've been spending my time there."

He scrutinised me, eyes narrowed. I sighed.

"I'm going to Tiffany's."

"Will there be boys there?"

William's glistening green eyes flashed across my mind. "No."

I consciously kept my hands still and in plain sight. My face relaxed, my eyes steadily focused on him, but not too focused. It was a trick I'd learned from being a police officer's daughter. He was good at catching liars, so I had to avoid the physical signs of lying. He'd spoken of his work often enough over the years that I'd picked up on the habits to avoid: don't touch your face, stay calm, never look to the right.

He pursed his lips. "Okay, but be back before curfew."

Curfew was 10 p.m. but mercifully he usually had night

duty. He wasn't there to know whether I made it home on time or not.

I left before he changed his mind.

I stood before the woman of the ancient highlander's purlieu. She hadn't changed since the previous day. I tried to distract myself with the structure of her face: the high cheekbones, the square forehead, her pointed nose. William was late. What if he didn't come?

The sweet scent of blossom mixed with cinnamon hit me.

"Hello, Evelyn."

I wheeled around and there he was with those green eyes, holding a single musk-coloured peony. His chequered button up was immaculately pressed. His hair was combed back, eyes glistening just as I remembered. I couldn't help but smile.

"A beautiful flower for a beautiful lady."

The blood of the Irish rushed through my cheeks again. "You can't say that," I said.

I glanced uncomfortably about the empty gallery. The snooty security guard eyed us from his corner.

"Why not?"

Because you're not my boyfriend. "Because beauty is only skin deep."

He chuckled and shook his head.

"Where did you get it from?" I asked.

"My garden. Just like these."

He pulled back the towel covering the wicker basket by his side and revealed a generous pile of bright red strawberries. I glanced back at the security guard, who continued to watch us carefully.

"There's a soft grassy patch at the edge of the bushland," he said.

He turned and started walking away. I hurried to follow as he led me towards the glass door of the art gallery, holding it open for me. My heart pounded against my chest. Was this really a good idea? I really wanted to trust him. The heat of the sun hit me.

"So, do you have a garden or do you like to garden?" I asked.

"I live on a farm. So, both."

We cut through the stone path that went between the art gallery and the bushland. We continued all the way to the point where the path curved round and travelled deep into the bushes. There on the bend of the path we settled beneath a flaming red poinciana on the grass. An occasional hot breeze blew as a mum jogged past with a pram.

William picked a strawberry from his basket and held it to my lips, offering. The sweet aroma filled my nostrils.

My stomach knotted as I took a bite. My teeth couldn't cut through the whole way. After an agonising moment of my mouth being way too close to his hand, the strawberry severed in half and juices dripped down my face.

He flicked his mousy brown hair back and smiled.

"Here, let me get that."

He wiped the juices away with his handkerchief, leaving a sticky feeling. I smelt like strawberry and my skin burned like the flaming red blossoms of the poinciana above.

"You are cute when you are embarrassed," he said, pulling a spice shaker from his basket and sprinkling some cinnamon straight on the strawberry. He bit down and gave a goofy grin as the juice dribbled from his mouth. "What I meant before is I have lived and worked on a farm my whole life."

"What kind of farm?"

"I do a little of everything. I keep animals, but I also have crops and an orchard. My specialty is spices, cultivated to be the best in the universe."

"You're very modest," I teased.

"The spices speak for themselves." He sprinkled his spice shaker over another strawberry and offered it to me.

"What about you, Evelyn? You are a famous artist, are you not?"

I took the strawberry, the smell of cinnamon catching in my nose. It tasted good.

"Oh no," I laughed. "I'm still studying. One day, maybe. I want to travel and paint and see where that takes me."

He nodded knowingly and pulled out his art journal from the wicker basket. "I took some time away from the farm a couple of years ago to travel." He flipped open the art journal to the first spread. It was sparse and dry and the haze of a mirage hovered just above the surface of the charcoal land. "This was the first desert I ever saw with my own eyes."

Despite the barren emptiness of the scene, it held a certain living quality, as if life were hiding just below the surface. He turned the page.

"This was the first man-eating plant I ever saw. It actually was not a pleasant thing to draw, I can assure you. They are putrid-smelling things."

"I thought they didn't actually exist."

"Oh, but they do. The cry of a man stuck inside is the most horrible sound you will ever hear. It still haunts me sometimes."

"You saw a man being eaten alive by a plant?"

"No, I only heard his cries. It was too late by the time I found him."

I didn't know whether to believe him or not. He turned the page.

"And this was the first—and last—time I will ever go cave diving."

Amid the drawing of murky seawater were sparkling treasures and obscure creatures with tentacles, fins and eyes, an eerie yet alluring sight. I couldn't look away until he snapped the journal shut before my eyes.

"Didn't your family miss you while you were off exploring?" I asked.

He scratched his chin and thought for a moment, as though he wasn't ready to talk about it. "I do not have any family."

"Oh," I paused. "What do you mean?"

"My parents abandoned me as a child and I have no other living relatives. None that I know of, anyway."

"I'm really sorry."

"It is okay. I am used to it."

I couldn't imagine having no family. Even a father like mine was better than no one at all.

"It will not always be this way. I will start a family of my own one day."

"You want children?"

"Of course."

I hope he realised that this made him ten times more attractive. I nodded as though it was no big deal.

"It's just me and my father at home. My mum..." my throat caught on the words. I'd never said them aloud before. "My mum passed away earlier this year, in February."

He stopped picking at the strawberry seeds in his teeth and looked at me with steady eyes. "That is far worse than never knowing your parents—to have one ripped away. I am so sorry."

I shrugged my shoulders.

"Do not brush it off. She was your mother."

"She *is* my mother."

His forehead creased at my correction.

"I always wanted a father," he continued. "You are lucky to still have him."

I looked down and picked at the dried paint that flecked my hands. "Sometimes I wish that it had been him that died instead of her." I'd never said that aloud before either. I glanced up. His eyes shone with a thin film of liquid. He placed his hand on my strong one and squeezed. His touch sent goosebumps across my skin.

"I'm a terrible person," I said.

"No, no. She obviously meant a lot to you. Who could blame you for thinking such a thing?"

"But my father, well. He tries. It's just… it's just that I can't stand him sometimes. He's so suffocating."

"What do you mean?"

"He wants to know where I am all the time. Like, can't I just live my life already?"

William nodded. "That is the best part about my farm—there is no one there to tell me what to do or how to live."

"It sounds like a dream."

He picked up another strawberry and offered it. The juice dribbled down my chin again.

"Only if you do not easily become lonely," he said.

"Is that why you visit the art gallery?"

He smiled, his eyes lighting up. "Exactly."

He had such gorgeous eyes. They were the kind of eyes that could persuade me to do anything. Deep and sparkling and mysterious. I wanted to stare into them all day, like a painting at the gallery. He must have read my mind, for he flipped his art journal open again.

"Hold that pose," he said. He pulled a piece of calico from his pocket, unwrapped a stick of charcoal, and proceeded to sketch me. "Your face—it catches the light so wonderfully from this angle."

He traced his forefinger down the middle of my face from my forehead, over my nose, across my lips, and around my chin. His touch sent a new wave of goosebumps across my skin.

"Your silhouette is very elegant."

I blushed and tried to steady my expression until he was done. My heart pounded. I wanted the moment to end yet last forever.

"Now you may move."

I let out a breath and glanced at his work. He had made me more beautiful than I thought I could be, glazing over my abundance of freckles and my untameable hair.

"Now it's my turn," I said. I took out my art journal.

"How shall I sit?" he asked. From his weathered hands to his broad shoulders, strong neck, thick eyebrows, and shaggy brown hair, he looked every part a farmer. But his eyes told another story that I could not place. They captivated me. It was his eyes only that I wanted to draw, to unravel the mysteries that hid behind them.

"Relax, and just look at me."

"With pleasure."

I ignored the constricting feeling in my stomach at his compliment and sketched his glistening eyes. What was hidden behind those eyes? What wonderful secrets were waiting to be found? How I ached to know him and his secrets. I turned my journal to face him, his almond eyes like a pair of opulent emeralds, filling the page. He smiled.

"Evelyn," he said, "may I see you again?"

My stomach constricted a second time in nervous excitement. All I wanted was to nod my head with a vigorous yes, but what about my father? What about waiting until I had finished school? It was his one rule, other than curfew: no boyfriends until I'd finished my studies. But there was still a whole year of school left. I couldn't possibly wait that long, or make William wait. He was so perfect. My father would love him, once he got over his anger. Once he could see that, for the first time since my mum died, I actually felt happy.

"Okay," I said.

What my father didn't know couldn't hurt him.

We continued to see each other for the rest of the Christmas holidays. William didn't have a phone, but it didn't matter. We shared a love of art, our favourite spot on the grass, and one another's company at the same time every day. It was the most perfect summer. By the end of it, joy had crept into my life and I found I could laugh again. I smiled constantly in William's presence, but when

I returned home at night, the joy always dissipated as my father met me at the door, ready to barrage me with questions about where I'd been, with whom and why. Of course, I never told him about William, repeating the same lie day after day.

"I was at the art gallery. I was alone, studying the paintings. I want to be an artist."

He never seemed entirely satisfied with my answers.

2

MY FINAL YEAR of school was well underway when I was met with the distressing reality that I might not graduate.

"Evelyn, your teachers are concerned about you," Miss Daniels said.

She sat across from me in her mismatched counselling office, sinking into a lumpy green sofa, whilst I rubbed the scars on my weak hand from a winged velvet armchair. Even if I wanted to be probed about my private life, the claustrophobic effect of the armchair would be enough to make me want to leave. Miss Daniels' eyes didn't help the matter, magnified through her oversized glasses. She failed to smile, the lipstick on her front tooth flashing at me momentarily. I looked instead at the fresh bruise on her left wrist.

"You're acing visual art, which no one is surprised by. But your basic subjects have taken a surprising downward turn since... since..." She trailed off.

I was glad she didn't have the guts to say it. I didn't want to hear those words said out aloud.

"Principal Gower feels, given your unique situation, that you and I would be best to journey together until things change. Would that be okay with you?"

I stared blankly at her pale face. She may have been one of the young, fun staff members, but it still sounded like torture. I nodded stiltedly in agreement, unable to produce a syllable either for or against the idea.

"He asked me to pass this along for your father."

She handed me a sealed envelope with the Mianjin Arts Academy emblem printed across the front in black and embossed with gold. It felt serious.

"He trusts that you will make sure your father gets it."

I nodded again, trying desperately to hold down the lump in my throat.

"Of course there is also the matter of today's significance."

The lump in my throat increased.

"Your mother's anniversary. How are you feeling?"

What did she hope would happen: that I would break down in her arms? That she could comfort me, and feel she had helped in some way? The reality was that she couldn't help. She couldn't bring my mum back.

"I'm fine," I said.

"Really, Evelyn? This is a safe space. You can be honest with me. Tell me how you are feeling."

"I really am fine. I don't need to talk about anything."

"Principal Gower has requested that we journey together, Evelyn. I cannot help you if you do not share with me."

From the light of the fluorescents above, the winged armchair cast shadows over me that felt like chains. I wanted to escape but my legs refused to budge.

"I don't need your help," I said.

"What did you say?"

Miss Daniels' face sapped of the little colour that remained. Her hands began to shake. Her voice caught. I hesitated before repeating myself less forcefully.

"I said I don't need your help."

A sob escaped her.

"I'm sorry," I said. "I didn't mean to hurt you."

She burst into uncontrollable tears and hid her face in her hands, making herself small enough that the lumpy green sofa might swallow her. Perhaps she wouldn't mind so much if it did. I instantly regretted my hostility.

"I'm so sorry, Miss Daniels."

She held a hand up and waved it at me as if to stop me, brushing away my culpability. She breathed in a snotty breath and shuddered. I escaped the chains of my winged armchair, grabbed the box of tissues on the coffee table between us, and sank into the lumpy green sofa beside her. She blew her nose violently and looked at me momentarily. Her glasses were fogged over and streaked by teardrops. Her layered brown dress was spattered and damp from where the tears had fallen.

"My fiancé, he…"

She launched into a new onslaught of weeping. I tried to fill in the blanks for her.

"Did he pass away too?" I asked.

Miss Daniels only howled louder in an uncontrollable, ugly cry. I passed tissue after tissue, soothing the gauzy back of her dress with my good hand. I wished I had kept my mouth shut.

"He… he is not dead, but he might die."

"What do you mean?" I asked. She sobbed a moment longer. What was wrong with me?

"Last night, I tried to break up with him. He said he'd end his life if I left him."

The bruise on her left wrist made sense now. It was just like the stories my father had told me from his encounters as a police officer. Of the women trapped in abusive relationships; of how they were stuck in a cycle of good days that kept them in the relationship and bad days that made them want to get out. But they never left, not until things went too far—murder, suicide, police intervention and often in that order. My father hated the messes he would walk into, too late to be of any real help. It was men like Miss Daniels' fiancé that had him banning me from dating whilst I was still at school. He hoped to delay the possibility that I might fall into a similar relationship, but I was smart. He had taught me the red flags; how to pick a liar, and to run for the hills if there were drugs or alcohol involved.

"It's all in the tells," he'd once told me. He'd looked haggard but triumphant after spending an entire day interrogating one man.

"He kept tugging on his ear. That's how I unravelled him," he'd said. "I walked him straight into a corner and he willingly went, thinking he had me fooled by his lies. But all I needed to do was ask him the right questions and watch what he did with his ear."

I'd known William for three months now. I knew he was trustworthy—my father would see that. But poor Miss Daniels, she didn't know the tells and now she was stuck in the cycle of good and bad days. I wished I could help. I wished I could get her out.

The bell rang, making me jump and setting Miss Daniels off on another onslaught. I continued to rub her back, trying not to look at the door or think of the next period I was missing. Visual art was the only subject I liked, but I couldn't just leave Miss Daniels in this state. I passed her tissue after tissue.

Her tears slowed to a hiccup and she rasped at me to leave her and get to class. When I didn't budge, she looked up at me, face red and streaked with tears, nose dripping, gazing at me through the one spot on her glasses that wasn't covered in tears and fogging. Then she burst into tears all over again.

I slinked into visual art just as Mrs Dawne entered the supply cupboard. The class stared at me as I made my way to the back where Tiffany sat, between the rows of paired desks. I dared them to look at my weak hand.

I desperately needed to tell Tiffany what had just happened in the counsellor's office. I needed to get it off my chest.

"Where were you?"

"The counsellor's office. It was horrible. I —"

"— Mrs Dawne is just about to demonstrate how to sketch another person's painting but she can't find the fake Monet."

Tiffany guffawed. The twins sitting in front of us turned around and stared for a moment. She smiled sweetly and fluttered her eyelashes.

"Eavesdroppers don't deserve kisses, boys. Remember that."

They nudged one another and turned away fast, faces plastered with goofy grins. Tiffany was bolder than I dared to be; yet I was the one with the boyfriend. She looked at me with hushed excitement.

I opened my mouth to explain again what had happened with Miss Daniels.

"Doesn't he look extra cute today?" Tiffany asked. She was looking two rows across and four down with a besotted smile on her face.

"Who?"

"Darius, of course."

"Oh, uh, I didn't notice."

She rolled her eyes.

"I just love the way he parts his hair down the side, and how it catches the light. He's like a Greek god or something, I swear."

I didn't understand what she saw in him. He was a self-absorbed womaniser who went to Mianjin Arts Academy simply because his parents could afford to send him to a fancy arts school.

It wouldn't matter though—neither Tiffany nor I were triple-threats. I had my art and Tiffany had her acting and though she tried, keeping a rhythm just wasn't her thing. Darius wouldn't look twice in her direction, despite her curves. He only mixed with triple-threats: music, dance, and acting.

"It's never going to happen, Tiffany."

She took her eyes off the back of Darius' head long enough for disappointment to flicker across her face. I opened my mouth for a third time to talk about Miss Daniels, but Tiffany's eyes lit up.

"Is that a challenge?" She stood up. "You and William are together, as unlikely as that is. Who's to say that Darius and I can't be together?"

"That's different. I wasn't competing against a school full of really talented, beautiful girls. It was easy for me to stand out."

"Are you saying I'm not talented or beautiful?"

"Are you kidding me? You know you're the pretty one out of the two of us. Guys drool over you. And you're gonna be a famous actor one day."

She shrugged her shoulders and made to walk towards Darius.

"I don't think you should go out with him."

Though I'd known Tiffany for years, it was still hard to be so brutally honest with her. I knew she wouldn't like what I had to say.

"Why not?"

How could I tell her that he just wanted to get in her pants, then move on to the next girl?

"Because… because he's not good husband material."

"Oh, and William is? He's some creepy guy who was lurking around an art gallery, preying on young girls. How does that make him any more husband material than Darius?"

"How can you say that? You haven't even met him yet."

"And whose fault is that? He doesn't want to meet me because he knows that I will tell you not to see him anymore."

"That's not true. You'll see—tomorrow on our

excursion to the art gallery. He'll be there, just like he promised. You'll see what he's like and you'll love him just like I do."

"You love him?"

"Well, yeah. I think. We've been together for three months now."

"You mean you've known him for three months now. There's a difference."

"Just wait until you meet him, okay. I promise you'll love him too."

She shrugged her shoulders again.

"Are you done?" she asked.

I nodded.

She turned on her heel and made a beeline for Darius. Cameron offered her his seat so that she could sit beside Darius. She flicked her hair and laughed in her unusual way. I tried to smile at her laugh but couldn't.

The empty chair by my side emphasised my loneliness. No one was likely to take Tiffany's place. It had been this way since my mum died. People started treading on eggshells around me as though I was fragile, as though they might break me if they said the wrong thing. Tiffany was the only one who had stuck with me through it all.

Cameron turned around from his standing place beside Tiffany. His dark eyes looked at the empty chair beside me. I made to busy myself, taking my art journal, and flipping to the next blank page.

Please don't sit next to me. Please don't sit next to me.

Having Cameron beside me was almost worse than having no one beside me. Out of my peripherals, I saw him approach my desk and sit in Tiffany's place. My heart sank and my stomach twisted into knots. He could only want one thing and I'd long given up trying to say no to him.

"Hey, Evelyn."

"Hey."

I evaded his gaze and focused entirely on the sketch of

the back of Tiffany's head that I'd begun.

"So we have an art excursion tomorrow."

"Yep."

"You'll help me with the assignment, right?"

This had been going on for almost two years now. Even though we weren't friends anymore, even though I had every right to be angry with him and never speak to him again, despite myself, I couldn't say no. Not to mention the fact that I needed the money so that I could go travelling next year. I'd already saved up four thousand. My father said I needed another four before he'd let me go, provided I booked return tickets.

"Sure, Cameron."

"Great. Thanks Evelyn. You're a real champ."

He lingered, looking at me expectantly. I wasn't sure what else he wanted so I glanced in his direction. The light through the classroom window that shone across his face illuminated the scattered freckles on the bridge of his nose. He scratched at his bark-like hair.

"What?" I asked.

A clattering sound came from the supply cupboard and a large foam-wrapped package emerged, followed by Mrs Dawne lumbering behind. She'd clearly found the fake.

Cameron sighed and left for an empty chair on the other side of Darius. It magnified how alone I felt without Tiffany beside me. How could she just ditch me like that? But Tiffany had been crushing on Darius for a while. If it were William, I'd probably act the same.

Maybe things would be better after Tiffany met William tomorrow? William seemed to be the only stable thing left in my life. Three o'clock couldn't come fast enough—I needed to tell him everything that had happened.

William was waiting for me on our little patch of grass as I came up the stairs from the gallery car park. He was sitting atop a tartan picnic rug, sketching. The fiery red blooms of the poinciana above had long died off but there was shade enough from the lingering summer heat. He stood as he saw me. I couldn't help but smile.

I ran into his arms, his body enveloping me. The smell of dirt and mint filled my nostrils. I inhaled deeply. I was home.

"I missed you so much," I said.

"You only saw me yesterday!"

"I know, but it feels like forever."

"Well, I am here now, and I have a surprise for you."

He led me to our spot beneath the poinciana and revealed a wicker basket filled with strawberries.

"They are the last of the season before winter. Not as big or juicy, but a pretty good haul considering how late in February it is."

He didn't seem to grasp the significance of the day— that it would require more than strawberries to console me. I burst into tears, falling into his arms once again.

"They are only strawberries," he said.

He was the only one I could trust, the only one who would listen. Fluid threatened to dribble from my nose as I wet his chequered shirt with my blubbering.

"Miss Daniels' boyfriend, he… and Tiffany… then Cameron made me… and I might not graduate."

He rubbed my back, hushing me.

"Like I keep telling you, you do not need school to be an artist, Evelyn."

"My mum died on this day last year."

William's hand stopped abruptly on my back and his arms squeezed around me a little tighter. I shuddered, the tears coming out hot and fast.

"I feel so stupid. Here I am, celebrating our three months together," he said.

I sniffed and let out a shaky breath. "Three months? But that's not for another few weeks."

"Three months since the day I laid eyes on you."

"Oh." I fell silent except for the occasional sniff as the

fluid threatened my nostrils again. I wiped the back of my hand across my nose and palmed the remaining tears from my face.

"Hence the strawberries," he said.

He drew back from me and gestured towards them.

"Like on our first date."

The humiliating memory of the strawberry juice dribbling down my chin sent heat to my cheeks. "You want to embarrass me all over again?"

"Embarrass you? No!" He hesitated. "Well, maybe— you are cute when you are bashful."

I pushed him away playfully and slumped down onto the picnic rug. He followed and picked up a strawberry, holding it up to the light and eyeing it. A golden glow surrounded it in the dappled light. His were the best strawberries I'd ever tasted. He looked at me squarely.

"But seriously, the way the juice magnified your sweet, red lips and perspiration glistened across your forehead? I decided then and there that I had to have you. So what better way to celebrate today?"

My cheeks flushed hot once more, but quickly settled down as the day just gone ran through my mind. I reached into my school bag and pulled out the envelope Miss Daniels had given me.

"It's for my father. I think it's to do with my grades." I passed the letter to William who scrutinised the front lettering. Like the strawberry, he held it up to the light.

"I do not think it is to do with your grades."

"What do you mean?"

He pointed at the light shining through the white envelope to the letter inside. I could just make out a dollar symbol.

"My school fees?" I asked.

"Open it and find out."

"No, I shouldn't."

"It is your school fees. Do you not have a right to know about it?"

"I guess."

He passed the envelope to me. I sighed and gingerly pulled back the seal. It was sticky. As I tugged at the last of it, the paper tore. I cringed, not looking forward to explaining the tear to my father.

The letter inside was formal and brief, stating the last date that my school fees had been paid—six months prior—and that without payment for both the previous semester as well as term one of that year, I would lose my enrolment in the school. The figure at the bottom of the page detailing the accumulated fees was a little over ten thousand dollars. The due date was a fortnight away.

A little squeak escaped my lips. William snatched the letter away, scanning it quickly. He shook his head.

"I told you," he said. "You do not need school. It is not worth the trouble."

"It's high school, William. I can't just not graduate."

"Look at me—I did not graduate and I turned out fine."

"It's not the same."

"I wish you would just let me free you from school and your dad and your stupid friends."

I ignored his insult directed at Tiffany.

"But how am I going to get a job if I don't even finish high school?"

"You do not need someone else to pay you money so that you can live. I have everything we could ever need on my farm. And you could paint all you wanted."

"That's not realistic, William. What about my father?"

"What about him?"

"He wouldn't like it."

"You would be doing him a favour by leaving school. Not that he deserves any favours from you, the way he treats you."

I sighed, thinking about what would be waiting for me when I got home that night. How his presence filled the space in the hallway, how he had a way of towering over me, eyeing my every gesture for a trace of dishonesty. How would he react to this letter? I dreaded the thought.

"Can we change the subject?"

William's face crinkled with annoyance, but something flashed across his eyes. A cheeky grin crept up his cheeks.

"But of course."

He turned my body around and pulled me down into his, wrapping his arms around me.

"The sun is setting," he said.

The light across the sky cast golden honey as the sun set behind the concrete art gallery, softening its harsh edges with a hazy glow. William ran his fingers gently across the back of my good hand. It sent shivers across my skin and down my back.

"Three months, huh?" I said.

He kissed my neck in reply. A new wave of shivers ran across my skin. He continued his kissing and pushed me onto my back. My stomach constricted in fear and excitement. Our lips met. His hands travelled up and down my body. My stomach continued to tense but my body responded to him. I wanted him more than anything. Our breathing grew fast and I ached to continue but I pulled away.

"What is wrong?" he asked.

I held my breath in an attempt to slow it.

"Evelyn, have I done something to upset you?" he asked.

I turned away to look at the sky that had now turned obsidian. Stars speckled across it faintly. Heat flooded my cheeks. I couldn't look at him.

"I want to wait," I said.

I chanced a glance up at him. I could only just make out his silhouette, his eyes catching the starlight and glistening ever so slightly. He nodded in understanding and scratched at his chin.

"We will not go any further than you want to go."

I was grateful for the darkness, as my cheeks continued

to burn. I looked away, picking at the dried paint on the back of my hand.

"Okay," I said.

He lifted my face up, forcing me to look him in the eyes again.

"Evelyn, I will wait for you."

He wouldn't leave me?

I couldn't believe how lucky I was to find such a guy. Unlike Darius, who would use Tiffany until he got what he wanted, William would wait for me.

3

THE LOUNGE ROOM light was on when I pulled into the driveway several hours later. My father was probably asleep in front of the TV. The two-storey Queenslander glared down at me accusingly. I'd missed curfew. By a long shot. The time on the dashboard of my car showed an angry red glow of 3:12 a.m. I closed the door as quietly as I could, a soft metal click echoing across the quiet country street. I crept up to the front veranda and across the wooden boards that creaked beneath my feet.

The house wasn't quiet. There was a strange rustling coming from inside. My heartbeat quickened. Was it the TV?

I pushed the front door open and it scraped along the ground. The rustling stopped.

"Evelyn? Is that you?"

My father's gruff voice drifted into the entrance hall. I tightened my jaw and my back drew up stiffly. I stopped dead in the doorway.

"Evelyn?"

I let the door scrape closed behind me, shook my shoulders loose and walked casually into the entrance hall.

I turned and looked into the lounge room. He had a disheveled, slightly manic look about him. It was rather at odds with his usually composed policeman posture. A crease was furrowed into his forehead, his chin was rough, and his eyes were wide and wild like a kangaroo caught in the headlights of a car.

He was sitting on the carpet, TV off, surrounded by mountains of boxes. He was suspended, hands halfway out of an old document file. He glanced at what he was holding, then back at me.

"Your mother's old pay slips," he said.

I eyed the rest of the belongings. He was clearing out mum's stuff. Why was he doing that today of all days? He had no right.

I opened my mouth to accuse him but he jumped to his feet, pointing at his watch in shock.

"What time do you call this?" He raised his voice. "Evelyn! Where have you been? Why didn't you answer your phone? Didn't you realise it was a school night? Did you even notice you missed curfew? How could you do this to me, today of all days?"

What a hypocrite.

"How could I do this to *you*? How could you do this to me?" I gazed about the room pointedly. "What are you doing with Mum's stuff?"

"I thought it might help us to move on if we got rid of some of it. Maybe even sold some."

He put his hand in his pocket and pulled out a piece of gold jewellery. It had a long, delicate chain with an ornate oval locket hanging from it. Mum's locket. She used to wear it beneath her nurse's scrubs at the hospital and cling to it when she was nervous. Each inside face of the locket bore a picture of me and a picture of my father—her most prized possessions. He placed it down on a teetering pile of gardening magazines and stepped towards me, holding his hands out defensively.

I shook my head in fury, suppressed anger bubbling up

inside of me.

"You have no right. It's all your fault she can't wear that herself anymore."

He hung his head in shame; clearly the thought had crossed his mind too. But I'd never been bold enough to say it aloud until now.

He took a deep breath in and out and lifted his head again.

"It's not important. What is important is that we try to move on from it. It's been twelve months, sweetheart —"

"Don't call me that."

He sighed again. He looked tired. "It's been twelve months. Don't you think it's time we let her go?"

"You know what I think? I think you're using this as an excuse. You really just want to sell her stuff because we're broke."

He stepped back and cocked his head to the side, pretending he didn't know what I was talking about. But it wouldn't work. He'd taught me too well how to pick a liar.

"Yeah, I know all about it," I said.

I whipped my backpack off and rifled inside for the letter from school.

"I'm not an idiot, you know."

I threw the opened envelope at him, not daring to set foot in the lounge room. The envelope flitted in the air and dropped to the floor at his feet. He bent down slowly and picked it up, scouring the lines of the letter, his eyes widening as he went.

"It's not what it looks like."

"It looks like I'm not graduating. That's what it looks like."

"Your mother wanted you to go to Mianjin Arts Academy as much as I did—as much as I do. We'll make it work. I'm taking extra shifts at work and if we sell a few things..." He trailed off.

"Why don't you just sell the house while you're at it."

"You know I can't do that."

"But you would if you could."

"No, I wouldn't want to, Evelyn. This is your house. Well it will be, one day."

"Mum made sure of that much."

"No, your grandparents made sure of it."

"Same difference."

"Look, Evelyn. Since we lost your mother's income and the insurance money has run dry, your school fees are hard to keep up with."

"Well then, maybe I'll just drop out of school and solve everyone's problems."

His face turned from frustration to desperation.

"No, Evelyn. Your mother would have wanted you to finish. She believed in you so much that she went back to work to help cover the cost. Don't let it go to waste."

"Stop assuming what she would have wanted—she's not here to speak for herself. You made sure of that."

Stony silence filled the house. A dog barked a couple of streets away. I gathered up my school bag and made to head for the staircase.

"I don't need school anyway."

My hand reached for the railing.

"Yes, you do."

His voice had cracked slightly, a hint of emotion behind it. He cleared his throat. "You need a high school certificate to get into art college. And your report card at the end of last year was not promising. You need to put less time into your art projects and more time into your other subjects, Evelyn."

I turned back to him, huffing.

"I want to be an artist. I want to get as far away from here as possible and travel the world and paint what I see. I don't need some stupid piece of paper to tell me I can do that."

"You're going to finish school and go to university. That is that, Evelyn."

"You can't make me."

"Yes, I can. I'm your father."

"Not in three weeks' time. I'll be eighteen."

"I will always be your father."

"But you won't be able to tell me what to do."

He raised his voice. A sense of finality clung to it.

"Legally, right now, I can. And I forbid you from spending any more time at that art gallery."

William's face flashed through my mind. If I couldn't go to the art gallery anymore, how would I see him without my father knowing?

"What?" I asked.

"That's right."

"You can't do that."

"You need to work on your other subjects."

"But…"

He rubbed his face, exasperated. "Sometimes I wish we'd never bought you that paint set for your fifth birthday."

I scowled at him. "Sometimes I wish you'd died instead of Mum."

His mouth bobbed open and a wounded look flashed across his eyes. He changed the subject.

"Where were you tonight?" he asked.

"What?"

"You couldn't have been at the art gallery—it closed hours ago."

I stumbled, caught off guard. "I was at Tiffany's."

"No, you weren't. I called her mother when you wouldn't pick up your phone. Tiffany was out."

"I mean, I was with Tiffany."

"At her boyfriend's house?"

Tiffany was at her boyfriend's house? Could that mean that her and Darius were a thing? Why hadn't she told me? I ignored the stab of hurt.

"So you were at a boy's house?"

"Yes. I mean, no."

"What is it, Evelyn? Yes or no?"

I started to pick at the dried paint on my hands.

"I was at the art gallery."

"The art gallery closed hours ago."

"I was outside the art gallery. With my boyfriend."

He wavered on the spot. The little colour in his cheeks sapped away, turning his olive skin a sickly yellow.

"Boyfriend?"

"I'm not so hideously ugly that I can't convince a guy to like me."

"You know how I feel about boyfriends."

"You don't know William. He treats me right, which is more than I can say for you."

"If you would just finish your high school first."

"And then what? University? Owning an art gallery of my own? It will never be safe for me to date, in your eyes. But I'm almost eighteen. I can decide for myself now."

"While you're living under my roof, you will follow my rules, young lady."

I stamped my foot in frustration.

"I'm not a child," I said. "Ugh. I'm sick of your rules. And I'm sick of you keeping tabs on me all the time. I feel so trapped every time I step through that door." I pointed towards the front of the house. "I can't do this anymore."

I ignored the mounting protest as he opened his mouth to speak and turned on my heel, running up the stairs, taking them two at a time. Ducking left towards my room, I slammed the door behind me. I heaved for breath, dumping my bag on the bed and pacing the room.

I couldn't do this anymore.

If I wasn't living under his roof, I didn't need to follow his rules. I grabbed my clothes that scattered the ground and stuffed them into my school bag. I collected my toiletries and hair straightener from the ensuite and pulled the plug of my phone charger from the wall. With difficulty, I zipped up the bag and hauled it back over my shoulder, giving my room a quick once-over to see if I'd forgotten anything. The flowers William had given me now sat dried up in a vase by my windowsill, his notes in the small chest on my dresser. I wouldn't need these memories because I was going to be with him, all the time.

I turned to the door to leave. My father's footsteps approached. I froze as he knocked on the door.

"Evelyn?"

I held my breath and waited.

"Evelyn, can we please talk?"

Moments passed in silence. He shuffled away to his bedroom in front of the staircase landing. The door of his bedroom clicked shut. I waited a few more seconds before opening my own and slinking past his bedroom, down the stairs. As I passed the lounge room, I chanced one last look at Mum's things and saw her locket on the pile of magazines. I stretched my arm into the room, still refusing to set foot inside, and pocketed the locket.

I started my car and reversed out of the driveway before my father could catch on to what I was doing. I needed to get away. Far away. Perhaps it would solve all our problems.

4

THE SCHOOL CHARTER bus chilled my skin, the air conditioning pumping from above as I waited for my classmates to join me. My lumpy schoolbag filled the seat by my side. I should have put the clothes and hair straightener into my car, but it was now parked on the other side of the school and there was no way I'd miss this art excursion. I needed to see William.

Tiffany's puffy brown hair bobbed into view as she stepped up onto the bus. She looked straight past me towards the back and her face lit up. She waved. Darius. Glancing in my direction she gave a half smile and made her way over to me.

"Why did you have to sit so close to the front?" she asked.

"What do you mean? We always sit here."

"It's embarrassing."

She looked over to the back of the bus again and smiled apologetically. She tugged at my school bag until it fell off the seat and onto the floor with a thud.

"What the heck have you got in there? Bricks?"

She claimed the seat for herself. I opened my mouth, desperately needing to download the fight I'd had with my father.

"You were right about one thing," she said. "Darius does have a type, but it's not triple-threats."

She paused for effect.

"Me. I'm his type. He said so."

She lifted her chin with pride.

"Last night he messaged me, invited me over."

"I know. You're his girlfriend now."

"No. He's my boyfriend. And how did you know?"

"My father called your mum when I didn't come home by curfew."

I waited for her to quiz me on why I didn't make curfew.

"Aren't you going to ask me what happened with Darius?" she asked.

I ignored her question.

"I was late for curfew last night. My father flipped out," I said.

"Evelyn. Aren't you going to ask me what happened with Darius?"

I picked at the dry flecks of paint on my hands.

"I don't want to know," I said.

She narrowed her eyes. I sighed.

"It's Darius," I said. "I told you—he's just going to use you to get what he wants."

"It may not have occurred to you that it's me that he wants."

"Yeah, your body."

"No. All of me. And you're just jealous because he's super hot and you're stuck with your nerdy farm boy."

"William is not nerdy. And you've never even met him. For all you know, he could be even hotter than Darius."

Tiffany looked at me pointedly. Heat crept up my neck and threatened my cheeks. The silence between us was more noticeable now that the bus was filling up. I started picking at the paint again.

"I told my father about William last night," I said.

Tiffany let out a frustrated huff.

"Everything isn't about you, Evelyn. Ever since your mum... Ugh. I've got parent problems too, you know."

"I know, but my father..."

Through her flawless olive skin, a tinge of angry red lit up her ears and forehead, filling the crinkle in her brow.

"You've got William. Now it's my turn, okay? Can't you just be happy for me?"

"But it's Darius," I said.

Tiffany stood up and turned in the aisle of the bus to face me, ignoring the people trying to get past to the back of the bus. The angry red had crept across her cheeks and down her neck, below the lapel of her tartan school dress.

"All you ever do is think about yourself, Evelyn. I'm done."

She leered menacingly at the people who were trying to push past her, turned towards the back of the bus, and walked away.

Some guys who had taken their places across the aisle sat gawking at me long after Tiffany had left. I was used to people staring at me because of my hand. I was used to people staring at me because they were really staring at Tiffany and her well-endowed rack. I was not used to people staring at me because I'd just had a heated argument with my best friend. Ex-best friend. Whatever.

I stared back at them.

"Mind your own business," I said.

They hurriedly turned away to make themselves look busy. The bus kicked into motion, vibrating violently.

She didn't even care about what happened with my father. What kind of best friend does that? If I was honest, it had been a long time since we'd been best friends. But she was right about one thing: I had William.

I stared at the empty seat beside me and with great difficulty pulled my school bag up so that it filled the space.

I couldn't believe she just did that.

I hugged myself. Despite being surrounded by the noise and bustle of the full bus, I felt supremely alone. It was going to be a long ride to the art gallery.

The white leather lounge was vacant when we entered the art gallery. I waited impatiently for Mrs Dawne to finish giving instructions so that I could make my way over to it—William had promised to meet me there.

I shifted from one foot to the other, eyes darting between Mrs Dawne and the lounge. An elderly man hobbled past us in the direction of the lounge. I clenched my jaw.

The class gave a collective, "Yesssss, Miss," drawing my attention back to the school group. I'd missed whatever the instruction had been.

"Lunch is at twelve sharp. We'll meet back here in the lobby for a headcount, then head to the bandstand outside to eat. Be sure you're here on time."

The elderly man walked straight past the lounge towards the painting of the ancient highlander's purlieu. I let out a breath I didn't realise I was holding.

"Yesssss, Miss," we said in unison.

Finally we were released to go freely about the art gallery and work on our assignment. I made a beeline for the lounge, noticing immediately the absence of charcoal fingerprints on the arm of the lounge. William had clearly not arrived yet.

I dumped my school bag on the ground and massaged my shoulder. Five minutes with that bag on was more than enough. My muscles tightened as Tiffany and Darius strolled past, hand in hand. Tiffany didn't even glance in my direction, too busy nestling herself into the base of Darius' neck and gazing up at him, all dewy-eyed. I watched them all the way to the side exit, watched how they scanned the room to see that Mrs Dawne wouldn't catch them leaving, and watched as they slipped out of the art gallery in the direction of the bush.

I was angry with Tiffany for ditching me, for accusing me of being selfish, for not caring about the fight I'd had with my father, but I was also sad for her. Darius would only use her. I shook my head and tried to forget about it. William would be here soon.

I pulled my mother's locket from my pocket and slid it around my neck for safekeeping. I re-did my ponytail, then picked at a particularly stubborn splotch of paint on my hand and quickly drew blood. I gave up and pulled out the assignment sheet from my bag, as I had twice the amount of work to do, after all.

The instructions were straightforward enough: sketch what you see whilst meditating upon what the artist was thinking at the time of painting. I put pencil to paper immediately, drawing from memory the landscape of the ancient highlander's purlieu. This one would be for me, not for Cameron.

As I finished the basic backdrop, the woman's face crossed my mind. She was forever attentive to those that gazed back at her. What did the artist mean by it? That she was always there when needed? That she didn't trust the competence of those around her? That she reprimanded with her eyes and not her words, or chose to stay out of things entirely?

I paused mid-stroke. Where was William? I wanted to collapse in his arms and hide from it all. From the troubles with my school fees and grades, from Tiffany walking away from our friendship, from the argument with my father and how there was no way I could return home after school. I had no idea what I was going to do: it was like I was holding a fistful of sand but the sand was running through the gaps of my fingers, and no matter how hard I tried to keep it all contained, the sand continued to fall, scattering in a mess on the ground. It seemed an impossible task to pick it all up again.

My palms were open before me when William slid his

hand into my good one, criss-crossing his fingers with mine.

"You're here," I said.

Calm washed over me as I launched into the enclosure of his arms. No one could touch me from here. I was safe in this stronghold.

"Something is wrong," he said.

I nodded into his chest.

"Everything is wrong."

He pulled away to get a good look at me as though it were written on my face.

"What is this?"

He picked the locket up from its resting place on my school tie. He gave me a cheeky grin, put the locket in his mouth, and bit it.

"It's real gold," he said.

"It's my mum's. My father was going to sell it because he can't keep up with my school fees. We had this massive fight last night."

He let the locket fall back around my neck.

"He was awake when you got home?"

I nodded.

"I told him about you."

William raised his eyebrows. He opened his mouth to respond but a shadow had fallen. Cameron was standing in front of us, head cocked to the side in confusion, his eyes squinting questioningly. His brow fell.

"Evelyn, leave this poor man alone. You've got work to do," Cameron said.

Only Tiffany and my father knew about William.

"For your information, this is my boyfriend."

Cameron scoffed. The passing security guard frowned in our direction and pursed his lips.

"No one would ever go out with you," Cameron said.

A heavy weight fell upon my shoulders and the colour drained from my skin. Hot tears appeared across my eyes, blurring my vision.

Why would he say something like that?

The tears threatened to spill out on my lap. I focused my attention on the white tiles at my feet but the tears only grew. I couldn't give him the satisfaction of seeing me cry. Avoiding all eye contact, I darted around Cameron and walked as collectedly as I could towards the side exit. I could feel the security guard's eyes on my every move, scrutinising my quick, echoing footsteps.

My vision became even more obscured as I opened the side exit and the glaring sun hit my tears. I wiped my face and followed the path that circled the art gallery back towards the front entrance and my favourite patch of grass.

What did I ever do to Cameron for him to treat me like that? Why did he have to be such a... a... an insensitive, self-seeking asshole with a silver spoon up his arse?

I kicked up the shrivelled and scrunched poinciana flowers at my feet. Tears dripped down my face and wet the front of my school dress.

I should know better. Cameron was always going to burn me eventually, just like last time. Yet I've never done anything but be nice to him. Heck, I've been more than nice to him—I've been doing his assignments without question for over two years now. And he just stood there and laughed at me. Was I really so unattractive that the idea of me having a boyfriend was so far-fetched?

A sob escaped my lips. Why did this hurt so much?

A rustling and giggle came from up ahead. I tried to stifle the noise of my sobs. It was a couple making out. The grey slacks and white button up told me he was from my class. He had her pinned up against a tree. It looked rough and rushed. Tiffany's brown hair bobbed into view as she turned them round so that it was him against the tree. Tiffany and Darius. I kept my head down and pretended I hadn't seen them, picking up the pace towards the front of the gallery until I was long past them.

I did tell her, didn't I? Why didn't she listen to me?

And she thinks I'm selfish? All I've done is look out for her. Well she can't come crying to me when he takes what he wants and leaves her to pick up the pieces. It'll only take a few days, if history was anything to go by. She can't say I didn't warn her.

The tears were hot against my skin, my jaw clenched. My weak hand formed a partial fist and collided awkwardly with the nearest tree.

"I hate you," I said.

I punched the tree again. My wrist jarred.

"I hate you."

Little fragments of bark crunched and fell as I connected with the tree again. My hand fell away, grazed, blood oozing out. It was just as well there wasn't much feeling in that hand.

"I hate you."

Screw Cameron. Screw Tiffany. Screw my father. Screw school. I quit.

I collapsed in a heap at the base of the tree; my head slumped against its trunk in the hope that it might wrap its branches around me in comfort. I couldn't contain my emotion any longer: the sobs came out loud and fast. I sucked in air between each cry. The tree refused to show any compassion.

"I can't do this anymore," I cried aloud.

Why did everyone have to be such jerks? Did they really care so little about me? What did I do to deserve all of this? Was William the only person in my life that I could trust? If only I could talk to my mum about it. Maybe I should just go and die too.

The tree's rough branches embraced me.

"There, there," William said.

I stared about through my tear-dripping eyelashes. William had his arms wrapped around me from behind. I fell into him once more.

"I just want to get away from all of this."

The tears welled up for a second time and burst from

me. William cleared his throat.

"You can," he said.

I choked back my sobbing. His face shone brightly, his eyes wild.

"What do you mean?"

"I know a place that we could go. Get away from your dad, Tiffany, Cameron, school."

I sighed with a deep shudder and sniffed.

"That sounds too good to be true."

"I could show it to you, see how you like it?"

He wiped the tears free from my face.

"What? Now?" I asked.

"Yes. You could stay as long as you like."

"And not go to school?"

He nodded, the wild look intensifying.

"What about graduation?"

"Evelyn, I have told you before: you do not need school to be an artist. You are already so talented."

Heat flooded my cheeks and I dodged his gaze at the compliment. It would mean that my father wouldn't have to sell Mum's stuff.

I sighed again. It sounded a whole lot better than going back inside and facing Cameron.

"So, what? We just leave and live like hermits?" I asked.

"We can live off the land."

A smile spread across his face triumphantly. In my opinion, it sounded like a lot of hard work.

"Please, come. We could try it, at least?"

There was no way I was going back home that night, and it sure beat the idea of sleeping in my car again. William scratched at his chin casually.

"If you do not like it, I can take you home."

There was no harm in just going to check it out, was there?

"Where is it?" I asked.

"Does that mean it is a yes?" he asked.

I picked at the dried paint, avoiding the spot where the

blood had clotted.

"Where is it?" I asked again.

"Not far from here," he said.

He lifted my chin and inspected my face with a grin.

"Yes?" he asked.

I hesitated. Those eyes. I would do anything for them.

"Yes," I said.

He jumped to his feet and whooped aloud. I'd never seen him so filled with joy, so enthused. I smiled to myself and allowed him to pull me to my feet. He grabbed my bag, which he'd brought from the art gallery, and swung it over his shoulder. The fingers of my strong hand laced together with his and he tugged me along, following the stony path towards our favourite patch of grass. Instead of continuing on towards the underground car park, we rounded the bend of the path and headed into the depths of the bushland, the smell of eucalyptus filling my nostrils.

William squeezed my hand. "I cannot wait to show you," he said. There was a slight bounce in his step. Why was he smiling at a time like this?

Fear of the repercussions gripped me. I'd never wagged before. What if I changed my mind and wanted to go back to school? How much could I afford to miss and still graduate? And what would Cameron do when I didn't hand him his assignment tomorrow? I could really do with the money.

Screw Cameron. He brought this on himself.

My father—would he yell or ground me? Would he stop me from seeing William again?

He'd already done all of that.

Even if I didn't go with William, I still wouldn't be going home tonight. And going with William was a much safer option than sleeping in my car in the school car park.

It would be nice to spend some time alone with William. Not surrounded by people at the art gallery, not subject to the stares of onlookers as we lazed on our grassy patch. Just the two of us.

I squeezed William's hand back and smiled.

The trees that lined the stony path cast shadows upon us, a welcome reprieve from the late summer sun. A hot breeze whipped through the tree tunnel, drying the front of my school dress.

"We're not going to hide out in the bush, are we?" I asked.

"Oh no, no. We must go through the bush to get there."

"A shortcut?"

"Yes, something like that."

We followed the path for some time, so that when I turned and looked at the way we'd come, there was only a small dot of light where the path turned towards the art gallery. William stopped abruptly and I stumbled after him. He scratched at his chin.

"We need to cut through here."

"Like, literally go through the bushes?"

"Yes."

"Oh. Okay."

He tugged me along through the gap in the brush on a well-worn trail. Dirt and snapped twigs and trampled low-lying plants covered the ground at our feet, but it was only wide enough for one to pass at a time. If he hadn't pulled me onto the path, I wouldn't have noticed it was there. William led the way, pulling at my hand to hurry up. The trees tumbled into one another with branches overlapping and roots weaving together. Just enough light cut through the canopy from the midday sun to navigate the treacherous path. Birds hid amongst the branches, twittering and rustling about, accompanied by a melody of wind whistling in the tree tunnel behind us.

Where was William taking me? A camping ground where we'd pitch a tent and start our own fires and live under the stars? Where we'd be far enough from civilisation that the stars would cover the sky and shine like diamonds? Or to a caravan park with rusty old picnic tables and tiny television sets from the eighties, where we'd walk around in singlets and thongs and people-watch from our creaking, rusting furniture?

Would the place we were going have running water? Showers? I could do with a shower. My palms, my back, between my thighs were sticky with sweat and my face was covered in the salty remains of my tears. Not to mention the dried blood on my hands. That would hurt to clean up.

"Are you taking me to your farm?" I asked.

William's hand slipped from my grip as he tripped on a protruding root and stumbled a few paces forward. He grabbed onto a tree for support and glanced back at me.

"Are you okay?" I asked.

"Yes."

He dusted his hands off on his pants and reached out for my hand again. He picked up the pace through the bushland.

"So is that a yes?" I asked.

"Yes. I am okay."

"No. Are you taking me to your farm?"

"Oh," he hesitated. "Yes."

His shoulders rose in tension, awaiting my response. He seemed nervous, apprehensive. Should he be?

His farm did make the most sense. With the juicy strawberries and the house he had grown up in, it could be the safe haven I was looking for. I could waste away the hours watching his animals frolic about, help him out in the garden, and we could cook hearty meals together. And paint. I wonder if he'd mind me exploring to find subjects to paint? But I'd left my paints at home. My brow furrowed at the thought. At least I had my sketchbook.

My school shoes were starting to rub from walking for so long when the trees grew less condensed. The bushland took on a magical quality, like an afterglow. Rays of light shone through the gaps of the canopy above, illuminating the path before us. Though it was lighter here, it felt uninhabited, like we had just stepped into an old and unchartered part of the bushland.

William slowed to a stop when two trees blocked our path. I stepped out from behind him to see that the two trees had intertwined with one another, forming an arch. They were old trees, grey and wrinkled, bent over like withering old men, leaning onto one another for support. A strange desire overcame me to walk through the archway between them.

William gave me an apologetic smile and took the few paces forward through the archway. He turned and waved for me to follow him, the light surrounding him seeming brighter on his side.

The bushland was silent, like it was holding its breath, waiting to see what I might do. I stepped through the archway. As I did so, a veil was lifted from my eyes, and where I had been surrounded by scattered, chaotic bush, now row after perfect row of trees on manicured grass welcomed me. The trees were immense in height and breadth; each the size of a small office building, their branches open wide in a neverending canopy above, protruding roots as wide as my body digging deep into the earth below. Despite their enormity, some of the trees were old and withered. They shrank into themselves like the archway trees. Others were bursting with life, displaying new branches and bright green leaves. No matter the age, they all stood tall and proud in their perfect rows, towering above us. All except for one tree, a couple of rows down. It had greyed and shrunk into itself so entirely that it now laid, half dust, half a carpet of moss, on its side. Its bark disintegrated as the wind blew, crumbling before my very eyes.

"What is this place?" I asked.

"The Hidden Grove."

"Grove? Is this your farm?"

William chuckled. "No, no. But we are not far."

He grasped my hand again and led me into the grove. It stretched for rows and rows in every direction, more than

I could count. We walked past tree after tree until William led me between the roots of one tree, its bark covered with white lichen. I looked around, noticing that the trees, though uniform in height, weren't just old or young but had little quirks about them too. The one to the left was covered in sand at its base. The one to the right was moist and water trickled down the trunk and along the protruding roots. I looked up to the rays of light peeking through the canopy. Where was the water coming from?

William's fingers slipped from mine as he reached up to the lowest hanging branch of the lichen-covered tree. He swung his body up onto the branch, which shuddered with his weight. He reached to the next branch above, ready to hoist himself higher.

"What are you doing?" I asked.

William turned around, eyebrows raised.

"Oh, sorry."

He lowered his leg back down and offered me his hand, his eyes wide with expectation.

"I thought we were going to your farm."

"We are."

I cocked my head to the side and folded my arms.

"Trust me," he said.

I looked up the trunk of the tree. It was really high. The fingers of my weak hand trembled. I sighed as he wrapped his hand around my wrist and tugged. I followed his pull up onto the first branch and watched as he hoisted himself up to the next one. The bark had worn thin where he stood, revealing a smooth, shiny surface.

"Shouldn't we be going to your farm?"

He continued up onto the next branch, then the next.

"William?"

I scrambled after him, slipping on the worn parts of the branches. My stomach dropped.

"We *are* going to your farm, aren't we?"

He continued up, loose leaves and the dirt from his shoes showering down on me.

"Come on. Quit playing."

I stood for a moment in defiance, clinging to the trunk, wondering if I should climb down and wait for him to stop being a child.

"William, I'm tired and I want a shower."

He kept on climbing, higher and higher, without any qualms about height or safety. I lost sight of him amongst the thicket of branches.

"Are you coming?" he called.

I tried not to look down to see how far I'd ascended. Every time the tree shifted under the weight of our movement, my breathing became more laboured, my feet released more sweat, the pounding of my heart more pronounced against my chest. A yelling male voice rang in my ears.

I shook the noise from my head, gritted my teeth, and continued up the tree. He was waiting for me several branches above. I wrapped my arms around the trunk for stability and screwed up my face in protest. His eyes glittered with excitement.

"Where is your sense of adventure?" he asked.

"I'm not going any higher until you tell me what we're doing."

A cheeky smile spread across his face. "Look up," he said.

I did. We were almost at the top of the trunk where the branches forked off to make the canopy.

"It is not much further."

"I don't understand. What is not much further?"

"The farm."

"William, if you're telling me that you live on top of a tree, I... I don't know what I'll do, but you won't like it."

He scratched his chin. "I do not live on top of a tree," he said.

I stared at him for a moment, waiting for him to elaborate.

"It is not something I can just tell you about. I need to

show you."

A breeze blew through the grove, sending a chill across my sweaty skin. The tree swayed in the wind. My heart skipped a beat as I grappled to clutch onto the trunk harder.

"I'm sure it's very wonderful but I'm not going any higher."

If I wasn't going to go up, it was time to climb down. I chanced a look towards the ground. My heart skipped another beat. I pressed my body firmly into the trunk of the tree. It would be a long way to fall.

William casually stood on the branch, arms up on the limb above and watched me with amusement.

"You just said you would go higher if I told you what we were doing."

"Well, I changed my mind."

"We are going to my farm, but the path is unconventional."

"What do you mean?"

"It would be best if I just showed you. We must go together." He reached out his hand for mine.

"Fine."

I gave him my strong hand and gingerly turned to reach for the next branch. We climbed the remaining two to the top of the trunk where a small flat space sat with branches forking out from it.

William squeezed my hand. "Come." He stepped slowly and purposefully the few paces across the top of the trunk and pulled me along with him. As I walked in his wake, crossing the centre of the trunk, bright and blazing light surrounded me like a flash of lightning on pause. It blinded me, the smell of eucalyptus replaced by crisp pine. I felt like I was everywhere and nowhere all at once, my body in motion, yet more still than if I were sleeping. As I passed the centre, the light disappeared and I could see clearly out onto the boughs and up to the canopy.

By William's side on the other side of the tree trunk, we

looked down upon the mass of branches below. As my stomach dropped at the sight of the ground so far below, the urge to clutch at the wood of the tree for support overwhelmed me, yet I experienced a strange feeling that I had crossed a threshold of no return.

"What was that?" I asked.

"An unconventional path."

He slid down onto the branch in front of us, pulling me after him. I tried not to look at the ground as we descended, bark and lichen covering my arms and my school dress as I scrambled from branch to branch, grateful that every bough brought us closer to the ground. My hands were red raw, my body covered with nervous sweat. It grew hard to hold on as we continued, the ground always within sight, making my heart beat faster in fear of falling. Finally we were but metres from the ground.

William skipped the last few branches, landing with a dull thud. I took my time, careful to grip the branches, my hands shaking profusely. He took my waist on the last branch and I slid slowly down into his arms.

"Please don't ever make me do that again," I said.

"I hope you never need to."

I raised my eyebrows. "You don't remember? I don't like heights," I said.

He shrugged apologetically and drew me into a hug. I concentrated on his steady heartbeat to calm my own. I took a deep breath and pulled away.

"There are showers on your farm, aren't there?" I asked.

He took my hand once more and swung it back and forth. He smiled and nodded.

"Nearly there."

We walked back through the rows and rows of the Hidden Grove towards the withered archway. He insisted that we step through the arch again. As I did so, I turned back to the Hidden Grove and the trees disappeared from sight, a pine forest replacing it.

"What? How?"

"Evelyn, welcome to Purlieu," William said.

I looked at the vista before me. Instead of scattered, chaotic bush, a few young pine trees dotted the path before us, abruptly ending in a clearing the size of several football stadiums.

Where had the bush gone?

5

F RUIT TREES AND small crop fields filled the clearing before us. To my right were several barns encased in wooden fencing. A lone tree as wide as a house towered from the centre of the clearing. Afternoon light refracted from its heights like it was covered in crystal, forcing me to shield my eyes. Wild, rugged mountains pointed to the sky in the distance.

How could this be?

"Evelyn, I have not been entirely honest with you."

My heart began to race once more.

"You know how I do not have a phone?"

I nodded.

"And how we always meet at the art gallery?"

I nodded again, my heart quickening.

"Well, it is because I am not actually from Earth."

A dull roar filled my ears. I scrambled to breath. What was he saying?

"At the top of the tree in the Hidden Grove, we passed through a portal to another world. We are in Purlieu now."

I could see his lips moving but I couldn't hear him. Memories flashed through my mind of the first time we had met. How I had offered him chocolate and it seemed as though he'd never tasted it before. How he had dodged conversation about his own schooling. How he didn't have a car to get around, yet he was able to meet me at the art gallery every day after school. How he had said that we were going to his farm by an unconventional path.

My breath came out quick and fast. It was all too much to take in. I turned on my heels and started running back into the pine forest towards the tree arch.

"Evelyn! Evelyn, wait! Where are you going?"

I went straight through the tree arch. The Hidden Grove reappeared so quickly that I stumbled into the tree that suddenly sprang up in front of me. I scrambled to my feet and ran back through the tree arch the way I'd come. The Hidden Grove disappeared behind me. I went back in and they reappeared. I doubled back around the side and went through the arch entrance again, standing just over the threshold. Nothing happened; there stood the perfect rows of vast trees, as before.

William ran toward me, halting at my side. I rounded on him.

"How?"

I jabbed my finger out at the perfect rows of trees.

"You really were raised here?"

"If you mean I raised myself, then yes."

"You really don't have any parents?"

"They are out there somewhere. I was abandoned here as a child." He nodded his head back at the clearing.

"Abandoned?"

Jaw tight, he nodded. "I came to terms with it a long time ago," he said.

Tears welled in my eyes as my brain failed to keep up.

"How did you know to climb up a damn tall tree and you'd be on Earth? And if you were abandoned, how do you even know you're human? How the heck does a kid survive without parents anyway?"

I knew I sounded insensitive—brutish even—but the words sputtered out, quick and hot as the tears that wet my face.

"Why did you lie to me? Why didn't you tell me who you were? Where you came from?"

I backed away from him, out of the Hidden Grove and into some vegetation. A strange melodic tune began to play behind me. I wheeled around and found a mushroom as tall as me rebounding like a jack-in-the-box from my touch. The tune came from white holes on its surface, the rhythm in time with the mushroom's movement.

This couldn't be happening.

I ran into the Hidden Grove, straight past William, to the tree with the white lichen. I reached out and grasped at the tree, adding to my already raw and bark-covered hands. It felt real.

I hurried up the tree as quickly as my raw hands would let me, sending bark and lichen and leaves scattering in my wake, ignoring the precarious sway of the branches beneath my feet. At the height of the tree I stopped and stepped purposely across the space atop the trunk, but no lightning-bright light hit me. Frantically I paced back and forth across the centre of the trunk. My heart raced, my breath shooting in and out in panic.

An image of Earth raced around inside my head, the planet existing in the blackness of space. Could I truly be in an entirely different world? Home felt so far away.

What if I were trapped here forever? How would I get home?

William called up to me, his voice echoing through the grove. "Evelyn? Come down, Evelyn. I have so much to show you."

Home. Why would I want to go back there? The thought struck me so sharply that my crying ceased. This was what William had been trying to tell me—no school, no Tiffany, no Cameron, and certainly no confrontations with my father. None of them could hurt me here.

I shuffled to the edge of the trunk on hands and knees and peered over the edge. Whatever I decided, for now I had to climb back down. I slipped down onto the first branch. The tree swayed and shuddered with my every movement, but branch by branch I neared the ground. I shared a collective sigh of relief with William when I looked below and could see his face again. He pulled me down into his arms from the lowermost branch.

I caressed his face in my hands. It felt real.

"I—I just don't understand. I can't believe it."

"I know. It is a lot to take in."

"If this is really real, how didn't I know about it?"

William slipped from my fingers' touch and turned about, looking up at the trees surrounding us.

"Every tree of the Hidden Grove leads to another land. This one just happens to lead to Purlieu. But all the people of all the lands originally came from Earth. It is just a well-kept secret. How many would think, like you said, to climb a damn tall tree, anyway?" he said.

He smiled cheekily. I nodded slowly.

"I believe it is desperation that drives people to such lengths."

I cleared my throat.

"William, where did the portal of light go?"

His smile changed to a grin.

"This tree leads to Purlieu. If you are already in Purlieu, it goes nowhere."

I took a breath, willing myself to remain calm. "I'm sorry I asked, and sorry for freaking out on you. But if I have no way to return home, I'm trapped the same as if I were back home with my father."

'Come, Evelyn. I will show you how to return, if you so wish.' William began to walk away, waving for me to follow. A few rows over to the left, he stopped. He took my hand and placed it on the tree before us. It was younger than any of the trees surrounding it, with new growth and bright green leaves. Old Man's Beard hung sporadically from its branches. He stroked the stubble of his own beard.

"This is the tree back to your world, back to Earth. No matter which world you are in, this tree will always lead you back to the same place."

I gripped at the tree, willing myself to remember its every facet. Not that I would need to remember it anytime soon.

"But Evelyn, you do not have to go back there. I have food, a hot shower, everything you could possibly need. No one will bother you here because I am the only one who lives in Purlieu. You can stay as long as you like and return home whenever you want, but none of your troubles will reach you here." He paused. "Please, will you stay with me awhile?"

Knowing there was a way home was enough for me. Still gazing up at the tree to Earth, I nodded. William wiped away the tears streaked on my face and took me in his arms.

"So, all these trees really lead to other worlds?"

I felt William nod as his chin touched my hair. Over his shoulder, I gazed at the endless rows.

How could there be so many?

William led me back through the tree arch, making a point to jostle the group of man-size mushrooms as we passed. A shiver ran up my spine at the sight of them rocking back and forth, but as they emitted their serene, childish pipe tune, I couldn't decide if they were freaky or cute.

We entered the clearing once more, the orchard to our left, barns to our right and crop fields ahead. William approached the corn crop and started inspecting the sheaves of corn. He pulled off a kernel and nibbled on it, nodding to himself. He looked at the mountains in the distance. I followed his gaze.

"The rain is coming." The sky was clear and the sun too hot and bright to look at. "We must harvest before it comes."

"Why?"

He pulled me through a narrow row of the field. The sound of dry corn sheaves slapping together filled my ears. His hand tugged at the dry hair protruding from the corn sheaves.

"See—they are all dry. They are ready for harvest. If it storms, the crop will be ruined."

He led me through to the other side of the field and into the open plain of the clearing. A crisp breeze met my skin. I wrapped my arms around myself.

An animal came bounding in our direction. A fox, bright red and limber. My heart quickened in panic and I made to turn back into the cornfield for cover, but it was too late. The creature circled round and round us, its tongue hanging from its mouth. It jumped up at me with its front paws. I screamed.

"Evelyn! Evelyn, it is okay. He is harmless."

William held me by the arms, trying to calm me, but all I wanted to do was run. He knelt down and the fox sprang into his arms, licking at his face like a dog. William ruffled up his fur and sank to the ground, the fox nuzzling into him playfully. "This is Bodie."

William rolled onto one knee and pulled at my hand, forcing it open in front of the fox's nose. I struggled against him in protest. Bodie sniffed my hand with enthusiasm, leaving a trail of cold wetness behind. He opened his jaws and licked at every dry patch of my hand. I scrunched up my nose and laughed nervously. William took me by the wrist and showed me how to pet the fox behind its ears. Tongue sticking out and panting, Bodie closed his eyes in contentment. The white patch across his chest was soft and fluffy, a stark contrast to the striking orange-red surrounding. Puffing out his chest, Bodie flicked and tucked his bushy tail around beside him, looking almost regal. He had such clean fur for a wild animal. This fox was clearly not wild.

"Come. I have so much to show you still," William

said.

He took me by my wet hand and led me towards the enclosed barns. Bodie followed along behind like a loyal dog. When he saw where we were headed, he dashed ahead, tongue wagging, pacing back and forth in front of the wooden gate of the enclosure.

William unlatched the gate and brought me inside the animal yard, leaving the fox outside. There were four individual barns lined up side by side in the yard, followed by an open space that carried on into the distance and down a vale leading to the mountains. Goats and ducks roamed along the wooden fence line that surrounded the yard. I had to dodge animal droppings and ducks alike as we drew close to the first barn. It had its own little enclosure out the front with a water bath and ramp that led up into the barn.

"The ducks live here." He leant on the woodwork and crossed his arms with a smug grin on his face. "I built it myself."

"Oh yeah?" It was pretty impressive. I marvelled at the handiwork. How could he have survived so long by himself? Didn't he get lonely?

"Yes. It took me the best part of a summer to build all four."

I surveyed the little barn, a miniature replica of its neighbours. The timber was stacked horizontally to eye level, with a hay roof that overhung the sides. There were no windows.

"I drew up the designs. Then I cut down the trees, dried them, broke the wood and constructed the barns. The most difficult part was calculating the ramp angle."

I stooped to peer inside the dark interior. William's voice became distant and muffled as he rattled on about the ramp angle. My eyes adjusted to the light, focusing on the wooden floorboards that were scattered in a mess of hay and mud down the middle aisle. Nesting boxes lined the walls.

"At first I thought I would need to apply trigonometry, but then I realised that if I only levelled out the ground—"

Between William's muffled calculations, a high-pitched distressed chirping cut through.

"William, be quiet."

"Excuse me?"

"Be quiet."

He huffed but remained silent. The chirping was coming from the back corner of the barn. I clambered inside towards the sound. My head collided with something solid and I fell to the floor with a thud, wet hay soaking through my school dress. I held my hands to my head to dull the pain as I looked up. There were rafters running along the ceiling of the barn with old bird nests nestled atop. The chirping stopped.

"Are you okay?"

"Shush."

I got on my hands and knees, the floorboards groaning beneath my weight. The chirping continued. It was coming from a small orange blur in the corner of the barn beneath one of the rafters. A little robin with musk-brown wings and a brilliant orange chest was thrashing about in distress. Its claw was hooked awkwardly between two of the floorboards.

"Oh, you poor thing."

I brushed the muck from my hands and reached towards the robin, but it flapped its wings wildly in protest. As my hand neared it, a stab of pain shot up my arm. The robin had pecked me with its beak. I pulled away, nursing my hand, watching a dribble of blood trickle across my skin. I screwed up my face in frustration.

"Hey—I'm just trying to help."

I grabbed a piece of straw and waved it off to the side in an attempt to distract the bird whilst my other hand edged towards it once more. It watched the moving straw cautiously. Just as I was about to grip my forefinger and thumb around its claw, it thrashed about even more frantically than before, chirping and pecking at me. I withdrew my injured hand for a second time and looked about the barn for something that could help. Sticking out of one of the nesting boxes was a long, sturdy twig. I pried it free and slowly moved nearer to the robin. Using the twig as a wedge between the two offending floorboards, I could just reach the robin. It flapped its wings and poked at the twig until, as the twig snapped, the robin became airborne, free from the hold of the floorboards. It plummeted into one of the nesting boxes, bouncing off the surface. It steadied and threw itself into the air, flapping its wings awkwardly.

I couldn't tell if it had never flown before or if it was injured. It flew up into the nest in the rafters, directly above where it had been stuck, and poked around in the nest for a few moments. It gave a small forsaken chirp before hopping up to the rafters' edge to eye me. The robin took to the air once more, clumsily flying out the open door, almost colliding with the wall on the way out.

I crawled out of the barn backwards and looked up just in time to see the robin flying off across the clearing until it was just a speck in the sky.

"You are a mess," William said.

I raised my eyes. "So flattering."

"Come on, let us get you cleaned up."

William slid his hand into mine and we continued to tread carefully through the yard to avoid manure and stray animals underfoot. We passed the next barn, a two-storey structure.

"This is the goat barn." He pointed ahead at the two remaining barns. "That one is for the cows and that for the pigs."

Sure enough, as we neared the next barn, a lone cow stood in the front yard, her calf suckling from her udder. In front of the pig barn, a sow, hog, and piglet were lounging in a muddy pool. The two barns were an odd pair side by side, not because of the animals that were housed inside them, nor their differing needs, but because they were worlds apart in design and age. The cow barn was rickety with old, greying timber. It had a high-pointed, tiled roof, unlike its neighbours with their hay-packed low angle counterparts.

"You made these, all by yourself?"

William rubbed at his jaw. "The duck barn is my crowning glory."

The piglet shook off the excess water and mud and trotted towards us, ducking easily beneath the railing of the enclosure. It sniffed at our shoes and rubbed mud against the skin of my ankle.

"Shoo, you." William waved him away and tugged my hand for us to continue walking down the yard, following the fence line.

"What was his name?"

William scoffed. "Why would it have a name?"

"Why not?"

"I tend not to give names to what will become dinner."

My stomach flipped over. "Wait—did you say earlier you're the only one who lives here?"

"Yes."

"This entire world and you're the only one?"

The image of Earth returned to my mind. I couldn't fathom it—an entire planet with only one inhabitant. It couldn't be. It wasn't possible.

"I am the only one, but I hope that it will not always be this way." He squeezed my hand.

"But how can you be sure? Have you travelled through this whole world? Maybe you're the only one here, on the farm, in this region, but there have to be others elsewhere."

"If there were others, I would know."

"How?"

He rubbed at his jaw once more. "Well, there is only one Hidden Grove in each world, so if there were more people, they would have lived as close to it as possible."

"But what if they didn't want to be close to the Hidden Grove, close to access to the other worlds?"

"They would be fools not to."

We reached the end of the yard, the final side of the fence blocking our path. William swung his body over and invited me to do the same. I ducked between the middle two railings and we continued down the last stretch of the clearing to a river that ran through the forest of trees.

The river was almost too wide to cross and utterly untameable, jutting with rocks, the water rushing over itself to get downstream. We trod carefully onto the basalt perimeters of the river, where it was shallow. I slipped quickly from my school shoes and socks and dipped my feet into the crisp, cool mountain water. It bubbled over my skin, massaging and tickling me. I crouched and let it wash over my hands, the blood and dirt and bark dissolving with the pull of the current.

William walked straight into the shallows and kept walking until it was up to his hips. He dipped his whole body, disappearing for a moment, and resurfacing, throwing his wet, shaggy hair from his face. The sun refracted off the droplets of water on his body. My stomach turned over.

I followed him into the water, the chill sending goosebumps across my body. He took me by my strong hand and rubbed his thumbs across the back, dislodging the last bits of debris. His hands travelled up to my face, wiping as he went. A new fit of goosebumps ran over me. He leaned in and his wet lips crushed against mine. He pulled me into his body, locking his legs around me, and continued to massage my lips. They tingled and swelled at his touch.

A screeching echoed across the clearing. I pulled away from William and whipped around but I couldn't see where it had come from.

"What was that?"

He wiped dripping water from his face and shrugged

his shoulders.

"Oh, just a bird."

It was louder than any bird I'd ever heard.

Sitting amongst the trees of the apple orchard, drying in the midday sun with a belly full of fresh fruit, the loud screech echoed across the clearing again. I twisted around, searching for the bird. Could it be supersized, just like the musical mushrooms?

The fox lazing across William's lap didn't even flinch.

"Why are you so jumpy?" William asked.

Oh, only because I travelled through a portal this morning to a whole other world. "I'm not," I said.

He eyed me. "How about a tour of the cottage?"

We gathered up our picnic and wandered through the dappled light of the orchard toward the centre of the clearing, where stood the lone tree the size of a house. We rounded the side until there, carved into the wood, was a door. William turned the knob and pulled it open. The light of the day cast down upon the inside of the tree, carved out to resemble a lighthouse. A staircase immediately to the right wound up the inner wall of the trunk. William entered before me and started lighting oil lamps that were placed throughout the ground floor, which was designated as a sitting room.

"This is the parlour," he said.

A pair of gold-rimmed, green velvet day beds sat opposite one another in the centre of the room, with a coffee table between them. A tasseled Persian rug with eddies of jagged burgundy, cream, and black shapes covered the floor. My eyes did not dwell for long on the furniture, for the walls of the room were covered in paintings. There was hardly a free space on its wooden walls to be seen, for the paintings hung in perfect rows vertically and horizontally across the curved insides of the tree cottage. I edged inside, drawn by the paintings. Some were done in acrylic paint and others in charcoal. Some were full of whimsy, bright colours, and joyfulness while others were dark, angry and gloomy. As I turned about the room, from sun-kissed landscapes my eyes fell upon windswept snowy mountains, then to flower-filled fields and back again to shades of bright yellow and burnt orange. The room was a visual depiction of the seasons.

I ended my circle of the room at the staircase where William was waiting for me. He reached out for my good hand and we made our way upstairs. Lost for words, I looked back upon the parlour. There by the door, hidden amongst the hats hanging from it, was the skull of an animal. It looked uncannily like the Pterodactyl skeleton at the museum next to the library.

On the first landing was the washroom, a dainty, lacy affair. The footed bathtub doubled as a shower. Besides the vanity, the room was empty and clean.

The larder on the next floor above was filled with food supplies dried fruits, jars of preserves, and drying spices. There were metal bins, filled sacks, and shelves lined with containers. A preparation bench ran across the wall of the room just below the windows. Neat stacks of boxes containing old tools and sewing supplies sat off to one side. I fingered through the contents of one of the boxes, finding empty sacks and strange metal contraptions.

"What's this one?" I held up an oblong-shaped metal loop with handles on both ends and a circle in the centre.

"A corn kernel cutter."

I tried to mimic cutting corn with it but looked at William in confusion.

"You place the corn cob down the centre circle and it slices the kernels off."

"Oh."

We continued up the neverending stairs that followed the inside of the tree up the trunk. The walls were smooth, the stairs at perfect right angles. We reached the kitchen, my breath slightly faster. The kitchen bench divided the room in half, kitchen on one side, dining room on the other. Like the furniture of the floors below, the kitchen's every object was carved from wood: the fireplace hearth, the countertops and chairs, crockery and cutlery, and even the sink.

"You cook?" I asked.

"Of course I do."

"We'll see."

He nudged me playfully.

"If you were abandoned here, how did you learn to cook? How did you build this cottage? Make all these things?"

I ran my finger across the bench top and stopped to survey a spoon. The curve of the mouthpiece was smooth like a river stone from years of wear and tear. Just like the walls of the cottage.

"I am well read."

He smiled as though he were waiting for an invitation to elaborate. I gave him a face. He chuckled.

"To make a spoon, such as this," William began.

He reached for the spoon and placed it on top of his nose, balancing it like a see-saw with arms spread wide either side.

"You must first chop down a tree and let it dry out for, perhaps, twelve months. Then it is only a matter of chopping it to the approximate size and carving it to shape. Then there is the process of fashioning a saw and chisels. Really though, when you break it down, it only takes a few short hours to make a spoon. Make a piece a day and, in a week, you have a full set to use at breakfast, lunch, and dinner."

"One bite at a time."

"I beg your pardon?" The spoon dropped from his nose and clattered against the kitchen counter.

My stomach curdled as I remembered my father's words. I was ten and he'd burnt the steak we were having for dinner. Mum was on my right, Dad on my left, at our sunny yellow kitchen table. I was on the verge of a tantrum. I hadn't wanted to eat the horrid, dry meat.

"How do you eat an elephant?" he'd asked.

My heart had constricted at the thought of eating an innocent elephant. I looked to mum for reassurance. She only smiled quietly to herself and continued eating as though it were the best food she'd ever tasted.

"One bite at a time, one bite at a time, Evelyn!"

I smiled at the memory but caught myself just in time. I was meant to be mad at my father. I *was* mad at him. My hand reached instinctively to the locket hanging from my neck. William's eyes shifted to the locket. I shrugged.

"Nothing. Sorry. It was just something my father used to say."

We continued up the stairs. I held my hands against the walls for support. We were climbing high up the trunk of the tree now. How much time did William have on his hands to construct this cottage so perfectly? It would have taken weeks, years to do all this work. He must have been incredibly lonely to throw himself into his work so entirely, to have no one else in the world to turn to for company or companionship.

It was no wonder he'd come to Earth.

"So, if all those trees in the Hidden Grove lead to other worlds, and you've already been to Earth, where else have you gone? What have you seen?"

"I only ever explore far enough that I can journey back to tend the farm the same day. It requires constant care and attention."

"Okay, but where else have you been?"

"I have seen a few other worlds, enough to know that I prefer Purlieu. When I learned that Earth was the first world, I stopped looking elsewhere for my answers."

"Earth was the first world?"

"Remember, all the people of the other worlds derived from Earth."

Heat crept up my neck. I felt stupid for forgetting he'd

said that already but it was a lot to take in such a short space of time.

"What kind of answers?" I continued on.

"To where I came from—who my parents are."

I nodded.

"Oh. So why did you keep going back to Earth, then?"

William stopped at the next landing and turned to face me, a cheeky smile spreading wide across his face.

"Your world was calling to me. You were calling to me."

The heat climbed up my neck and rushed to my cheeks. Before I could gather my lost breath from trudging the stairs, his lips crushed mine again. He pulled away and I sucked air into my aching lungs.

"I love you," William said.

The air whooshed out of me as quickly as it had entered. My heart thudded and skipped a beat. He'd never said those words before.

"I—I love you too, William."

He smiled again, his shoulders relaxing. He took me by the hand and opened the door behind him. "This is the boudoir. I prepared it for you, in case you ever came to Purlieu. You can stay as long as you want."

Relief washed over me at the thought of having somewhere private—somewhere entirely mine to hide away in while I sorted out my life. I smiled inside. At least one part of my life was okay. More than okay. William was such a blessing.

The thought dissipated as a pang of guilt hit me in the gut. I was doing the exact opposite of what my father wanted—effectively dropping out of school to live with my boyfriend. I waved away the thought. All I needed was time away from him, just for a while. William was offering a safe place for me to stay, with no obligations.

I crossed the threshold of the room and approached the centre where a four-poster bed with white breathy chiffon hung from the crown. Creeping vines were carved into the wooden poles and across the bedhead. The velveteen coverlet shone royal purple and gold. Behind the bed was one large window covered over with matching purple curtains. William walked past the freestanding wrought-iron mirror by the door to the towering wardrobe on the side.

He opened its doors. An array of muted cloth—dresses, blouses, coats—burst out of the confines of the wardrobe. He continued on to the dresser and opened the top drawer.

"Please do help yourself. I think I have thought of everything you may need."

He waved for me to join him. I flicked through the wardrobe, an abundance of lace and flowers and ribbon: a mixture of English garden party and vintage couture. Below the clothes was a neat row of shoes, including a healthy choice of heeled low-cut leather boots.

William looked intently into the wardrobe and tugged on a delicate periwinkle evening gown. "I would recommend the cream and blue hues. They would suit you best," he said.

"Okay."

He nodded and returned it to the wardrobe. "The items of this room belong to you now. I want you to wear them, instead of that dastardly tartan pinafore."

He dipped his head towards my school dress.

A gale rushed through the leaves of the cottage and the tree swayed slightly. William walked over to the window and peered beyond the curtains through the glass.

"The harvest must happen before the storm comes."

He returned to the dresser and opened the top drawer. Amongst the socks and pantyhose, he pulled out a latched wooden box the size of my hand.

"For your locket. For safekeeping, just in case."

I touched my mother's gold necklace, warmed by the heat of my skin. I didn't want to part with it. He gazed at it intently, as though it were a prize.

"The weather outside—I would hate for it to ruin something so priceless," he said.

He was right. I unlatched the necklace and placed it carefully on the velvet insert of the box. William snapped it shut and put it back inside the drawer. From the base of the wardrobe he pulled out another box. It was long and thin with a leather strap across the top held in place by brass studs. He slid the lid off and revealed an array of paintbrushes. My jaw dropped open. They were beautiful. I let the soft animal hair slip luxuriously between my fingers.

"I want you to paint the harvest."

"Really? Why?"

He ran his finger down my cheek. "Because you are an incredible artist."

Heat flooded my cheeks. With William by my side, encouraging me in my art, I would be unstoppable.

Unlike my father.

The bitterness flashed through me, making my spittle sour.

Outside on the grass by the cornfield, William pulled on a glove and set a large cloth on the ground. He frowned in concentration, taking a cob of corn in hand. With a quick flick of his wrist it broke free. He tossed it behind him onto the cloth. He moved onto the next stalk.

I watched closely from my place in the grass, blank canvas in hand.

Sweat gathered on his brow despite the cool breeze. I watched the repetitious movement of his hand, the bright yellow freshness of the corn lying in a pile on the cloth, and the light of the sky waning as the darkness of the storm neared. It was beautiful, but how could I capture all of that in one painting?

Perhaps I could focus on the motion of how swiftly William worked, racing against the oncoming rain. What was most interesting about a race? The finish line, the ending, the result? But the journey is what makes the result significant. Without the journey, there would be no ending.

What was his journey?

He was well practised. He clearly knew this journey well. It would have begun with the turning of the soil and planting the seeds. The shoots would have broken free of the ground and then groaned in anguish to reach the sun.

"Anguish to reach the sun," I repeated aloud.

What made the harvest so beautiful was this parallel to human life and to my own anguish. Not that I really knew what I was reaching towards.

I lay my first stroke: a vibrant yellow to portray the freshness of the corn, contrasted with a pale brown for the brittle, sun-damaged sheaf. Layer upon layer I worked, creating depth and life.

The darkness above grew. The moisture in the air caused the colour on my palette to mix in an interesting way. It added to the beautiful mess of it. I used it to my advantage, showing the motion of the corn mid-flight to the cloth on the ground.

It had been a long time since I'd painted so freely, though I'd often tried. Probably not since Mum had pruned back the rose bush at the edge of the patio. I had gazed down upon her, the delicate petals being my focus. I chose to leave the perspiration forming on her back out of the painting. It detracted from her elegance and poise.

I watched patches of perspiration form on William's shirt. I didn't want to leave it out this time. It was this anguish, this toil that I wanted to capture.

Thunder rumbled in the distance and the clouds cast dullness over our work. A storm was definitely starting to brew. I pressed on—it was a race now.

The corn stalks looked bare without the cob. The pile on the ground grew higher, cobs tumbling as fresh ones landed on the heap. William removed the glove, tossing it to the ground, and untucked his shirt, using it to wipe his face free of sweat. Judging by the dark skin at his navel, it looked like he had spent many hours in the beating sun. He caught me looking, so I hastily returned to finishing the painting. He raised an eyebrow in curiosity and edged towards the canvas, reaching for it. I held it close, careful not to stain my school dress with wet paint.

"It's not finished yet."

"You are running out of time."

A bird-like screeching filled my ears, coming from behind. I turned around and looked to the sky, my eyes falling upon the source of the bewildering sound. Several winged animals were fleeing the oncoming storm. Their beaks and heads appeared reptilian but their bodies were covered in bright green and red feathers that shone like metal as the lightning flashed. I craned my neck to follow them as they flew past, each wing spanning at least the length of a dining table—it was hard to tell from a distance.

Thunder rumbled again and the rain swiftly followed, rushing down upon us. I flipped the canvas over to protect it from the onslaught and threw the paintbrushes and uncapped paint tubes back into the wooden paintbox. I jostled the lid of the box, coaxing it to slip smoothly closed. Tucking it under my arm, I held the wire backing of the canvas while William grabbed the four corners of the cloth and hauled the cobs over his back. He reached for my hand and we sprinted towards the cottage, already drenched through from the rain. My hair was slicked against the skin of my neck and face, my socks sloshing in my shoes.

The storm ran wild above our heads. Cracks of thunder vibrated through my body. It had become dark all too fast and I could barely make out where we were going. I slipped in my shoes and felt William's steady hand grip tighter around mine. Another crack of thunder roared, lightning illuminating the way. The cottage was before us now.

William let go of my hand and rattled hastily at the

doorknob. The door flew back, smashing against the trunk of the tree, the wind so strong my feet slid across the grass. We dove into the cottage and William threw the cobs to the floor, turning to contend with the crashing door. He pulled it shut and the wailing storm became muffled. The tree groaned under the strain of the wind, rocking and swaying. William lit the lamp by the door, light falling on the animal skull. I wheeled on William, between short breaths.

"What was that? Where are we?" I pointed to the skull. "What year is it?"

William raised his hands and leaned back in defence. "We are in Purlieu."

"But when?"

"I do not know."

"What do you mean, you don't know?"

"How am I supposed to know? There was no one to tell me what year I was born. For all I know, it could be year twenty or twenty-five or thirty! I did not even know what a year was for the longest time."

"But there are dinosaurs." The word sounded clunky. How could there be dinosaurs?

"I have wondered about that too. Because they are extinct on Earth, correct?"

The lamplight cast shadows on the wall from the animal skull. I shuddered.

"My theory is that they came through the portal into Purlieu accidentally, many, many years ago, before they were wiped out on Earth."

My body started to shake. I leaned against the creaking trunk of the cottage for stability. My breath came out short and fast.

"They are perfectly harmless, Evelyn. You have nothing to worry about."

"But they're dinosaurs." My voice cracked.

"They eat fish and eggs, like scavengers. They are essentially just large birds."

I crouched on the ground and held myself tightly, letting the paintbox and canvas drop noisily beside me. William dashed up the stairs.

I was no longer on Earth.

I rocked back and forth.

I was far away from my father, from Tiffany, from Cameron, from school.

I slumped against the wall and looked up at the paintings that covered the walls. They were scattered with dull light, the lamp not strong enough to illuminate their contents.

I looked back over at the Pterodactyl skull.

No one could tell me what to do, here. I didn't need money to travel in Purlieu, to explore and paint foreign and wondrous things.

A smile spread across my face and my forehead relaxed. I let out a small laugh.

No one on Earth could ever imagine the things that I would paint.

My father had been wrong. I didn't need an art degree to say I was an artist. I would prove him wrong.

William returned and wrapped a towel around my shoulders. I shrugged it off and grabbed the oil lamp, moving to take a closer look at the paintings hanging on the wall. Water dripping from my body was the only sound to combat the storm outside.

Before the cluster of spring paintings, I saw the upside-down waterfall, a musical mushroom, a Pterodactyl.

I would be famous.

6

I STOOD AT the window of the boudoir watching the rain pitter-patter, the morning sun nowhere to be seen. The storm had not yet passed. Guilt ran through me at the thought that I had not gone home last night. Would my father have wondered where I was? He would have panicked, no doubt—called Tiffany and the school. How much trouble would I be in when I returned?

William came into the room and wrapped his arms around me from behind, resting his chin on the neckline of my white cotton nightdress.

"How did you sleep?" he asked.

"The same as usual."

I had woken in a cold sweat; my mother's pale, gashed body lying limp in the morgue was branded across my mind. Yet another nightmare to add to the list.

"It is still raining," he said.

I nodded.

"There will be no going out today."

I could easily dash through the rain to the Hidden Grove. It wouldn't be that hard to get back to school, to explain my absence.

"We can spend the day inside painting," he said.

My back tensed up at William making such a decision without even asking what I wanted, and assuming I would stay. I opened my mouth to protest but remembered how much I'd enjoyed painting the previous day. That peace and sense of purpose I had not felt in so long; it was exactly the way I wanted to spend my day.

"Well, I'd better get ready for the day, then," I said.

I slipped from his arms and made for the dresser, opening the sock drawer. The small wooden jewellery box was not sitting on top. I felt around for the jagged edge of the box amongst the soft fabric, but found nothing. Frantic, I hauled the contents from the drawer.

"What is wrong?"

William was by my side.

"The locket. Where is it?"

I had watched William put it back in the drawer with my own eyes. William held my hands to steady their search.

"I took it out. I put it away for safekeeping," he said.

"But I want to wear it."

"There are thieves that have been known to visit through the Hidden Grove."

I threw his hands away from mine and stepped back. "Thieves? You said I would be safe here, William."

From the fox to the dinosaurs and now thieves, perhaps I would be better off back home?

"Evelyn, Evelyn. Relax. I love you. I will protect you."

I pictured the Hidden Grove, just on the other side of the clearing, a stone's throw away.

"But someone, anyone, can just waltz into Purlieu from any of the other worlds? They're right there at our doorstep, William. How am I supposed to relax?"

"Yes, it is possible, but it is not something that happens often. There are very few who dare to leave the comfort of their home worlds to travel. Out of all the worlds to choose from, what would one gain by coming to Purlieu?"

He was right. There were a lot of trees in the Hidden

Grove to choose from.

"But once you found out that Earth was the original world, why did you stay in Purlieu? Wouldn't it be safer to leave?"

"Evelyn, I have seen your world. Government, war, money. Why would I ever want to live amongst it when I can live freely in Purlieu? You will always be safe here so long as you are by my side."

He took me in his arms and held me close. "I love you."

"I love you, too."

"You have nothing to worry about. Please, relax and enjoy yourself, yes?"

I nodded into his chest.

After breakfast, William took me up past my boudoir to the highest landing.

Was it his bedroom?

He opened the door to reveal another short flight of stairs. Crossing the threshold of the landing, I stopped abruptly before the three steps up into the room. All four walls were made of glass. The ceiling too. It was like a giant had taken a greenhouse and placed it amongst the canopy of the tree. Beyond the glass, the branches of the cottage swayed and rustled with the wind. The sky above was gloomy, drizzling down onto the ceiling. Each droplet that connected with the glass roof dispersed into a quick circle before trickling down the walls of the room.

Like iron drawn to a magnet, I took the three steps up into the room and closed my open mouth. Through the rivulets of water, the swaying branches and the raindrops descending upon the clearing, I could just make out the horizon in every direction. The forest that concealed the Hidden Grove surrounded the clearing entirely, stretching on as far as I could see on three sides. On the final side, the river wound back and forth all the way until it fed through the valley. Its course led between the mountains, which seemed less towering from this height.

My nose was pressed up against the glass, staring out until my breath fogged up the view. I stepped back and looked directly down on the farm. We were really high up, eight storeys, if I'd counted correctly. I crouched and held onto the floor, feeling the sway of the tree.

"At certain times of the year, on a good night, you can see the craters of the dwarf planet." William nodded towards the telescope and armchair that sat in the centre of the room. The rest of the room was bare.

"It is a conservatory first and foremost but sometimes I like to come here to paint."

"This room—this cottage—is incredible. How did you make it?"

"I did not. I cannot recall a time in my life when it did not exist. It must have been someone before me. I wish I knew."

I pressed my lips together grimly. It must be so hard to have all these unanswered questions about where he had come from.

He shook his head. "Anyway, shall we?"

I crawled to the centre of the room and nestled into the armchair. It was high-backed and winged. It reminded me of the velvet chair in Miss Daniels' office back at school, except it felt safe, unlike the velvet prison.

William and I quietly set to work on our respective paintings. I wanted to catch the depth of field of the glass wall, the branches beyond, and the horizon beyond that.

I focused my attention on the branches, turning the chair to find the best angle. To my left, shadows cast amongst the canopy. I edged closer for a better look, searching for detail in the shadow. Large, hunched silhouettes took shape. Three of them. The Pterodactyls' wings were collapsed against their bodies, beaks nuzzled beneath. Their feathers were slicked down, no longer metallic and shining but deep shades of burgundy and emerald, water dripping off them. Huddled into themselves, they were each the size of a small car. My breath fogged up the glass again.

My heart quickened, being so close to them. I grabbed my canvas and began to paint, bringing one of the oil lamps over to cast light on my work and further illuminate the bodies of the great birds. No one would ever believe that these were real.

The better my eyesight adjusted to the light, scrutinising the detail, the more pronounced the wet bark of the tree became; the dripping leaves; the subtle shine of the Pterodactyls' feathers. Amongst the branches nearest the conservatory, a dot of orange caught my eye. I peered closer. Perched in a small, scraggly nest was a robin, its bright orange chest rising and falling quickly. Could it be the same that I had set free the previous day?

Bang. Bang. Bang.

I jumped. The robin took flight. Someone or something was banging on the door downstairs. William looked concerned and dashed from the room. His footsteps thudded rhythmically down the stairs until they became distant soft patters like the rain. Muffled voices floated up the stairs. The front door slammed shut.

I pressed my nose against the glass wall of the conservatory and peered down below once more. Through the branches of the tree, a man with platinum hair and stark white skin that reminded me of my mother's was backing away from the cottage. The sight of him made me shiver.

He was wearing a soiled yellow jumpsuit, like something from a prison. It was drenched from the rain, making the fabric and stains more pronounced. His body was shivering, but whether it was from fear or cold I could not tell.

William moved into sight below. He was angry, hostile, pointing and waving his arms in an attempt to send the stranger away.

I couldn't hear what they were saying but the stranger was pleading with William. That I was sure of. His hands were in front of him, palms showing, a sign of sincerity and truth, so my father had taught me.

My breath had fogged up the glass once more. I looked about the room for a window but the glass walls looked entirely impenetrable. In the corner nearest me, a brass lever jutted out from the base of the glass. I pushed down upon it but it wouldn't budge. I pushed again and it groaned in protest from disuse. I put my bodyweight onto it and, with a drawn-out screech that sent a shudder down my spine, the lever moved down towards the floor. The glass wall nearest me tilted a few centimetres inwards. At the noise of the brass screeching, a loud squawk erupted from the branches beyond. The Pterodactyls flapped their wings and took flight, the branches springing back from beneath them and sending a rocking sway through the cottage. The rain drilled down on the glass, splashing through to the inside of the conservatory, wetting my feet.

At the sudden squawking and flight of the Pterodactyls, the stranger stopped his pleading long enough to look up. Even from eight storeys above I could see his piercing blue eyes and the glint of a gold chain around his neck. He held my gaze for a moment. He looked not much older than twenty. William never stopped staring at the stranger.

"I can force you to leave," William said.

The stranger looked back at William. "No, you can't," he said with a thick accent that could have been German or maybe Icelandic.

"You think that gold chain will stop me?" William asked.

The rain continued to pound down upon the clearing.

"Bodie!" William yelled. The fox was by William's side in an instant, his fur slick against his body. The stranger took a step back, his hands up again in defence.

"Bodie, attack," William said.

The fox snarled and pounced forwards. The stranger

turned and ran for the Hidden Grove, Bodie nipping at his heels. They passed under the cover of the forest but I heard no cry of pain.

When William entered the room a few minutes later, my heart was beating fast, my skin prickling with heat, my cheeks flushed. He wiped away at the water that dripped from his face.

"I told you there were thieves," he said.

"What did he want?"

The stranger had looked, to me, to be seeking refuge. "What all thieves want: what does not belong to them."

"He looked homeless."

"He probably was."

"Couldn't we have given him shelter for the night or some food or a warm shower?"

William raised his eyebrows and wiped the water from his face. "He is a thief, Evelyn. Why would we welcome him into our home?"

He didn't look like a thief to me. He looked like a desperate man in need. I couldn't help but feel as though William was withholding something from me. Just like my father had two nights ago when he wanted to sell Mum's things.

William sighed in frustration. "You are letting all the rain in."

He dripped water across the floor of the conservatory as he traipsed over to the brass lever and pulled it up in one swift movement, closing the glass wall.

It was bad enough that my own father would lie to me, but now my boyfriend too? I thought he loved me. I thought he cared enough to tell me everything. But if the last twenty-four hours were anything to go by, William was a very prolific and skilled liar. I hadn't seen that one coming.

"I need a shower." He left the room, the door swinging shut behind him. With the Pterodactyls and the robin and the stranger gone, loneliness washed over me and I felt supremely far from home.

If only Tiffany were here. But Tiffany was not here. Even if she was, she would not be talking to me. She'd made it very clear that she wanted nothing else to do with me. William was the only one left in my life to talk to, but I could hardly discuss my boy troubles with the boy who was causing me troubles.

I knelt down and grabbed the paints once more. My father's lying face flashed before my eyes. I put brush to canvas, remembering his cold, sad eyes. I saw the guests at my mother's funeral pass by one by one, shaking his hand, whispering condolences, dabbing tears from the corners of their eyes. They tried to be sincere, to share in even a fraction of our pain, to say helpful words. Yet my father had stood there, stiffly grunting to each, dismissing them.

How could he be so callous, so disrespectful to them, to the memory of my mother?

My brush hit hard at the canvas as his face took shape. His lips were downturned, his eyelids drooping.

I had stood by his side the entire time, forcing myself to hold the tears back, following his lead. But I wanted to cry. I so desperately needed to cry. The pain had been so unbearable that I just wanted to crumple in a heap under the weight of it, and for him to fall with me.

Instead, my mother's death was brushed under the carpet. He expected me to carry on as though nothing had happened, as though I was unaffected.

Heat bubbled under the surface of my skin. Sweat gathered on my brow as I remembered that day and how he had failed me. I needed him to show weakness. I needed him to turn to me and cry with me, to reach out and touch me. But instead, though we lived under the same roof, I'd never felt so far from him since that day.

How could he not be there for me when I needed him most? How could Tiffany just leave me like she did? How could William lie to me?

The paint went on thickly, my paintbrush digging and

scraping at the canvas as hot tears trickled down my face. I slapped down the staring eyes of the unfamiliar faces passing by as we stood at the entrance of the church. Those eyes, forever staring. They burned through my face as I evaded their gaze.

I pressed so hard that the metal holding the bristles scratched a chasm into the canvas. It fuelled my rage. I grabbed at the tubes of paint and squirted fire engine red onto the surface, scrabbling at it with my hands, rubbing it until every white patch was covered. A sob escaped me. I yelled. I picked up the canvas, banged it against the floor and threw it against the glass wall of the conservatory, to which it stuck.

My chest heaving, thick tears falling, I tried desperately to calm down.

In every one of those situations, I had failed to stand up for myself. No wonder my life was such a mess. Things needed to change. I needed to change.

I took a few deep breaths and gathered up the paints, placing them neatly into the wooden box. I went over to the canvas and pulled it away from the glass wall, its heavily painted surface dragging from the suction. I wiped away the paint left behind on the glass just as William re-entered the conservatory.

"Time to eat," he said.

His shaggy hair was now combed back, his flannel dry and tidy. He remained at the door, surveying me.

"What is it?" he asked. He was looking at the canvas in my hand.

"The day of my mother's funeral."

His forehead crinkled. "Oh. I thought you would be over that by now," he said.

My mouth dropped open. How could he be so insensitive? We'd been together for three months now, but the man he'd been two days ago seemed very different to the one before me now. Where had this all come from?

I tried to form the words to defend myself, but nothing

came. He pursed his lips and left the conservatory.

I turned his words over in my head. Was I over her death? It wasn't why I had painted her funeral. Or was it? Perhaps that was what this whole episode was about.

7

I T WAS EARLY afternoon of the next day when the rain finally stopped. The clouds gave way for warm sunshine and a cool breeze so I took my chance to hang my clothes out to dry. Once they were ready I could leave, maybe live out of my car for a few days, go to school and hope they hadn't noticed my absence. By then I hoped to feel better about returning to my father. As for William, I really didn't know what to think anymore. He had been the last person left in my life I could trust, but now? He was different, and I wasn't so sure I liked the side of him I'd seen since we arrived in Purlieu.

Waiting for the clothes, as William hung the corn up to dry in the larder, I wandered into the forest, away from the clearing. The smell of pine was overwhelming, intoxicating. It was so unlike the vegetation back home that I couldn't help but be mesmerised by it. Tall, thin pine trees rose high into the sky, the ground covered with their browning needles. Despite the occasional bramble and oversized mushroom, the forest floor was quite empty of vegetation. I could see off into the distance in all directions.

I didn't wander too far. Purlieu had foxes and

Pterodactyls. Who knew what else lurked, hidden between the strangled shadows of the forest? Paranoia washed over me and I turned full circle, unsure whether it was safer to have my back to the clearing or the depths of the forest. A glint of light caught the corner of my eye. I wheeled to the right. There it was again. Light, refracted from something in the shadows.

I hid behind the nearest tree, its pockmarked bark catching on the skin of my hands. I dared a glance out from behind the tree and peered off to where the light was coming from. It was deep inside the forest.

I moved from tree to tree, stopping often to peek out until I was close enough to see what lay ahead—the light glinting off the glass window of a small wood cabin.

What was a cabin doing in the middle of the woods?

I edged closer, a little less apprehensively, until it came into full view. It was the size of one room, with a pile of firewood leaning against it. It was constructed the same way as the oldest of the barns. The cabin looked empty, abandoned, but not unkempt.

I knocked gently on the door.

"Hello?"

I waited.

I knocked a little more intensely, the door latching open as I did.

"I hope you don't mind. I was just in the forest and I saw your cabin," I said.

I wasn't sure if I expected to find anyone inside. William had said that he was the only inhabitant of Purlieu but who's to say he wasn't lying about that too.

I pushed the door open and peered inside, but it was empty. I let out a breath. The inside of the cabin was bare—a single bed with no sheets, a table and chair, and two buckets by the door. I ventured inside for a closer look.

The table was worn and well-used. Scratch and scuff marks marred the surface. An ink stain had dripped across the left-hand side of it. The chair had a crack across the seat. There was no dust. I moved to the bed, which supported a modest, timeworn mattress. The walls were blank and there were no cupboards or drawers.

The cabin didn't make sense. It was clearly uninhabited yet cared for, but why?

I stuck my good hand between the crack where the mattress met its wooden bed frame, tracing along its four sides. Nothing. Not even crumbs or dirt or a stray button.

I sank onto my hands and knees and scanned the floor. There, beneath the headrest, wedged between the floorboards and the leg of the bed, was a piece of scrunched-up paper.

I wrestled with it until it came loose, then smoothed it out. It was two pieces of paper, pulled from a notebook and crumpled into one. I laid them out on the table side by side. The first depicted a pocket watch in charcoal sketches across the page. Alongside the sketches were calculations and a list of parts with names I didn't recognise. The second piece had an ink-scratched list of items in eloquent handwriting. It was so scripted and curled that the words themselves were hard to decipher. I spent a few moments going over the list.

- *Master of a land*
- *Sustainable living*
- *Modern lodgings*
- *Provide basic needs*

Was it William's list? Was this William's cabin? Or did it belong to a long-forgotten occupant, one that William did not even know existed? But surely he knew the cabin was here—how else would it remain so clean?

The notepaper was the type of unusual find that I had hoped to come across in my travels, after completing school. An item that would provoke new ways of looking at the world and give me an edge over other artists. I turned around and pulled my phone out, taking a photo of the cabin with its bare bed. I returned to the papers, poised to take a photo of each when footsteps approached the cabin from outside. I wheeled to face the door, stashing my phone and the nearest piece of paper in my pocket just as William entered the cabin.

His arms were laden with bed sheets and a pillowcase. Clearly he was shocked to see me.

"What are you doing in here, Evelyn?"

"I—I—I…"

He raised his eyebrows, waiting for an acceptable excuse.

"I was just curious, and bored."

He dumped the sheets on the bed. "It is not polite to snoop. What did your parents teach you?"

Heat flooded to my cheeks. I felt small, like a child being scolded. My father's face flashed through my mind—how he had yelled at me, how he had made me feel so stifled.

"What?" William asked.

He was looking at the piece of paper on the desk. It was the strange list. I grabbed at it and balled it in my fist.

"I found it on the floor."

"You should put it back where you found it."

"But it was scrunched up, like it was rubbish."

"Put it back." He jaw was tight, his look stern. I gritted my teeth but complied, ceremoniously scrunching it up and wedging it back between the floorboards and the leg of the bed.

"Now go and collect the eggs from the duck barn."

My mouth dropped open. Where did he get off ordering me around like this? He started to make the bed with the fresh sheets, ignoring my response. My legs moved towards the door. I needed to stand up for myself, but I couldn't, almost as if a voice was whispering in my ear, telling me to do as I was told. I walked all the way to the duck barn and collected the eggs.

It wasn't until I had finished the task that I relaxed on a wooden bench beneath a trellis of hanging strawberries. Someone cleared their throat. I jumped at the sound.

"I wondered when I might finally see you here."

From beneath the shadow of the apple orchard, a greying man appeared. His double-breasted black coat was emblazoned with gold stitching along every edge, complimenting the solid gold chain that hung from his neck and into his pocket. He was swinging a carpetbag at his side, approaching me.

Was it another thief?

I edged back towards the clothesline and made to make myself busy, pulling down the mostly dry clothes, keeping him within eyesight.

"Hi," I said.

"You must be Miss Evelyn O'Shea." He gave a slight bow. "Mr James Cuthbert, Esquire. Pleased to make your acquaintance."

I stopped unpegging my school dress and faced him. How did he know my name? He smiled encouragingly, baring a glint of gold that replaced his right canine.

"William has told me all about you."

He didn't appear to be a thief, but William had said that no one else lived in Purlieu. Had he come through the Hidden Grove?

"How do you know William?" I asked.

He stroked his beard. "Oh, we have been business partners for many a year now."

"Business partners?"

He nodded. "How else do you think he fitted out his cottage? I make trading between the different worlds possible."

He looked about the clearing and pulled the watch from his pocket, checking the time. The watch was covered in an array of woods of different colours and textures overlapping with one another, rather like the sketched image currently scrunched up in my pocket.

He frowned. "William has not told you about me?"

I shook my head.

"Understandable, I suppose," he said.

"You trade between the different worlds?" I asked.

"I do."

"So you've seen the other worlds."

He chuckled. "Why yes. How do you suppose I could trade with them otherwise?"

"Oh. Yeah." Heat flooded to my cheeks. "What are they like?" I asked.

"What?"

"The other worlds. Are they," I hesitated, "safe?"

"What do you mean by safe, exactly?"

An idea was forming in my mind. "Are there many thieves?"

He smiled to himself. "They are safe if you know the rules."

"Oh." Did he mean that literally? How much more had William not told me about these worlds?

"And not many are game enough to thieve," he added.

Why not, I wondered.

He looked about the clearing and checked his pocket watch once more. I remembered the stranger from the previous day and the glinting gold chain that hung from his neck.

"Does everyone have one of those?" I asked.

He grinned. "Certainly not. This is a custom piece."

He looked at my neckline, searchingly. "But I never travel without it," he said, "and neither should you."

His eyes flicked over my right shoulder and he straightened his coat. Footsteps were approaching. I turned to find William upon us. Mr Cuthbert reached out and shook William's hand.

"Mr Cuthbert."

"Master William."

They drew back from one another.

"You are early," William said.

"I am afraid that it is you who are late."

As Mr Cuthbert drew out his pocket watch for a third time, William put his hand into his pants pocket and did the same, pulling out an identical pocket watch.

William looked at his pocket watch and raised his eyebrows in a mix of surprise and concern. "Yes, I am late after all." He turned to me.

"I see you two have met."

I nodded.

"Mr Cuthbert and I have some business to tend to. You can take the clothes upstairs."

A mixture of shock and anger ran through me at his third direct command for the day. Where was this coming from? I wanted to protest. I wanted so badly to finally stand up for myself. But despite myself, I obediently unpegged the remaining pieces from the washing line, dumping them into the clothes basket. I tried to will myself, instead of walking towards the cottage, to turn around and walk straight past him into the Hidden Grove. To leave him, because he was not who I thought he was and I'd had enough. But the muscles in my legs took control and walked me all the way to the cottage and upstairs to my boudoir.

I threw the contents of the basket onto the bed, seething. How dare he boss me around so blatantly—and in front of someone else! I slumped onto the bed.

Was I really so weak that I couldn't even stand up to him? That I couldn't say no? That I couldn't just leave? What was wrong with me?

As I played back over the scene in my mind, I realised that in that moment, a part of me just wanted to do as I was told. Was I really so pathetic?

I unzipped my bag and started folding and packing my clothes. I needed to get out of there. I just had to wait for the right moment.

I watched William and Mr Cuthbert from the boudoir window as the sun began to set behind the mountains off to the right. The men hadn't moved for a long time, deep in conversation.

The mountains mirrored the two men, standing tall and proud, hidden by heavy black silhouettes. Above the mountains, fluffy, sparse clouds filled the sky, blue and green light catching their expanse. Mere moments passed and the green intensified, emerald and jade filling the sky beyond the mountains. The tufts of cloud blossomed like sugar being spun. A perfect, entirely extra-terrestrial, green sunset. It was eerie but undeniably beautiful and emphasised my feelings of disconnection from this place, and from the bond I thought I'd had with William.

William and Mr Cuthbert's silhouettes finally moved towards the cottage. I heard their distant footsteps in the parlour below, then two sets of steady, trudging feet coming up the stairs. A door opened and one set of footsteps ceased but the other continued up.

I cringed, thinking about having to face William. I threw my bag under the bed just as he opened the boudoir door.

"Hello, gorgeous," William said.

My father had always said that you couldn't trust a man's words. It was their actions you had to judge. Tiffany could attest to that with her dad and the number of breakfast dates and drama productions he'd missed in her life, despite his promises.

I folded my arms in protest at his so-called compliment. He wore a grin, completely ignorant of the fact that I was planning on leaving. He came into the heart of the room and wrapped his arms around me in a warm embrace. My body was stiff, tense, my arms still folded. He didn't seem to notice.

"I missed you," he said.

He stroked my back gently in wide, sweeping strokes. It sent goosebumps up my spine. I shivered in response and he pulled me in closer, sighing into my ear.

I'd missed this side of him.

"I am so happy you are here," he said. He pulled back and smiled. "For you," he said. He held up a magenta flower with cascading petals and tucked it behind my ear. "Mr Cuthbert is staying for dinner. He always does. Come, help me to entertain him."

His eyes were pleading and his stare intense. How could I walk out now? I hated that he'd put me in this position but that small voice whispered in my ear once more. I moved into step with William down to the kitchen.

Mr Cuthbert was looking out the window as we entered. The soft, green glow of the sunset remained, illuminating him. He turned and raised his eyebrows, flicking from me to William and back again.

"You know, I tend to prefer Italian sunsets, but Purlieu does have its share to offer," he said.

I smiled. "What? Aren't you green with envy that William has this to enjoy every day?" I laughed and gave him my best smile. "Do you get it?" I asked. "Green with envy?" I laughed again. What was wrong with me?

Mr Cuthbert eyed William and let out a soft snicker. "Very good. I see what you did there."

"Shall we eat?" William asked. He quickly set the table, laying out a mountain of cold steamed potatoes and fresh, crunchy bread, nudging me to ladle the stew from over the fire into three bowls. It had been brewing for hours and now smelt of smoked ham, celery, and mint. The meat fell apart as the ladle nudged at it. It was exactly the kind of comfort I needed right now.

"So, Miss O'Shea —" Mr Cuthbert said.

"— Evelyn is fine," William said.

Mr Cuthbert watched William for a moment. "Evelyn, then. Please, tell me more about yourself."

I ladled out the last bowl and served it to him. "I'm from Earth." It still felt strange to think that this was a significant fact.

"Yes, I know as much. But you have gifts and talents, no?"

William's hand formed a tight fist on the table. "Time to eat," he said.

I took my place beside them and dunked a piece of bread in the stew. "I suppose so," I started.

"Evelyn, do not presume that Mr Cuthbert is so noble and trustworthy. You do not have to share such intimate facts of yourself."

Mr Cuthbert scoffed. "I taught you everything you know about being noble and trustworthy, boy."

William clenched his teeth and looked at Mr Cuthbert piercingly.

"I am not a boy anymore." He turned back to me. "He is a good-for-nothing merchant who cares only about what is in it for him. He will only use you for his trading."

William and Mr Cuthbert eyed each other steadily. I took up the breadbasket in case it went flying and tried to breath as little as possible.

Mr Cuthbert cracked a smile and started laughing raucously. "You know me too well," he said.

William smiled, shook his head, and hoed into the potatoes. I let out my breath and relaxed.

"I like to paint," I said.

"Ah, so you have the creator's eye like Master William."

"I hope so. He's very talented," I said. "I'd like to be an artist one day."

"Do you have anything to show for it?"

"I've done a few things."

"Alright, alright, that is enough. Do you want me to send you off to your shack before dessert is served?" William asked.

So it was Mr Cuthbert's cabin, then. How did he have the gall to order Mr Cuthbert around? Who was this merchant, really?

"What about you, Mr Cuthbert? Do you have any skills or talents?"

It was William's turn to scoff. "What? Other than thieving and pillaging?"

Thieving and pillaging? Was he being serious? If this merchant really was so dangerous, why would William welcome him into his home?

Mr Cuthbert cracked a cheeky smile. "I am very skilled at finding out what people need most and giving it to them," he said.

"The truest thing you have said tonight," William said. "The only problem is that you do not always give people what they want."

"But I always get paid."

William shook his head. "Here we go."

Mr Cuthbert ignored him. "Take, for instance, the time a witch doctor employed me to gather dandelions from a neighbouring world. When I found out it was to heal a feverish child, I brought him penicillin from Earth instead. They weren't too impressed and refused my wage, until the next day when the child started getting better.

"And speaking of sickness, there was the time I stumbled upon the violently ill Nori people. They besought me to find a cure for their curse, promising me all their pearls, but threatened me with stone-carved knives when I started poking around their campsite." He shrugged. "I couldn't just treat their symptoms. Fortunately, it didn't take me long to find out the cause. I returned to the people and told them not to let their cattle walk through the river upstream. It was like talking to a brick wall. I needed to have several sittings with their chief, taking him to where the cows were shitting in the river, before he understood.

"Or what about the time I was banished from Celoso?" Mr Cuthbert said.

William rolled his eyes and grunted into a spoonful of stew. "Alright, that is enough. They were all fools for doing business with you," William said.

"But *you* do business with him," I said.

Mr Cuthbert laughed jovially. "I like her," he said.

"She is very disobedient."

I scrunched up my forehead. Disobedient? Is that what he really thought, that I should obey him? I thought of my packed bag hiding under the bed upstairs. If that was the way he thought things should be, it would be better if I left without him knowing.

"People have always had minds of their own," Mr Cuthbert said. "It is how the worlds of the Hidden Grove became populated."

"What do you mean?" I asked.

"Over the years, through good or bad luck, people have stumbled upon the various Hidden Grove locations on Earth and made a home for themselves in the new worlds. Fast-forward a few generations and now they are heavily populated by entire civilisations."

"Excluding Purlieu," William said.

"It must be the sunsets," Mr Cuthbert said. He gave me a cheeky grin. "It is these people, dissatisfied with their place in life," he continued, "who enable my trade to exist and I give them the means to stay."

"But why is Purlieu so under populated?" I asked. I wondered whether it had something to do with the terrible company.

William scratched at his chin. "I guess no one chose to go through its portal," William said. "Until my parents."

"As people entered each land at different points throughout the history of Earth, some worlds are stuck in the dark ages. Yet others are technologically advanced, like Purlieu," Mr Cuthbert said.

I looked at the lantern lighting our table, and baulked. How could Purlieu be considered technologically advanced?

"But there's no electricity. No phones. I can't even use my hair straightener."

It was starting to show, too. The humid weather had made my hair wiry and more uncontrollable than usual. It was embarrassing.

"Most do not even have hot, running water," William said.

"If Purlieu is so great, why did you keep coming to Earth?" I asked.

William's eyes softened. "Because I was looking for you," he said. He reached for my good hand and rubbed it affectionately. I tried my best to appear receptive but I wasn't buying it anymore.

"What was the real reason? For choosing Earth and for choosing me over all the other girls out there?" I asked.

Mr Cuthbert shifted in his seat. This conversation had become way too personal.

"It was Mr Cuthbert, actually, who encouraged it," William said.

"I did no such thing."

William pulled his hand away and looked at Mr Cuthbert. "You told me that was where my parents came from. Of course I would go looking for them." William looked into his lap. For the first time the cockiness washed away, a hint of sadness and missed opportunity weighing upon him.

"I know it was foolish and impossible, but I had hoped to run into them one day. That they might remember me and beg my forgiveness for leaving me all alone in Purlieu. I had no idea that Earth was so large."

Mr Cuthbert scratched at his chin. "The possibility of finding them was dismal," he said.

William nodded his head. "I spent weeks, months probably, waiting at the art gallery, looking up every time the door opened, asking complete strangers if they had accidentally lost a boy sixteen years ago. Finally, I realised that if my parents really wanted me, they knew where to find me—exactly where they had left me."

I looked to Mr Cuthbert for confirmation but his face was unreadable. My heart was heavy with sadness. I squeezed William's hand. He smiled weakly. "It is why I only ever leave Purlieu for short amounts of time."

"But you were sixteen—that was four years ago. Why did you keep returning to Earth after you gave up on finding them, if you knew it was impossible?" I asked.

He sighed and looked off over my shoulder. "The day I decided I had to stop looking for them, I was about to leave the art gallery for good when I saw a mother and father with their little boy. I realised I did not need my parents. I needed to start a family of my own." He looked at me now and squeezed my hand back. "Then I met you."

Mr Cuthbert cleared his throat and started gathering up the dishes from the table. "Tell me, Master William, are you having a successful season?"

William pulled back from me and replaced the half-empty bowl of potatoes with strawberries and cinnamon sugar. "It has been a good season. The spices are coming along nicely. Ginger and cumin in particular thrived. I changed the ratio of manure to soil and moved the bulk of the cumin crop next to the river. It loved its new location. I am also in the process of producing a headache soother that I think several dignitaries will find interesting."

As William droned on, the reality of what he had said hit me. He wanted to start a family with me. I wasn't sure if I should be flattered, think him more attractive for wanting something so honourable, or if I should run for the hills.

Nerves washed over me, making my stomach churn, the thick cream of dessert sitting uneasily.

Tomorrow. Tomorrow I would leave him.

8

S TANDING BY THE musical mushrooms at the
entrance to the Hidden Grove, the dappled light of
dawn peeping through the branches and dotting our faces,
William and I bid Mr Cuthbert goodbye.

"Are you going home?" I asked.

"Home? I live everywhere." he said. He gave a cheeky
grin, dismissing the question.

"But where did you grow up?"

"I try not to meditate upon it."

"Why not?"

"Because when I was a boy, the one that ruled my land
also ruled the ocean. There was no escaping him."

"Oh. I'm sorry."

"You were not to know. He is long gone now. The
current monarch takes life," he hesitated, "a little more
lightly."

I raised my eyebrows in query. Mr Cuthbert let out a
disparaging breath.

"For instance, she lawfully changed her name to
Sovereign Sovereign." His lips drew thin. "But I do not
mind her horseplay. Because of my position as trader, she
gives me the autonomy to come and go as I please. I have

a warehouse by the beach that I visit every so often."

"And do your family live nearby?"

He looked away, stroking at his beard. "I have none."

My cheeks flushed hot with embarrassment, but I could not help but feel this was a lie. "I'm sorry," I said.

"Stop bothering him, Evelyn. He has work to do," William said.

My eyes dropped to the ground and a new flush washed over me.

"Well, until next time," Mr Cuthbert said. With a quick nod of his head, he turned and walked beneath the tree arch and into the Hidden Grove. I glanced to the side of the tree arch. It was strange that I couldn't see him, just the thin pine trees. Yet as I returned my gaze through the arch, there he was, amongst its towering trees. He walked into the depths of the grove until the trees hid him from sight.

William turned and walked back out through the forest.

"Where are you going?" I asked.

He huffed. "So many questions."

I cringed. His face softened. He had noticed.

"To make an early start on the chores," he said. "I want to check the cumin by the river."

I nodded. It was a fifteen-minute walk to the river alone. Here was the opening I was looking for.

He turned and continued through the forest to the clearing. I waited a few moments and followed after him, turning towards the cottage when he continued past it to the river.

Upstairs, I grabbed my bag from beneath the bed, my heart pounding. It was time: I was leaving him. What would he do when he couldn't find me? Would he search for me and promise to do better? Did I want him to find me and prove he wasn't who he had been the last few days?

Didn't he at least deserve me to tell him to his face, to not leave him wondering? But I knew what would happen if I said it aloud. He was too persuasive. He would never let me leave, not unless I forced him to, assuming I could. No, it would be better this way. A clean break.

I scrounged around in my bag for a piece of paper and a pen and scribbled the words 'I'm sorry' on a scrap, leaving it at the foot of the bed. My feet made to turn for the door but I changed my mind, flipping over the paper and adding, 'I just need some space.' After thinking for a moment, I added three big crosses.

My bag securely on my back, I went down into the clearing, headed for the Hidden Grove. I checked over my shoulder. Twice.

As I stood in front of the tree arch, looking into the Hidden Grove beyond, I knew there was no going back after this. Was I sure I wanted to leave William? Our relationship would never be the same once I left. I still loved him, after all. At least I think I did.

No. This was it. I was leaving him. I may not have had the strength to say it to his face, to say no to him and defy his commands, but this was my way of making a stand. The only way I knew how. By walking away.

I crossed beneath the tree arch and into the Hidden Grove. A weight fell off my shoulders. Clouds cushioned my feet. The further I walked away from the arch and into the grove, between those towering trees, the lighter I felt. I stood up straighter.

I was leaving a weight behind, but what was ahead of me was just as heavy. I would have to face the school, Tiffany, my father. What would they say? What would I say?

The weight fell back upon me.

I passed row after row of trees, looking for the one with the Old Man's Beard hanging from its branches. I hadn't taken enough notice of exactly where it was in the grove when William had showed me.

How was it that the trees could be of different ages yet all perfectly uniform in height?

There, to my right, stood the one covered in white lichen, the one that had brought me to Purlieu. I wasn't far from the tree to home. It was somewhere to the left and a couple of rows across. Old Man's Beard hung sparsely from the branches of a young tree six rows from the Purlieu tree. It had to be the one.

I began the arduous climb up the tree, each elevated branch making my stomach knot and quiver. I tried not to look down but instead focused on what was ahead of me. Given my history, I was pretty sure I could convince the school to put my absence down to home troubles and let me off scot-free.

Reaching the top of the tree trunk and passing through the portal of light, that strange feeling of everything and nothingness washed over me once more. The light disappeared as quickly as it came and I was down on the ground of the Hidden Grove in what felt like mere moments, surrounded by the familiar grassy acres and perfectly lined trees.

I hurried through the rows, looking for the tree arch that marked both the entrance and the exit to the Hidden Grove. I waited for the smell of eucalyptus to smack my nostrils but when I found and exited through the tree arch, the smell didn't come. There was no bushland. A slate wall stood a few paces in front, towering over me, higher even than the tops of the Hidden Grove would have reached. The wall surrounded me in a perfect circle, encapsulating the tree arch. The only light came from directly above, like a wide well.

What had happened to the bushland?

I approached the wall and touched the matte black rock face. It was warm. On the wall at eye level was a metal warning sign in strange curling script stating that visitors were not welcome.

I wasn't on Earth at all. I had climbed the wrong tree.

I traced my finger along the strange script of the sign in front of me. The sign shifted beneath my finger. I flinched—it was on a hinge. I prodded the sign and it swung open to reveal a small cavity in the wall, wide enough only for a hand to fit in. Light streaked from a small gap in the other side of the wall. I reached inside and prodded the back wall. Another hinge. It creaked as it swung open, golden afternoon sun blinding me in my dark well.

As my eyes began to adjust, through the little window I could make out vast, green rolling hills and vineyards. The shadow of a city marked a distant hill. It was breathtaking, like I imagined an Italian countryside to be. I had to capture it. I put my phone into the empty cavity and took a picture of the view before closing the windows on both sides of the wall.

This wasn't home, so it was time to leave.

Turning to the tree arch, I made my way back towards it.

What secrets had passed through that little cavity over the years?

The rusty creak of metal sounded behind me, like a letterbox being opened. Metal clinked. The metal scraped again, sending shivers up my back.

I returned to the sign and put my ear as close as I dared, my heart beating uncomfortably in my chest. Footsteps rustling through grass were moving away from the wall. I waited until the sound disappeared and carefully swung open the metal sign. Someone had placed a package in the small cavity in the wall.

I reached through to the other side, dodging the package, and carefully swung the window on the other side. With her back to me, an aging woman hobbled away with the help of a gold cane. She wore a caped velvet gown in royal purple, a crown on her head, and a heavy chain around her neck. Despite her hobbling and the obvious weight of her jewels, she had perfect posture.

I'd never seen a woman like her, the perfect subject for a future painting. I stole a photo of her, then pulled closed the metal sign at the back.

Who was she trying to reach with her secret door? I picked up the package, metal clinking inside. A note sat beneath it. It was unaddressed. I unfolded it and found a scrolling, ink-inscribed letter.

I have but few days left in me on this sun-kissed country. Though I loathe to leave this life knowing that none shall care for the child hereafter, I have no choice in the matter.

You will find enclosed my final, most generous payment. You are free of our bond, sir. I do not begrudge you. May you yourself have a happy and long life with the remaining gold. I trust that with my generosity you shall honour it by continuing to see to the child's needs.

It was unsigned.

Feeling dirty, I hastily folded and replaced the letter and package, heat spreading up my neck. I closed the door and returned to the tree arch, the Hidden Grove unveiling itself before me.

It was none of my business who she was trying to communicate with or about whom. I needed to return to Earth.

I searched again, finding the tree covered in white lichen to Purlieu, and looked about at the trees in the rows that followed for that young tree with the Old Man's Beard, the real tree to Earth.

It tickled my shoulder before I noticed it. I jumped back in fright. The time it took for me to recognise its familiar grey tendrils was enough for me to regather myself and leap onto its lowermost branch. I scaled up the tree; putting aside my fear of heights, ready to return to Earth.

Why was she paying someone to look after a child? Whose child was it?

I passed through the light portal at the top of the tree, that strange feeling enveloping me for the infinitesimal moment it took me to step from one side of the top of the tree trunk to the other. Keeping my eyes on each branch below me and not the ground, I climbed down until I reached the grass of the Hidden Grove.

Who was the letter addressed to?

No. I would not be distracted by the mysteries of these strange worlds. William and I were over. It was time I returned to the real world; time I forgot about all this nonsense. It would be far easier to lie and say that the images I painted were of my own imagining than of hidden worlds, if—and only if—I could put this crazy escapade behind me.

I shifted into a run, determined not to delay my return to Earth any longer. I exited the Hidden Grove through the tree arch, anticipating the harsh dirt of bushland at my feet, but instead found nothing. My stomach dropped. I was falling. I grappled about around me as I slid down the side of a damp mountain face overlooking a deadly fall into mist and jungle. My hands connected with a thick green vine and I began swinging across the face of the cliff.

The sensation jolted my memory and all I could think of was Cameron, his face growing distant as I swung from the flying fox. His eyes were wide in horror as though he'd pushed me. But he hadn't, I'd volunteered. We'd been trying a high ropes course on grade nine camp, back when the three of us were friends. Tiffany had gone first, cool and fearless as usual. She hadn't hooked her carabiner to the zip line, and when she'd started gliding one-handed, she'd fallen to the ground.

The fastest way to get help, to find a teacher, was down the flying fox. The only problem was that the handlebar was now down the bottom of the line and it would waste too much time to pull it back up with the line. It took only a moment for me to follow her. I hooked my carabiner onto the zip line and jumped from the platform at the top of the tree, hands and legs flailing. The wire took my weight, bowing slightly.

Cameron called my name. He yelled for me to stop. His

voice became a ringing sound in my eardrums.

A blur of leaves whizzed past my face and I shifted my focus from Cameron to the ground, searching for Tiffany. I spotted her ahead, facedown, unmoving. In the space of the breath I refused to take, I passed over her, the platform of the next tree fast approaching. Without the handlebar of the flying fox, I had no way of slowing down.

The further down the line I travelled, the more speed I gathered. I started to panic, reaching my right hand up behind me to the wire and grabbing it as hard as I could to slow down. Heat seared through me. White-hot pain blinded my sight, soaring through my hand and down my arm. My outstretched feet connected with the tree of the next platform. The next thing I knew I was in a hospital bed with third-degree burns to my hand, Tiffany by my side with a broken arm and a crooked smile. We didn't see Cameron until the next week at school, but it was as though he didn't see us at all. That was when he'd ditched us for Darius and the others.

The same feeling of sickening fear washed over me as I swung down the mountainside of this jungle-filled foreign land. Where was the bushland? Where had these mountains come from?

I wrapped the arm of my weak hand around the vine, the memory of pain still fresh, turning my stomach. A clear space in the jungle opened ahead. I'd reached the centre of the arc and began to swing upwards. If I didn't let go now, I would miss my opportunity. Holding my breath, I released the vine, aiming for the edge of the grassy opening.

I fell the length of my body down into thick scrub. Bracing for pain, I lay, unable to move, but pain didn't come. I slowly stirred, moving my hands, my head, my legs, my whole body. Awkwardly I crawled backwards out of the scrub and raised myself to my feet.

The vine swung back towards me like a pendulum, until it settled in the middle of the clear space where I now stood. I looked up at the jungle-covered mountain above, shrouded in mist and low-lying cloud. In every direction I turned, identical mountains sprouted up from the earth at sharp angles.

I pulled my phone out and took a photo, returning it to my dress pocket. Surely I hadn't climbed the wrong tree again? I was certain it had been the one William showed me: the young one, with Old Man's Beard hanging from it. Had the one I'd just climbed been very young, though?

Sweat gathered on my back. How was I going to get back home now? I let out a long breath and started looking over the mountain for a clear route of ascent. Slitted eyes and red faces appeared between the tangle of trees and vines. I wasn't alone.

"Hello? Who are you?"

Voices in a foreign tongue yelled and half-naked tattooed men rushed at me, brandishing pointed wooden poles. I sucked in a breath, frozen in terror.

They bound my wrists, spittle flying in my face. The biggest of them lifted me over his shoulder. I thrashed about and screamed as they filed downhill, chanting to a beat set by a bone flute.

"No! Put me down!"

I clasped my hands together and beat my captor on his back. The men following directly behind pointed their sticks in my face until I stopped. I looked past them just in time to see the mountain up to the Hidden Grove disappear as we rounded another mountain. Dread washed over me. I thrashed about, turning and slipping in the man's grip as sweat covered our bodies. I had to get home. I couldn't lose track of which mountain to climb.

Pointed sticks were shoved into my face once more. I fell limp in the man's arms, defeated. I was unarmed and outnumbered, a tiny girl in the strong grip of a man four times my size.

We passed by yet another staggering mountain jutting sharply from the ground. I smelt smoke. It wafted around us. I coughed and spluttered, my eyes starting to water. The humidity mingling with the dry smoke was unbearable. I held my breath.

We were heading down a slope between slashed jungle. The smoke cleared and the jungle parted. Women's voices mingled with the men's. Their faces emerged, painted in black ink, widening their slitted eyes. They looked even more intimidating than the men.

The procession drew to a stop and I was hauled to the damp ground, mud soaking into my clothes. Hundreds of half-naked bodies lined the edge of the clearing. So many hungry eyes stared at me. Fingers were pointing. Poles were raised.

In the centre of the clearing was a wide hole the width of a house. Smoke filled the sky above it, permeating the surrounding jungle. In the distance, more turrets of smoke rose into the sky, dotting the valley landscape. Beside each of the turrets, bamboo huts with palm frond roofs clambered over one another in a mess of flaxen and green.

Were they savages? Cannibals? Would they sacrifice me to their god? My heart beat hard against my chest. I choked on bile.

From behind a mud monument in the shape of an orb, a girl dressed in nothing more than ornate gold jewellery approached. The best part of her neck and chest was covered in tattoos, a stark contrast to her yellow skin. She couldn't have been older than ten. The chanting dropped to a melodious whisper. The flute fell silent.

She started to speak in a foreign language to the man who had carried me. He held up his hands in defence, cowering. The people shifted away from him, leaving him exposed to the girl's anger, alone in the clearing like me.

The girl glared at him for a long moment, the chanting fading out. She said something softly and the blood drained from his face. The people behind him shifted even further back. He turned and started walking towards the fire pit. There were two bamboo towers either side of the pit, with planks held by vines running between them through the smoke. He climbed the nearest one; it swayed beneath his weight. A shiver travelled across the vine bridge, the sound of rattling filling the clearing. Dry bones hung from the centre of the vine bridge, hidden amongst the smoke. My heart skipped a beat.

The haze enveloped the man as he reached the top and dropped to all fours, crawling on the plank like a child, coughing and choking as he went. The vine bridge swung precariously. He reached the middle, barely visible for the shroud of smoke that encircled him, and he wrapped his ankles in vines. The bridge shook as he shifted. A moment later, he was hanging upside down from the bridge, attached at the feet, writhing and swinging. His yellow skin glowed red from the heat. He gave a chilling scream that sent more bile up my throat. He choked and coughed, thrashing about, making the bamboo towers quiver. The smell of burning skin filled my nostrils, an overwhelming acrid stench that made my stomach turn. He fell silent and still. Slowly his body came to rest, turning black from ash and burnt flesh.

A little bit of vomit came up as I stared at his corpse. My mother, lying dead in the morgue, flashed across my mind.

Through the silence, the girl turned to me and raised her voice in her foreign tongue.

"I don't know what you're saying," I said, my voice pleading.

That voice in my head returned, telling me to get up. I struggled to my feet, ignoring the mud that stuck to me.

She yelled at me and pointed to the fire pit. My legs started to move towards it. Where was I going? What was I doing? I tried to stop walking, the fire pit ever closer, the smoke and heat increasing. I screamed internally for my muscles to stop moving but they ignored me.

I didn't want to end up like him. I didn't want to die. A shiver went up my spine at the thought of choking on smoke, of my skin burning like his still was.

The heat of the fire scorched my face, hot and dry. Too hot. I wanted to stop walking. I wanted to turn around. The tower was mere metres away, the fire pit just before me.

A man's voice sounded from behind me. It spoke in the foreign language, but sounded old and familiar. The girl responded to him, her voice muffled, her back to me. He spoke again. She yelled in my direction. The muscles in my legs finally responded to my screaming: my feet stopped moving. I could turn away from the flames.

I fell to the ground and crawled away from the pit, away from the smoke, sobbing, clutching at the ground in relief.

Mr Cuthbert stood at the edge of the clearing. The people parted to let him through. The girl yelled again and pointed at me. One of the men stepped forward and pulled me to my feet, unbinding my hands with a stone knife. He bowed his head slightly to me as he returned to the mass of the crowd.

Mr Cuthbert approached the girl and placed a hand across his heart, then bowed to her. They shared a few words. She smiled and nodded. He bowed again and motioned to me.

"Evelyn, bow to the empress." He had a smile on his face but his tone was icy.

I copied him, placing my hand on my heart and bowing to her. She nodded her head in acknowledgment.

"Time to get you home," Mr Cuthbert said.

I didn't need to be told twice. While my body still obeyed me, I scurried forward, past the empress, accompanying Mr Cuthbert to the edge of the crowd. They watched in silence as we passed. I dared not look at any of them, focusing uphill as we re-entered the jungle.

Mr Cuthbert hiked several strides ahead of me, slashing at the thick jungle with a dagger the size of a ruler. His shoulders were tense, his breathing laboured. The silence was heavy. I felt like a naughty child being given the silent treatment.

We were now far enough into the jungle that the smoke was smothered by humid air. The scent of burning flesh disappeared with it. I shuddered at the image fixed in my mind of that blackened body hanging upside down from the bridge, lifeless. Bile threatened my mouth once more.

"Thank you for saving me," I said.

The silence continued for a few moments, Mr Cuthbert hacking through a particularly tough branch. His body wasn't young anymore but he moved with ease. He stopped and heaved a long sigh.

"I can assure you that I did it for my own good rather than yours," he said.

I couldn't tell if he was just trying to avoid becoming emotional.

"I mean it,' I said. 'I'd be dead right now if it wasn't for you."

Tears trickled down my face.

"Again, my actions were more for my benefit."

"I just don't understand—how did she make that man burn himself alive? And I—I was going to do the same. I couldn't stop myself. What is she, a witch?"

"Something like that," he said.

"But why? Why would she do that?"

"Foreigners often carry disease with them. He should have known better than to bring you into the camp."

"So she killed him?"

"She cleansed the camp of any disease he may have picked up from you."

I hastily brushed the tears away.

"I don't have any diseases."

He sighed.

"To you, it looks like a heinous crime. To her, she is merely protecting her people."

He severed the branch and we continued trudging up and around the mountain. How many of these staggering mountains had I passed on the way down?

I sucked in a deep breath and changed the topic.

"How did you find me?" I asked.

Silence ensued once more. He cleared his throat. "I saw you, in the Hidden Grove."

"Were you coming to trade?"

"In a manner of speaking, yes."

"I'm sorry I got in the way."

"I can return after I take you home."

"But will they trade with you now?"

"There is no reason not."

"Why would you trade with such savages anyway?"

Mr Cuthbert stopped walking and looked back at me. "I believe we are talking about two very different things."

I thought for a moment. "You saw me in the Hidden Grove of the world with the impenetrable wall."

"Celoso."

"Celoso?" I had heard that name somewhere before.

I thought back to the curious world and its tall black, well-like wall.

"There was a little window, behind the sign," I said.

Mr Cuthbert stumbled on a tree root but quickly found his feet again. A small animal leapt from the branches of the tree above and ripped Mr Cuthbert's pocket watch from his neck. Mr Cuthbert fell forward into the tree from the force. It wasn't an animal, but a child native. The boy dashed away into the jungle, swinging through the trees as though he were a monkey.

Mr Cuthbert quickly regained himself and launched after the boy. Though he didn't move as effortlessly, his legs were long. I ran after them both, conscious of the fact that we were moving down the side of the mountain, away from our destination.

"It's just a child. His family probably needs the gold more than we do," I called ahead.

Mr Cuthbert ignored me.

Leaves slapped my face, my feet slipping on the moist

ground.

The boy moved erratically through the jungle, zigzagging unpredictably. We were going to lose our way, I just knew it. I began to panic. Visions crossed my mind of never finding our way back to the Hidden Grove, lost in the jungle forever.

Mr Cuthbert's coat grew more and more distant with every step. It would be far worse to be lost in this jungle without Mr Cuthbert than with him. I forced my body to push through the stitch that was developing in my chest and the chaffing of my backpack thumping against my back, rubbing on my shoulders. My heaving lungs protested as I took quick, small steps over protruding roots and under low-hanging branches.

What if we were running into a trap? What if the child was instructed to trap us in a corner, or over a cliff, or into a pit? What if he was from a different faction to the ones we'd previously encountered and they were less accommodating to Mr Cuthbert's charms? What if they burnt us alive or wanted to eat us?

I agonised over ever step, sure that with each one would come my demise.

Ahead, Mr Cuthbert stopped running. A few moments later I caught up with him. He had his pocket watch back around his neck. Holding the child by the hair, he raised a dagger up above the boy's chin.

My eyes widened in horror. "What are you doing?" I yelled.

Mr Cuthbert looked up. The child wriggled from Mr Cuthbert's grip and dashed away into the shadows of the jungle. Mr Cuthbert turned around just in time to see him disappear.

I keeled over, heaving for breath. Sweat dripped down my back like a waterfall, my school dress wet and sticky, the stitch finally lessening. He rounded on me, brandishing his dagger in the air. The blade, along with the stingray handle, was night black. The bubbled surface of the stingray skin and the sheen of the sharp blade caught the light that seeped between the trees.

"You let him get away," he said,

I took a deep breath and stood up straight again. "You were going to hurt him," I said.

Mr Cuthbert cursed. "You know what he is doing right now? Going to tell his whole clan about us. If we get burned alive, it is entirely your fault," he said.

"You were the one that started chasing him."

"He took my pocket watch."

"That's no reason to kill him."

"When it's my life on the line, yes, yes it is."

I pursed my lips and folded my arms.

"We need to get out of here before he returns with his clan," Mr Cuthbert said.

I turned and looked back up the mountain we'd just descended. It was a long way up. Mr Cuthbert waltzed past me, not even glancing back. My already hot cheeks flushed with embarrassment.

I followed him up and around the mountain, trying to keep up with the pace his long legs set. We walked in silence, filled by the sound of our huffing breath, the scratching of our feet hitting the scrub, and Mr Cuthbert's excessive hacking at the jungle with his blade. It had probably been about an hour and there wasn't a dry patch left on me, yet my throat ached for water.

We had reached the mountain base, jutting up in a hazardous mess of pointing rock and cliff faces. There to the right was where I'd landed in the thick scrub some few hours ago, the long swinging vine hanging limp against the mountainside. I slumped onto a mossy log. It took Mr Cuthbert a few paces before he noticed I wasn't following him.

He doubled back and reached into his carpetbag for a flask of water.

"Thank you," I said. I took a long, greedy swig as he paced back and forth, waiting for me. I breathed out. My muscles ached with weariness. I didn't want to get up again.

"What's the big deal with your watch anyway?" I asked.

"William has not told you?"

"Told me what?"

Mr Cuthbert let out a long sigh and turned away from me. "I need it because of the time differences between the worlds."

"What do you mean?"

He pointed through the jungle towards the setting golden sun. "It has been only a few hours since dawn in Purlieu, when you saw me off through the Hidden Grove. You recall?"

I shrugged.

"So what? There are different time zones on Earth too, and no one puts their life on the line for the sake of their phone or watch."

Mr Cuthbert looked at me now. His stare was cool and serious. "Zones between worlds would better be described as date zones that fluctuate."

He pulled out his pocket watch and joined me on the log. "See here."

The watch had hundreds of tiny arrows made of different shades of wood. Each was pointing towards the circumference where the numbers one to a hundred were inscribed in a brass setting. A few of the miniscule hands moved to a consistent beat, while others remained still. The vast majority pointed up to the number one, in line with one hairline arrow made of brass. It was impossible to read.

It reminded me of something. I reached into my pocket and pulled out a damp, scrunched-up piece of paper. I gently flattened it out on my knee.

"You made that watch, didn't you?" I asked.

"Where did you get that?"

"I found it."

I blushed. He watched me steadily.

"A week has passed in Purlieu in our absence," he said.

He indicated an arrow pointing slightly to the right of the brass hairline arrow. It was speckled with minute white lichen. My stomach dropped.

"But we've only been gone a few hours!"

"That is why I need my watch. It is essential to my trade." He sighed. "And now I am behind schedule."

I cringed, feeling the accusation in his words. I looked at his watch again. The Purlieu hand ticked over. My heart was beating uncomfortably in my chest. Surely it couldn't be true?

"Morning," he said.

I raised my eyebrows.

"It is now morning in Purlieu," he said.

"I don't understand." My heart beat harder against my chest and my stomach started to churn. If just a few hours had passed since I left Purlieu and yet it was a week later there now, what time—what day was it back on Earth?

"How fast can a world's time pass in comparison to the others?" I asked. The words tumbled out of my mouth too fast. I waited with baited breath for Mr Cuthbert to explain, watching the steady rhythm of those few hands tick-tick-ticking by.

"Some worlds are years ahead of others."

My heart skipped a beat.

"That is why my watch is so important. If I were to visit a new world and did not know it was so far ahead, if and when I tried to leave, even after just a short visit, I would find that years had passed elsewhere."

Hot shivers ran across my arms, my cheeks, and down my back.

"It happened to me once." He clenched his jaw and looked away. "That was what drove me to design the watch. That is why I could not let the child have it."

My face became sickly hot.

"It is essential that I make my trades on time," he continued. "My clients rely on my punctuality, especially given that their worlds move at different paces."

What if time passed that quickly between Earth and Purlieu? What would I find when I arrived home? Would I be that girl who got lost in the bushland and reappeared decades later? Would my dad be an old man?

The last thought sent shivers up my back. I needed to get back home as soon as possible. Ignoring the droning headache that had set in, and Mr Cuthbert snatching the paper away from me, I stood to continue climbing the mountain.

Darkness began to fall. Mr Cuthbert had retaken his place as leader, setting a mean pace with his long legs that I was now only too glad to match. The mountain had become so steep it felt like an endless staircase through the obstructing jungle.

Even if I couldn't stand my father at the moment, I didn't want him to be an old man already. I'd figured that I'd have time to sort things out with him, eventually. But not on his deathbed.

Light was fading fast from the gaps in the jungle. It was becoming hard to navigate through the scrub. Mr Cuthbert stopped abruptly and turned around. His eyes were wide, almost fearful. He put his carpetbag down and started rummaging through it, pulling out two rocks and some paper. He struck the rocks together. The paper lit.

"Get some rocks," he said.

I hesitated. He looked like he was settling us down for the night.

"But I need to get home. My dad—"

"Rocks. Now," he ordered.

I searched about beneath the trees, gathering as many into my arms as I could. He had transferred the flame to some brown leaves and was trying to catch them on a moss-covered twig. It hissed and crackled as the moss connected with the flame. The jungle was just so damp. The rocks cascaded from my arms, clanking and clunking by his side. He shushed me, looking about the jungle in alarm.

"Would you keep it down?" he said.

My cheeks grew hot as he formed a base with the rocks. "Why are we stopping?"

"I need more," he said.

I let out an annoyed breath and searched a little further, bringing back four piles before he was satisfied. He'd managed to start one fire with the kindling and logs, and was starting another.

In mere minutes, he had slashed back at the jungle and arranged five fires in a wide circle around us. They hissed and smoked from the damp wood. Mr Cuthbert sat down in the middle of the fires, pulling his carpetbag close into himself. The sun had set, the jungle now thick with darkness. The firelight licked at our faces, throwing disproportionate shadows around our little clearing.

I slumped down beside him. Dad wouldn't have given me the silent treatment. He tended to over communicate. I think I preferred that.

"Why did we stop?" I asked.

"Lower your voice," he said. He let out a long breath and continued in hushed whispers.

"The jungle of Bayartai is dangerous at night. Mercifully though, if the clan were trying to hunt us down, they will have given up by now and be returning to their village."

"So why don't we keep going? Get out of here as soon as possible?"

"Miss Evelyn, it is pitch black out there. Not only could you walk off the side of the mountain at any moment, but there are the night dwellers to contend with."

My heartbeat quickened. "Are they dangerous?"

"The people of Bayartai are nothing compared to what lurks in this jungle at night."

My ears pricked up at the sound of rustling as the nocturnal jungle started to wake. A white light poked through the trees. We watched it in silence, my heart beating uncomfortably, my breathing constricted. Moments passed and the white light took shape, finding a space between the jungle to reveal itself. It was a moon, large and bright like a beacon, rising across the mountain face, sending a silver film over everything it touched.

My shoulders relaxed. I reached into my backpack and pulled out the muesli bar I'd packed several days prior for the art gallery excursion. Mr Cuthbert snatched it from my hands before I had the chance to open it. He threw it into the darkness, sending creatures scattering at the disturbance.

"What did you do that for? I'm starving."

"It would be safer to go hungry."

"But —"

"Do you have any more food in there?"

"No."

"Are you sure?"

"Yes."

He sat up straight and watched the jungle, scrutinising every movement and sound.

"You would do well to get some rest," he said.

I sighed and leant back into my backpack, trying to relax. I didn't want to sleep, the hanging burnt body above the fire pit still fresh in my mind. I feared it would only exacerbate my already vivid nightmares of my mother and her death.

A clicking sound came from behind me. Something screeched in the distance, projecting an echo through the jungle. The tree to Mr Cuthbert's right rustled. My heartbeat picked up once more. I stared about, waiting for something to jump out at us.

"How do you know that William's parents are from Earth?" I asked.

"You should sleep, child," he said.

I recoiled at the insult. "I can't," I said.

He remained silent.

"That's what William said last night. That you'd told

him they were from Earth."

He continued to ignore me.

"Because if you knew that they came from Earth, then you probably knew them. So I can't help wondering why you haven't told William anything about them—even their names."

"Discretion is what my clients pay for," he said.

"Did they pay you to take him to Purlieu?"

Mr Cuthbert's lips grew thin in the silvery moonlight. He scratched at his chin.

"William has a right to know," I said. I no longer wanted to be with William, but that didn't mean I'd stopped caring about him.

"Telling William that his parents do not want him is not going to help him."

"So it's true, then? They paid you to abandon him in Purlieu, to fend for himself as a baby."

"I did not say that," he snapped.

His fervour shocked me. I carried on feebly. "You said they don't want him."

Mr Cuthbert wiped his face with both hands. "If they have not looked for him, they probably do not want him," he said.

"But maybe they do want him now, they're just afraid to reach out after all this time, afraid of how he might respond," I said, my voice rising. "Families need each other, even if they don't always show it."

My dad's face flashed across my mind. The rustling in the bushes to the right of Mr Cuthbert started up again.

"Shush," he said. He waved his hands at me to settle down before continuing in a whisper. "Get some sleep."

I closed my eyes, keenly aware of the jungle noises. Footsteps padded on damp leaves and trees groaned in every direction surrounding us. My heart resumed its quick pace.

I tried to focus on the steady whistle from Mr Cuthbert's nose instead. I breathed in time with his breath, my hand over my heart, waiting for the throbbing to slow down, pushing away the images that threatened to overtake my mind—images of the cut up body of my mother in the morgue. A monkey shrieked. Another responded. A chorus of shrieking began and the padding feet moved with greater intent. I braced my body, waiting for impact, for certain death. Any breath could be my last.

If only it were dawn already. If only it were time to finally go home.

This was going to be a long night.

I woke to the sound of a baby's cry. It was soft, distant and persistent, like it was in distress. Like it wanted its mother's milk but the mother wasn't there. Like it was cold and needed the warmth of a father's skin. Where were the parents?

The moon had moved behind the mountain, making the jungle surrounding our dwindling fires impossible to see.

I waited for someone to pacify it but the baby cried on.

Who would leave their child so high on the mountain, away from the village, in the middle of the night? Could this be the child that the old lady was referring to in her letter?

No one was coming.

I couldn't just lie there. I had to do something.

Mr Cuthbert was asleep now, arms wrapped protectively around his carpetbag. I reached over to shake him awake and saw my art journal hanging loosely from his hands, open on my sketch of the ancient highlander's purlieu. I pursed my lips and left my unzipped bag behind for him to continue snooping through, if he so pleased.

The cry was coming through the trees directly in front. I slipped between two of the fires and followed the call. Despite the humidity, it was cool in the jungle now. Thick mist clung to the trees. The poor thing could catch a cold.

I hurried on, stepping over protruding roots and slithering between vines and obtrusive branches. But with every step I took, its cry seemed no closer.

I was distracted by every sudden movement and unusual sound, equally conscious of how much noise I was making as I tripped and stumbled through the jungle. I felt as if every creature was staring at me. Cold sweat gathered on my back. At any moment I could be assaulted by one of the faceless creatures of the night. I was exposed, away from the safety of Mr Cuthbert's side and our firelight. The scrub was difficult to navigate without Mr Cuthbert's slashing or the sun lighting the path. A twinge of regret hit me as I realised I should have brought a lit branch from the fire for light and warmth and safety.

The baby stopped crying. What could that mean? Had it fallen asleep or had someone else answered the cry? Or was I too late? I gulped.

I tripped on another vine and lost my footing, thumping to the ground. My body skidded down a steep slope. I screamed and thrashed about, looking for something to grab onto, but the cold, wet ground was slick like oil. The slope ended, sending me over the edge of a cliff. My hand connected with a tree root and I wrapped my arms around it, body dangling. The tree groaned under my weight.

My heart moved uncomfortably in my chest and my breath came out unevenly. The baby cried out in one defeated shrill and fell silent. I was too late.

I whimpered, taking another deep breath. My arms began to shake. I shuffled up the tree root until I reached the base of the skinny trunk, sitting precariously on the edge of the cliff. I gulped down air and unwrapped one arm from the root to clutch it around the trunk. I swung my body up over the ledge, hugging the tree with quivering determination. My whole body shook. I scrambled to flat ground and fell in a heap, catching my breath. Tears welled in my eyes as the reality of almost falling to my death caught up with me. But what about the baby?

I crawled up the slippery slope until I was surrounded by jungle once more. I had to find the child. Remembering the phone in my dress pocket I pulled it out, using the torch function to light the way. It cast a ghostly blue light onto the trees that blocked my path, but there was nothing ghostly about this jungle. It was alive and buzzing. I ignored the creatures that scampered from my light and picked up the pace. It had been several minutes since I'd heard the baby last. What if I found the child and it was too late? What if it had died of starvation or illness?

I reached the location from which I thought I'd heard its last cry, shining my light on the crooks of trees and between the roots that tangled across the ground. I tripped again and my phone flew through the air, sending light scattering. Eyes between the trees reflected back at me. Red eyes, yellow eyes, big and small.

The baby cried out again in one long scream that transformed into a wild, cat-like shriek. Creatures scampered and scattered from my light, dashing away into the jungle, the sound of the shriek growing distant with them.

It hadn't been a baby at all, but an animal's cry.

Heat rushed up my neck. I was stupid and now I was lost.

A vicious call replaced the sound of the animal's cry. My heart skipped a beat. I fumbled, picked up my phone, then shone it about, turning in circles. Which direction was the campfire?

Footsteps were coming towards me. I backed into a tree and sucked in a breath. I flashed my phone back and forth in the direction of the footsteps and roared out with my best impersonation of a tiger's growl. The footsteps continued towards me.

Mr Cuthbert's blue face appeared in the light from my phone and he cupped his hands over my mouth, shushing me. He was tense, his eyes wide and livid. He swung me over his shoulder and slunk through the jungle back the way he had come. He didn't stop until we were in the middle of the fires again. They were a welcome sight, even if they were waning.

He set me down and crossed his arms. I tucked my phone back into my dress pocket and hugged my backpack, which was now zipped closed. My body shook violently and tears welled up in my eyes. The tears overflowed and I sobbed into my backpack. Mr Cuthbert stayed still and silent, watching me.

I sucked in a breath. "I heard a baby crying," I said.

"You fell for the mimicry of the margay."

"The what?"

"The margay. They mimic sounds that lure their prey into a trap. Once their prey has fallen to their death, they feast."

It was such a shocking statement that it cut through my sobbing. I looked up, wild-eyed and horrified.

"They lured you away from the fire."

I trembled. I had thought it was a baby, a child in trouble. I'd been so sure. What was wrong with these worlds? Why would anyone want to live here? Why would they leave Earth for this kind of life? I needed a hug.

If only Mum were here.

"I want to go home."

He nodded his head. "Whilst all worlds may have derived from Earth, not all worlds are alike."

He sat down beside me and we watched the trees take shape again. When the light of sunrise split through the jungle, we stood and gathered our bags, kicking out the fires, and continued up the mountain.

"It is time I took you home," he said.

Relief washed over me at the thought. A warm shower, cheesy toast, straightening my hair. Even seeing Dad's face at this stage wouldn't be so bad.

My hand became clammy. I'd forgotten about the time difference. How many years had passed? I needed to know. Could he ever forgive me for being gone for so long, without any warning? Without any goodbyes? And what if so much time had passed that he wasn't even alive anymore? I wouldn't be able to apologise.

We climbed up and up, slashing through the thinning jungle, when the tree arch appeared round a bend. Tears formed in my eyes at the sight. Home was not so far away.

We stepped through the arch and the Hidden Grove appeared, an impossible sight on the small pinnacle of the mountain. I followed Mr Cuthbert down the alley of trees.

"I'm really sorry for last night. And for yesterday," I said.

He nodded in acknowledgement.

"Thank you for saving me."

"There was nothing in it."

We continued on in silence once more.

"Thank you for being my friend," I said.

He looked sideways at me. "I am just doing my job," he said.

I stumbled on a dense patch of grass. My body ached with exhaustion. I just wanted to lie down and close my eyes again. Tears of tiredness dribbled down my face, blurring my vision. I followed Mr Cuthbert blindly, the blur of his form always just ahead of me.

We reached the tree and climbed in comfortable silence. Mr Cuthbert sprang up the branches with ease as I struggled along below him, still quavering at the height. At the summit, he linked his arm with mine and we crossed the trunk together. The light flashed through me and disappeared as soon as it came. I was more than happy to leave Bayartai behind.

Relief washed over me once more. I would never have to do that again.

Mr Cuthbert helped me down the tree. When we reached the bottom, he dusted the bark from himself, his black coat free of dirt. He looked me up and down, raising his eyebrows. My body was covered in a cracked layer of mud, my school dress soaked through with it.

"You are a mess," he said.

I wiped the tears from my face and sucked in a deep breath.

"I don't care. I'm just glad to be home."

He nodded. We began the final walk through the Hidden Grove.

"I will never forget what you've done for me," I said.

"I have done nothing."

The tree arch was just ahead. A frosty breeze blew, ripping through me. I shivered. A knot formed in my stomach. Something wasn't right.

Through the tree arch I couldn't see the brown and green of the Australian bushland. Only a wall of white. Was the exit from the Hidden Grove blocked?

As we neared the tree arch, the white wall began to take shape. It was snow covering the ground and the trees and everything else in between. But it didn't snow where I came from.

Mr Cuthbert encouraged me across the threshold first, my shoes crunching on the sprinkling of fresh snow. My body shivered again.

"What happened?" I asked.

"A substantial amount of time has passed since we left."

My heartbeat picked up. What had happened to Earth? It was like the end of the world. How much time had really passed since I left? My dad's face flashed through my mind.

The trees ended and opened onto a clearing. We weren't on Earth at all. We were back in Purlieu. We had climbed the white lichen-covered tree. I had been so tired that I had unthinkingly followed along behind Mr Cuthbert, never questioning his direction. I had trusted him entirely to get me home.

I turned on him. "You tricked me!"

"What do you mean?"

"You said you would take me home."

He stroked his beard. "I thought this was home for you." He took a step back in defence, his jaw hanging loose. He looked sincere. I had no chance to question him further, for William came running from the cottage, wearing the same look of fury that Mr Cuthbert had given me the previous night.

"Where have you been?" William asked.

My mouth bobbed open but I failed to formulate a response.

"Weeks have passed," he said. "How could you do this to me?" He looked from Mr Cuthbert to me and back again, his eyes covered with a film of liquid.

Mr Cuthbert set down his carpetbag on the snow and pulled a brown package from it. He offered it to William. William looked at the package for a long moment, his face screwed up in a mixture of disgust and distress. He roughly pulled it from Mr Cuthbert's hands, then waved Mr Cuthbert away, dismissing him.

"I will deal with you next time," he said.

I found my voice. "Mr Cuthbert saved me," I said. "Twice."

"Saved you? He kept you away from me. Weeks have passed since you were here last."

Weeks? My heart skipped a beat. If so much time had passed in Purlieu, how much more could have passed back on Earth?

William looked back at Mr Cuthbert as though he wanted to express the fullness of his rage, but thought better of it. Mr Cuthbert picked up his carpetbag and nodded his head. I took the few paces between us and wrapped my arms around Mr Cuthbert. He tensed up.

"Thank you," I said. "Again."

He patted my back. I couldn't help but like him, despite his coldness.

I pulled away and he walked back the way we'd come, toward the Hidden Grove. William and I watched until he disappeared into the forest. Then William turned on me.

"You have no idea how worried I was," William said. "How could you?"

The reasons ran through my mind. Wanting to leave William—having left William—was trumped by the more pressing point that I needed to find out how much time had passed on Earth.

"I know I just got here, but I need to leave. Right now. I climbed the wrong tree last time. Can you please show me the right one?" I asked.

"You are going to leave me again?" William asked. "But I need you. I have been a mess without you." He burst into tears, collapsing on the snow at my feet. He buried his face in his hands and sobbed, his whole body shaking.

Had he read my note?

I felt awkward touching him. In my mind, we'd already broken up. Despite myself, I crouched down and placed my hand on his shoulder, rubbing back and forth.

"I cannot leave Purlieu, you see," he said. "What if my parents were to show up and I was not here? All those times I visited you on Earth, in the back of my mind, I could not help but think of the risk. I am trapped here."

If his parents were from Earth, wouldn't they be dead by now anyway? Because of the difference in time?

My skin flashed hot with embarrassment. How stupid could I be? William had travelled to and from Earth daily for the past three months we'd been dating. The time difference between Earth and Purlieu couldn't be that different. Relief washed over me. My dad wouldn't be an old man yet. I would be able to see him again. When I was ready.

William pulled me into him, wrapping his arms firmly around me, sobbing into my neck. "I need you, Evelyn. I would kill myself if you were to abandon me too. Please, never leave me like that again."

He threw me away from him erratically and pulled the pocket knife from his belt. Fear rushed through me. What had I done? I looked about for something to defend myself with.

He turned the knife on himself, holding it to his neck. "I will do it," he said. His face glistened, wet with tears. His eyes were serious and desperate. Despite the cold, sweat gathered across my forehead. I couldn't breathe.

"I cannot live without you," he said.

My mouth fell open again, my chest constricting. "Don't do it," I said. The light hitting the snow was too bright. I felt suffocated, just like I had at home with my father.

I reached out to William and gently placed my hands on his shoulders. "I won't leave you. I promise," I said, quivering. What had I just agreed to?

William's hand loosened on the pocket knife and his arm dropped to his side. His face unfurled and tears dribbled over his cheeks. He fell into me once more.

I couldn't just leave him in this state. Maybe I didn't love him like before, but I still cared about him. He obviously needed help.

And now I was sure that Earth time passed no faster than Purlieu time, I didn't need to rush home anymore. I could afford to stay a few more days, make sure William was okay. Wait until he was more stable.

9

M Y PHONE WAS almost out of battery.
I sat on the bed in the boudoir, the blanket
wrapped around me. In my absence from Purlieu, winter
had arrived and I had brought no clothes with me to
prepare for such icy weather.

Though William's demeanour hadn't changed, swinging
from one emotion to the next, my bag lay packed by the
bed, ready to leave at a moment's notice. I'd experienced
the full brunt of his anger, offence, and misery in the past
twenty-four hours. When would it pass? I sighed.

I flicked back through the photos on my phone,
looking for ones of home. A shiver ran up my spine as
images of the jungle of Bayartai filled the screen. I'd taken
them moments before being accosted by the natives.
Before I would be scarred forever by the images of a man
burning alive.

I swiped to the next image of the old woman walking
away from the impenetrable wall of Celoso. I kept swiping,
seeing the strange curling script message on the metal sign
with the window through the wall.

Why hadn't I been more attentive when William had
showed me the tree to Earth? I never would have ended

up in either world and back in Purlieu again if I had.

I swiped across again to Mr Cuthbert's cabin and the images of the notes I'd found beneath his bed. That was the day that William had started bossing me around. I swiped again and my stomach knotted. It was a selfie Tiffany and I had taken not long before we'd fallen out. We were at school in art class, goofing around with pigments, using them like henna. We'd struck a Bollywood pose.

I sighed again. If only Tiffany were here. If only we were still on speaking terms. I wouldn't even mind if she said, 'I told you so' about William. She had been right, after all. Tiffany would say it, then hug tackle me and vow not to move until it was fixed—even if talking through our disagreement took all night. She was always there before I even knew I needed her to be. Like the time I'd stayed over at her house and we'd hidden in her room, the music turned up loud to drown out the sound of her parents fighting. We'd talked all night beneath her bedcovers about our mutual crush on the new sports teacher, until I finally relented at dawn and opened up about the bad mark I'd gotten in Sports Ed.

Shortly after her parents had gone through their divorce, it was mum's funeral. Tiffany hadn't left my side, even skipping out on her weekend with her dad to stay with me. She had always put me ahead of her own problems.

No wonder Tiffany had blown up at me on the bus.

I wracked my brain but couldn't recall even one time when I'd dropped everything for her like she did for me. Heat flushed my face. She deserved better. Guilt ripped through me.

I was such a bad friend.

William walked through the door of the boudoir without knocking. I hid my phone beneath the covers, but I couldn't do anything about my packed bag on the floor.

He was dressed in a navy suit and bowtie and carried

the package Mr Cuthbert had given him. His face was wide in a big smile. He followed my gaze to the bag. The smile dropped.

"You have not unpacked yet?"

"I was just —"

"Never mind, never mind." He waved it away and sank into the bed close to me. Internally I sighed with relief that he wasn't going to blow up over the bag.

He placed a hand on my knee. "I should not have yelled, yesterday."

That was his idea of an apology? What about how he'd threatened to kill himself? I pursed my lips and held my tongue. Retorting was not going to help him to find stability.

"Can we put it behind us?" he asked. I nodded.

"Good. Good."

"Why are you all dressed up?" I asked.

His smile returned. "I have something I want to show you." His hands were shaking. "I arranged a trade with Mr Cuthbert the other day. It is why I sent you away that afternoon—I did not want to spoil the surprise." He motioned to the package in his hands and passed it to me. "Could you put this on and meet me downstairs?"

I nodded again. What was I agreeing to? I didn't want to do this, but I was reluctant to give William another reason to go off at me.

He left, glancing back at me when he reached the door, a look of hope in his eyes.

That day when I first met Mr Cuthbert and William had sent me away, I thought it was because I wasn't mature enough. But all he had wanted was to arrange the trade, because he wanted to surprise me. I didn't know what to make of it. Had I misjudged William?

I unwrapped the package and pulled back tissue paper to find soft, champagne chiffon. I lifted it gingerly. A satin covered, bone-lined bodice led into a chiffon full-skirt. Sparkling jewels dotted the fabric in sweeping lines of lace that pulled across the body.

I left the warmth of the bed covers and stripped, stepping with care into the ball gown. I twisted to zip it up. It fit snugly around my torso, draping to the ground. It dragged as I shuffled towards the wrought iron mirror, trailing behind me gracefully.

The dress was stunning. I smiled, despite myself, and smoothed out my auburn locks, patting down the fly-aways.

A shiver hit me, the cold climbing up through my feet. I didn't own any shoes suitable to wear with it, let alone having brought anything with me to Purlieu. I shuffled back over to the package and rifled through the tissue paper. A pair of matching satin-heeled boots lay tightly enveloped in the tissue. I laced them up and let out a long breath.

I stood for a moment, gazing at my reflection in the mirror. I longed to go home but couldn't deny how much I loved the way the fabric fell softly against the skin of my legs.

What could William possibly have planned? If it would help him to put his anxieties behind him and allow me to leave quietly, I was all for it.

But I couldn't deny the flutter that his gesture rekindled in my stomach. This was the William I had fallen for in the beginning. The thoughtful, romantic man chasing after my heart.

Careful not to trip on the voluptuous gown, I turned from the mirror and made my way downstairs, holding both walls for balance. Orchestral music drifted up from the clearing.

I was about to exit the cottage when a glint of light caught my eye. Hanging on the coat rack was a glistening black masquerade mask. It was simple in design, tracing only the tip of the nose and across the eyes. It was covered in black glitter. I leaned in to inspect it and realised that it wasn't glitter but hundreds of tiny black gems, hand-stitched to cover the entirety of the mask.

There was a note attached to it in William's handwriting. 'The final touch' it read. I followed the unspoken instruction and slipped it easily onto my face.

I stepped outside the cottage. My breath caught.

Bouquets of white roses and glowing lanterns were dotted across the clearing. The flowers were fashioned from snow and shimmered in the lamplight. William was standing, chest puffed out beside the nearest bouquet.

"Hello, Evelyn." He smiled a crooked smile, eyeing me up and down. "Tonight, the masks come off, he said.

I reached up to the mask across my eyes but he shook his head.

"Not that mask." He took a deep, shaky breath. "I have been keeping something from you, Evelyn."

An overwhelming sensation washed over me that I didn't want to hear what he was about to reveal.

"I am the master of this world. I have the power to will anything to do as I please."

I stared blankly at him. What did he mean?

He pulled one of the roses from the bouquet nearest him and held it in his open palm.

"Every land has one master, well, except for Earth of course. Some worlds call them kings, emperors, chiefs. Each has the ability to control anything in his, or her, world." He looked at the rose in his hand. "Melt," he said.

The snow flower immediately liquefied, melting and dripping from his hand until the flower no longer existed. He shook the excess water away.

"I am the master of Purlieu."

My heart beat uncomfortably in my chest. William was delusional, surely. His hand was just really warm.

"Come." He took my hand and led me around the side of the cottage. The clearing was filled with ice sculptures; people in suits and ball gowns and masquerade masks fashioned from snow. The faceless men and women were paired up, waltzing in perfect unison to music being played by an ensemble of snow-formed instruments.

The hanging lanterns threw light across the clearing and glistened off their icy backs. They moved without fault, eerily focused on their partner, devoid of emotion and voice.

Heat gathered around my neck and my heart quickened. They were dancing. They were made from ice and they were dancing. How could this be?

William looked at the ice men and ice maidens. "Stop," he said. They halted in their dancing simultaneously, sending a crackling echo through the clearing as the music also drew to a stop.

He glanced at me with a smile. I smiled weakly back. He looked at the ice sculptures once more. "Dance, double time," he said.

The music started up again to a fast beat. The ice sculptures continued to waltz, keeping in time with the orchestra's pace. "Triple time," he said.

The tempo increased. They moved unnaturally fast, not missing a step. The beat of the music made my heart palpitate. I clenched my teeth in terror. I needed to get out of here. But William couldn't know. I put on a false smile and squeezed his hand.

"I formed each one of them. It took hours," he said.

"They're amazing," I said, trying not to choke on the words.

"I did it all for you. Your inauguration to Purlieu."

Did he really believe that I intended on staying? Especially after this? I didn't just need to get away from here; I needed to get away from him. He was crazy, and maybe dangerous.

"Slow down," he said. The ice sculptures resumed a natural pace. The way they reacted without hesitation reminded me of how William had dismissed me from Mr Cuthbert's cabin. How despite myself, I had walked out of there, compelled to follow his instruction. It reminded me of the way the empress of Bayartai, despite me not understanding her language, had managed to force me towards that fire pit.

What William was saying was true. He had the power to make me do what he wanted, and he had used that power on me already.

The truth was too much to comprehend. How could he have done that? He said that he loved me. Why would he try to control me? And I had thought it was me who was weak, unable to stand up to him and say no, but all the while he'd been using his power over me without me even knowing.

How could I ever forgive him?

My breath came out short and sharp. I glanced about the clearing for an escape route. I needed to leave now—but how?

I tried to take quiet, deep breaths. I needed to think straight, to plan this out before William used his power on me again.

"Evelyn, are you okay?"

He was looking at me. I needed to control myself. He couldn't know how I felt about all this. He couldn't know that there was no way I was staying with him now. I put on my best expression of fascination.

"In Bayartai I saw a girl convince a fully-grown man to tie himself upside down by his toes above a fire pit," I said. "It makes sense now."

He opened his eyes wide and nodded knowingly. "Each world can have only one master, a title that is passed down through lineage in death or by declaration. Some masters are better than others." He watched the ice people for a moment. "I encountered a vast array of them in my travels."

"How did you become the master of Purlieu, then?"

"I am not actually sure. I have always been the master of Purlieu, at least for as long as I can remember."

He took my good hand and looked at my weak one. "Heal," he said. My hand started to itch and tickle. Before my eyes, the twisted scars across the palm of my hand melted down into the surface of my skin. The patches of calloused yellow disappeared until an even hue of pasty white remained. A cold breeze blew through the clearing and I felt the tingle of it across my palm.

My mouth dropped open. I flexed and stretched my fingers and they were able to straighten fully.

William smiled and took my healed hand in his. He had never touched that hand before.

"Dance with me."

We moved forward into the throng of dancers, my body complying without hesitation. I didn't know the steps but my feet somehow stepped in time with the perfect waltz of the sculptures, mimicking the movement of the ice maidens.

Horror ripped through me. He was blatantly using his power on me, not even trying to hide it. No hesitation, as if it was a perfectly normal, sane thing to do. As if it wouldn't destroy all sense of trust and affection that remained in me for him. Did he really believe it wasn't morally wrong?

I mirrored the ice sculptures, removing all emotion from my face. I allowed my body to move unobstructed to William's instruction, all the while wracking my brain for how I could escape. After an hour of uninterrupted dancing and turning over scenarios in my mind, I threw caution to the wind.

"I'm thirsty," I said.

He abruptly stopped dancing. My body echoed his. His face dropped.

"I thought women loved dancing," he said.

I shook my head. "It's not that—I just need a break."

He scrutinised my face for a moment, looking for the faintest hint of a lie. I kept my face steady, unreadable, just like I had trained myself to under my father's scrutiny.

"Okay. I will be right back."

He let go of me and slipped past the other dancers. I

watched him round the cottage until he disappeared. I waited a few moments and looked around at the ice people. They continued their perfect dancing, unperturbed by William's absence. I started walking casually in the general direction of the Hidden Grove, skating around the creepy dancers. I held my breath. Would they react if they realised where I was going? Or were they just as subjugated by William as I was?

What was I thinking? They weren't real people. They were made of snow. I threw the masquerade mask from my face and moved into a run, ducking in and around them for the Hidden Grove.

"Evelyn?" William called.

I sucked in a breath.

"Evelyn, where are you?" He sounded panicked. "Stop the music, stop dancing," he said. "Find her."

The music stopped and the ice sculptures stepped away from their partners. They moved to create a corridor, exposing me.

I was sprinting now. I had no choice. There was no going back, now that William would know I wanted to run from him. If I couldn't escape now, I never would.

"Evelyn, where are you going?"

I ignored him, pushing my body to move faster, my dress dragging.

"Stop her!" His voice was desperate.

I was mere metres from where the clearing ended and the forest began. The ice people moved again, forming a blockade. They linked arms and towered over me. I swung around to the right, hoping to find a gap or reach the end of the line and dodge around behind them. My heels stuck in the snow as I ran. I kicked them off, feeling the cold burn the soles of my feet.

"Take her!"

They unlinked their arms and lunged out, their cold hands grabbing at me, pulling and ripping at my dress. I'd run so far to the right that I'd swung back, facing the clearing and the cottage. William stood by the cottage, two mugs hanging by his sides, eyes wild. He watched me as I ran past, the ice people just steps behind.

They wouldn't relent in their chase. But what would they do once they caught me? What would William do once they caught me?

Images of the man in Bayartai burning alive flashed through my mind. Was William capable of such malice? Was he so cruel and immoral? Or would he entertain reason and allow me to leave if I simply told him I wanted to?

The last time I had tried that, he had threatened to end his life.

The moon reflected off the icy landscape, lighting my path. My body screamed at me to stop as I pushed myself up the little hills of the clearing. I was running out of breath. But, like a dull roar in my ears, the sound of footfalls crunching on the snow behind me drove me on.

I had a feeling that the ice people would not stop until they'd done what they were told to do—catch me. It wasn't an option. I pressed on.

The river came into view: a dead end. Forest lined the clearing to my left and to my right. Where should I go? I was headed straight for the water and the ice people were neither closer nor further from me. I had little chance of shaking them off.

I slid down the icy bank to the water's edge and sprang as far into the water as I could. It splashed into my face as I sank knee-deep. The cold ripped through me, my limbs instantly tensing, resisting my struggle forward. I used my arms as paddles as I waded through the water. The current was mercifully slow. Now the water reached up to my chest. I kicked and splashed and forced myself through, pulling the dress along behind me. I ignored the pain of the cold and the sounds of splashing coming from behind me, eyes fixed on the embankment on the other side. By the middle of the river, the water rose to my chin. I could do this. I had to do this. Just to the other side, then I'd figure things out from there.

My body jerked back in the water. I wheeled around in fright.

One of the ice men had caught me. He, in his glistening ice-fashioned top hat, was tugging on my dress. The mass of white figures was looming behind, like a tsunami. I was swept off my feet and pulled back through the water, my head falling below the surface.

I had no chance to breathe, but righted myself, finding I had moved slightly downstream. The ice man's arm had ripped off in the water. It washed downstream, disintegrating before my eyes. As he lumbered after me, his body melted and collapsed. The tsunami behind him lost momentum, sinking.

I swam for the other embankment and pulled myself from the water, gasping for air, aching for warmth but coercing my limbs to move. I had to get away before William tried to use his power on me again.

I took one last look behind me. The ice men and ice maidens hadn't made it past the middle of the river. Body parts were floating and disintegrating downstream, heads bobbing above the water before sinking. A few remained intact on the bank I'd come from. No sign of William.

I reached the top of the embankment and hurtled on into the forest beyond, heading for the mountains. The forest was eerily empty and solitary, silver trees stood motionless and the underbrush was minimal. My path was clear. The sound of my short sharp breaths, my feet thudding, and my dress slithering across the icy ground filled my ears. It was quiet, too quiet.

Surely I hadn't evaded him? Surely William and his ice sculptures had crossed the river somehow? I tensed my body, bracing for him to jump out from behind every tree I passed, fully expecting that the next moment would be my last moment of self-determination before he had me under his power again. I recoiled at the sight of a mound of snow, half expecting the ice sculptures to grow before my eyes, formed by the snow at my feet.

I dodged around a tree, then another, to confuse him with my trail. He wouldn't find me. He wouldn't catch me. I couldn't let him. I could not let him. Terror gripped me and I began to hyperventilate.

Snow fell through the gaps in the trees of the forest. Wind whipped up my sodden hair and sent a shiver down my back. My body started to shake. I couldn't keep running. I slowed to a jog, feeling the burn of the icy ground intensify on my feet. I needed to find shelter.

The snow came down more forcefully, obscuring further the path through the dark forest. My body shook violently from the cold. I pulled the top layers of the dress up and around my shoulders, hugging it tightly.

William loved me. At least he said he did. My dad had been right about judging people by their actions, and maybe he'd been right about not dating while I was at school, too, though surely not all men were like William. I wasn't old enough, strong enough or wise enough to deal with this.

William had controlled me. Intentionally. Why would he do that? What had happened to my boyfriend, the gentleman? Had I been such a bad judge of character? Had this side of him always been there, lurking below the surface?

I thought back over the last three months but failed to see how any of his words or actions had hinted at this other side of him before I'd come to Purlieu.

But the day we'd first met, he'd been very persuasive that I should see him again. Not to mention that he'd lied about where he came from. I had thought it flattering that he wanted to sketch me. Maybe it was his obsession, instead? And he had said such nasty things about Dad and Tiffany. It had been him that convinced me to leave school, always telling me that I didn't need it.

Maybe the signs were there, I had just been too blind to

see them. Tears welled in my eyes. How could I have been so stupid? I began to sob, clutching at myself for warmth and comfort.

The snow was thick and cold as it fell over my skin. The wind ripped through me, a constant barrage that I struggled to move against, stumbling along in the dark. Snow clouds obscured the moon and the forest became hard to navigate. I stretched my arms out blindly, looking up and about for a source of direction or providential sanctuary.

Dark shadows clung to the branches of the trees above. I stopped walking to take a closer look. The long body and nestled wings of Pterodactyls took shape. My body tensed. I stifled a scream, which abruptly ended my sobbing, holding my breath instead.

I stepped slowly, quietly, making sure not to disturb their sleep. One Pterodactyl back at the cottage I could handle, but a whole drove of cold, hungry dinosaurs was an entirely different matter. They were scavengers after all, and all they needed to do was wait until I collapsed on the ground, unable to carry on any longer, ready for them to pick at the meat between my bones. I shuddered at the thought. It sent a new wave of shivering across my body.

I pushed against the wind, passing hundreds of them, determined not to give them any reason to wake, to see me, to attack me. Tears welled in my eyes once more. I suppressed a whimper. There was no way I could survive this. Between frostbite, being eaten alive, and falling under William's power, I was surely done for. No one back on Earth would ever know what had happened to me. Tears trickled silently down my face, freezing before they dripped from my chin.

I felt so cold it burned. I was going to die in this forest.

The path before me rose higher with every step. I looked up. The mountain towered above, its cliff face before me. The trees were sparse here, the Pterodactyls behind me now. Snow inundated my face. I'd run out of forest to hide in, the mountain blocking me from placing greater distance between myself and William. I stumbled up the mountain instead. My teeth chattered. I whimpered, not knowing what to do.

Darkness lay ahead, a patch of shadow across the face of the mountain. Were there more Pterodactyls hiding? I stumbled at the thought, feeling utterly trapped, with nowhere left to run. I slumped down into the snow and sobbed, not caring anymore. Perhaps the Pterodactyls would be a better death than hypothermia. If they were Pterodactyls, then I'd surely woken them by now.

I sucked in a breath and looked up at the shadow, scrutinising it through the flurry of snow. It was too perfect a semi-circle. I got to my feet and staggered towards it, my frozen body screaming out in protest at every movement. It was a cavity in the mountainside, dark inside. Did I dare venture in? My teeth chattered. I had to at least try.

I stepped out of the brunt of the blizzard and into the relief of the cave, my hands out in front, waiting to feel the back wall of a shallow fissure. The sound of the wind whistled against its opening behind me, growing distant and echoing as I edged away from it. The cave kept going, deep into the mountain.

My back loosened, no longer tense and shivering. I collapsed against the cave wall and wrapped the skirt of my dress around me into a makeshift pillow and blanket. Sleep overcame me.

10

THE WHISTLING OF the wind outside heightened the silence of the cave. I lay in a pool of water. The snow that had covered my dress, my hair, my body, had melted. I stretched out my stiff muscles and shuffled down deeper into the cave, its warmth surrounding me. I must have been out for a few hours, for the light of morning refracted around the corner into the cavern where I lay.

William had been in control from the start, I could see it now. From trying to convince me that I didn't need school, to bringing me to Purlieu under false pretences, to how he forced me to dance against my will. I'd been making excuses for him, as if it would be more loving to accept him as he was. Bullshit. It was he who had failed to love me.

The best I could do was run away, just like I'd run from my problems at school and with my father. All I ever did was run. It was time I stood up for myself. Time I said the things I was too afraid to say. Time I stopped being a coward and faced my problems.

I needed to confront William, even if he had some crazy powers that I didn't understand or fully comprehend.

If I could just appeal to his compassionate side and give him no reason to control me, help him see that I wasn't the one for him. That I was leaving him for good and returning to Earth. I could do that, I think. What I would do once I reached Earth, I'd figure out when I crossed that bridge.

The strength of determination sent warmth to my cheeks, my hands. I rose to my feet and made my way back through to the cave entrance. The blizzard had passed. I edged forward eagerly until the mouth of the cave was in sight, looking out over the forested valley.

The ground began to shake beneath my feet. The stones on the ground rattled. I stepped back and crouched for stability. Had William seen me and sent an earthquake my way? The shaking intensified and snow and branches came pouring into the cave. Fear gripped me and all too suddenly a pine tree rushed at me, riding the snow. It swept me to my feet and pinned me to the ground. I threw my arms around my head and lay as still as possible, bracing for pain as snow and debris poured around me.

The shaking reduced and stopped. The snow settled. I waited. The shaking didn't return. I tried to get up but the trunk of the tree ran right across the back of my legs. I twisted and struggled, trying to manoeuvre out from under it but it was too heavy to budge, and there wasn't enough room for me to slip out.

I was trapped.

The weight of the trunk was crushing my legs, its bristles jabbing into me through my dress. I could barely breathe, and it hurt when I tried. I needed to escape but the more I struggled, the heavier the trunk weighed on me and the more suffocated I felt.

I cried out in frustration, grief and anxiety. Hot tears spilled onto the ground. If only I had faced William when I'd had the chance, instead of running away, this never would have happened. How stupid it would be if I died here, where nobody even knew I was. No one was coming to save me.

Here was my end: in a mountain cave of a faraway world. Generations from now, someone would stumble upon the cave and they would find my dry bones and wonder who I had been. They would conclude that if I had died here, all alone, then I had surely been no one important.

I wept inconsolably, lowering my face into the dirt and snow.

My breath settling down into a hiccup, through my tears, I saw a small frosted daisy sitting propped up in the snow. I hadn't looked around to properly gauge the debris brought into the cave with the avalanche. The little flower seemed like a miracle or maybe a sign.

It reminded me of the first sign of my mother's oncoming death. I'd found her in the backyard one afternoon, lying flat on her face in the garden. The memory sent a shiver of dread across my skin.

I placed my finger into the dirt of the cave floor and traced the outline of her body, surrounded by the flowers. I wiped the floor clean and traced her body again, this time out the front of the house with a nosebleed. She'd run into the front door. I wiped the floor clean again and placed her on the gurney in the morgue with cuts across her face and arms. She had been so lifeless.

I'd rushed in, wide-eyed and numb from my father's phone call, not really believing it. Until I saw her. My father was just standing there, looking at her dead body, covered in scratches and cuts from the car accident. He seemed entirely unable to process it. He said nothing, not even acknowledging my presence.

The coroner was saying something about how she had crashed into a ditch, minutes from the hospital. That she'd been going home early from her shift because she had a fever. No one else was on the road, so she must have gotten distracted. He couldn't be sure. He'd need to do an autopsy. My father signed some forms and we left together, driving all the way home in silence.

We'd later found out that she had contracted a disease from a tick in the garden. Which was why she had passed out in the flowerbed, why she'd banged into the front door, and why she'd had a fever. They were all symptoms and she would eventually have died from it. They said the car accident was a mercy.

Only it didn't seem like a mercy to me. I didn't get to say goodbye.

My mother, who was so beautiful, so perfect in every way, lived her whole life doing only one thing wrong—dying. Dying too soon. Dying when her daughter needed her most. Dying because of what she loved to do—gardening. Dying when her husband and daughter would live on and miss her every day.

Tears streamed down my face in a constant flow, dripping onto the dirt. I heaved for breath, not caring how loud I cried. No one would hear me up here. No one would try to console me, or tell me whether it was good or bad to cry. I let it all out. All the emotion I'd bottled up since she'd died, all that I'd held inside because I felt like I wasn't allowed to express my feelings, because my father hadn't even shed a tear.

Yet I'd wanted to cry every day that she was gone. Every time I turned to share something with her and remembered she wasn't there. Every time I'd sworn I'd heard her singing from the garden but it had just been the wind. Every time I'd sat at the dining table with my father, only to eat dinner in silence. I missed her smile, her dirt-smeared face, contented from spending the afternoon in the garden, and her warm hugs. I missed her so much.

I continued to trace across those red lips, that small freckle in the shape of a flower below her ear, those delicate hands covered in blood. I dug my finger into the dirt, rapidly drawing out the scene in the morgue, the cold, hard dirt ripping into my frozen finger; the sterile plastic chairs, the bleached white cloth that covered her naked body, the blank look on the coroner's face and the goosebumps on his arms from the cold, cold room. Through the blur of the dirt, I could see the image perfectly as though I were back there, the smell of chlorine still fresh in my memory.

A stone lay nearby. I picked it up and carved the image deeper into the dirt, tracing continuously around the shape of her body in a frenzy of anguish. I needed to get the image out of my head, the strange way she had lain there on the gurney, lifeless, legs at odd angles, head tilted slightly, mouth agape.

She had died too soon. She had a husband and a daughter who needed her. She had abandoned me.

Anger boiled within me, fuelling my crazed sketching until the picture before me was indecipherable. Deep troughs criss-crossed over each other and piles of dirt and dust lay before me. The stone clattered from my hand as I broke down once more. I was all out of tears. Thirsty and tired and aching, my sobs rasped and croaked, echoing about the cave.

My confidante, my greatest fan, my wise counsel, was gone. I needed her. How could she just die like that? How could she leave without saying goodbye? How could she leave me alone with my father?

If she hadn't died, my dad and I would never have argued, and I would never have run away from home to seek comfort in William's arms.

I wouldn't be here now, trapped and dying.

My fist slammed into the ground as I cried out in self-pity. Shaking my head, I sucked in a deep breath and closed my eyes. I took another deep breath, steadying myself, then another.

She had loved the garden. It was better that she had enjoyed her garden and died for it than if she'd never had it at all. There was no one to blame. Not the hospital, not my father for suggesting she work that shift, not myself for disregarding the signs of the disease. It was just one of those things that happened. People die. I needed to accept that.

My breath came out shaky, so I took another deep gulp.

Though dehydrated and weary, I didn't feel numb. A weight lifted from my shoulders. My head felt less cloudy. Tension released from my back.

She was gone but it would be all right. I opened my eyes, looking at the trenches in the dirt before me. An idea struck me and I seized the stone again, twisting my body as best I could, driving the stone into the dirt around my legs. A long trench beside my body would create a pocket of space for me to move freely—to escape.

I dug away at the ground, piling loose dirt around me. The piles grew steadily higher. My arms began to ache. Would the trunk just lower with my body into the cavity in the ground? Or was there enough of the tree's weight being taken by its branches to hold it in place and allow me my freedom?

I had to take the risk.

The stone in my hand clanged and vibrations shot up my arm. I'd hit rock. Digging around it, I tried to find where it ended so that I could lift it from the ground, but I couldn't find the edge. My plan was foiled. I threw the stone away in frustration. It clattered across the ground out of reach. I instantly regretted it.

Not much dirt had been moved by my efforts, but maybe it was enough? My legs were scrawny, after all. My hands brushed away the loose bits around me, giving me room to move, and I sucked in a deep breath. Pushing up against the trunk with my hands, I wriggled my body beneath it. The dress tore, catching on the bristles of the trunk, grating across the surface of my skin. I cried out in pain, but my legs scraped free. Releasing the trunk, I rolled away as it collapsed, catching the top two layers of my dress. On my back, panting, exhausted and aching, I smiled and whooped aloud. Maybe I wouldn't die here after all.

Taking the ensnared fabric in my hands, I ripped it free, determined not to be trapped any longer. My legs were red-raw and covered in scratches. Droplets of blood dotted the skin where the bristles had skewered me. I stretched out my legs and found I could move them freely. It was going to be okay.

My head slumped back into the dirt as I contemplated my next move. To stay any longer in the cave, I knew I would starve, yet I had little desire to head out into the snow.

I looked over to the cave entrance. It was obscured by the pine tree's thicket of branches. Boulders and snow filled the spaces between. Light seeped through the gaps, making a diamond-filled cave out of the snow. A breeze blew in and chilled my face.

How could I get out of the cave without it collapsing further, or instigating another avalanche? My heart skipped a beat at the thought of being caught in the snow itself, unable to breathe. I sucked in a deep breath—I could do this.

Taking my dress in my hands once more, I ripped some more fabric, this time creating long strips, and wrapped my hands until they were covered. Cupping my hands together, I shovelled the snow away and tossed large and small rocks behind me. My hands followed a rhythm of shovelling and tossing, shovelling and tossing. It was quick progress, creating an Evelyn-size hole through the snow.

A rock came loose at the base of the pile, just to my left, tumbling out and down onto the cave ground. It sent an echo up the mound, rocks shifting and rolling to fill the empty space below. They thundered and scattered around me. My feet were swept out from beneath me. My shoulder hit the ground hard and I immediately whipped my arms up around my head, bracing for a crushing blow.

The cave fell silent as the rocks steadied.

I slowly unravelled myself, feeling the pain swell in my shoulder. Where there had been small gaps through the cave entrance, now rocks interlocked with one another and entirely obstructed my path. I let out a shaky breath. Would I be trapped in this cave forever?

A sat in a moment of despair.

Breeze picked up my hair and blew it in my face. There was a draught, but it wasn't coming from the cave entrance. Instead, it was as if it were being blown into the avalanche of snow and bouncing back at me. But where was it coming from? Could there be another opening?

I focused on the draught's flow over my skin and followed it towards the back of the cave, past the pool of water I had left behind previously. The passage continued to twist and turn, growing darker with every step. My hand gripped onto one side of the passage and, through my makeshift glove, I felt the jagged edges of the rock, following them deeper and deeper within. The draught increased as the passage narrowed.

Was I walking into a passage that would become too narrow to navigate? My heart pounded against my chest. I sucked in quick, sharp breaths. Left and right, the passage continued to zigzag in a shroud of darkness. I lost track of time. If I let go of the wall, I would surely forget which way was up.

The draught was a rushing wind now, whipping my face, my cheeks smarting with the cold. I rounded a corner and the darkness seemed less gloomy. With the next turn, and the next, my surroundings grew lighter until I could see my hand upon the jagged rock wall, the grey of the granite tunnel illuminated, a golden light to follow.

Hope grew inside me. Had I found a way out of the cave? I wasn't going to die here! I could still make it home.

The light became blinding. I let go of the wall and shielded my eyes. Around the next corner the sky was unveiled, blue and clear and magnificent. Relief washed over me.

I reached the end of the passage, stepping into a cavern. I edged towards the mouth of the cave eagerly. My stomach dropped. I was on the precipice of a mountain, far higher up than I'd climbed on the other side.

Mist clung to peaks and valleys that swept across the landscape. Young forests lined the river where it forked, one course flowing around the mountain to my right.

Who knew what lurked in those forests? It was beautiful yet terrifying, just like Bayartai. Low-lying cloud parted to show mist filling the valley. I looked down the mountain to find the best path to take into the veiled valley.

A shock ran through my body. I stepped back in horror. There on the lower mountainside stood the remains of a village. Some of the little buildings were more intact than others, with four wooded walls and a roof, while others were covered in char marks, roofs caved in, walls missing. An entire village had been set alight.

How could this be? William had said that no one had ever lived in Purlieu. Was it possible that there were many nations across this world that he wasn't even aware of? Or were they all long gone?

I moved down the mountain. The smoothest path led me straight into the village. All I wanted was to reach the bottom, to find my feet safely on flat ground.

The buildings on the periphery of the village were the worst off, nothing more than piles of rubble and splintered logs, covered in black burn marks where flames had licked them. I walked through what was left of the village, my curiosity growing when I passed a building that had remained intact. I doubled back.

Snow covered its roof, but an entire wall was missing. I poked my head inside. It was a modest dwelling with no internal walls or doors. The floor was covered in a carpet of snow. I stepped inside and recoiled immediately, screaming. On the floor, curled in a ball, was the skeleton of a child.

I took a slow breath in and out, for my heart had started racing. It was just a skeleton. The child had died a long time ago. Not even the clothes on its back or its hair remained.

The poor thing. Had the child died before or after the fire came through? My heart wouldn't let up as I left the house and continued down to the valley.

What had happened here, and when? Was it long before William's time? How could one fire wreak havoc on an entire village, erase an entire civilisation?

The mist that had filled the valley started to lift. More buildings took shape. Two-storey, sandstone buildings clustered around a town centre. In the heart stood a turreted castle. Maybe there was food, or clothes? Or maybe I could stay the night?

I entered the town centre. The buildings were made of stacked sandstone bricks, with what looked to be shopfronts at the bottom and lodgings at the top. Char marks covered the stone façade of building after building. Fire had come through here too.

I imagined trinkets and spices, tailors and blacksmiths, fresh fruit and vegetables, meat and grain, all overflowing from the shopfronts in piles of wealth and abundance. Clothes were sold from the windows upstairs and seasonal banners lined the streets. Bustle and chatter filled my ears of a pretend marketplace made up of colour and life and laughter.

What I saw before me was the absence of these things: long, empty, grey streets, missing doors and windows, utter desolation. My arms gripped around me tighter as I continued through the town.

A high wall surrounded the castle, a wrought-iron gate the only entry, standing wide open and unattended. I entered the drive and approached the castle. Two turrets flanked either side of a central chamber. The same sandstone bricks were layered atop each other in concentric circles, creating a sun-shaped pattern around a grand gunmetal door. The great door was ajar, snow spilling inside.

I pushed it open with a grunt. It creaked and groaned, but eventually gave way. I gritted my teeth, my shoulder crying out in resistance. The door opened onto a long, carpeted hall. Tattered yellow banners hung from the ceiling and chairs lined the two walls.

I stifled another scream. On every chair sat a skeleton, dressed in decaying finery. Their clothes were made of different hues of velvet, with capes and bonnets and gloves. Their heads lolled to the side or back or had fallen entirely forward. My heart pounded. I stared at the sea of empty eye sockets that appeared to be staring back at me.

How could so many have died in their very seats? This destruction had to be orchestrated by an enemy of some sort, an enemy who had come to wipe them all out in one fell swoop. But the fires had not reached the castle, so how had they died? Could it have been of boredom, or a lethal gas, or poisoning? Or had their master ordered everyone to die and so they promptly did? Did a master possess that level of power?

William's face flashed through my mind. I shuddered. Perhaps this was the real story of how William had come into his power, that he had killed all these people to become master of Purlieu. It wouldn't be the first time William had lied to me.

My stomach grumbled. There was nobody living here, so there was no hope of food. I was unsure why I thought there might have been food—wishful thinking, perhaps. But did I dare take clothes from the back of a corpse?

I stepped into the hall. At the end was a throne with a host of smaller ones either side of it, about a dozen in total. Each chair housed another skeleton. They were dressed to the hilt in matching, embroidered silver thread and green velvet fabrics with varied amounts of puffiness overflowing from their thrones. Several more skeletons lay at their feet. Could the master not have stopped the attack by simply commanding the adversary to stand down?

I passed the courtiers and headed straight for the master and his warm cape. His skeleton eyes stared back at me strangely. Something wasn't quite right.

I pressed closer, the silence of the hall loud in my ears, then flinched as dread washed over me. A small dagger stuck out from his eye socket. An instant death. Each of his offspring or concubines, or whoever they were by his side, shared identical blows.

Someone had murdered them.

I edged closer still. The daggers were night black. Had the king been a master? Was that why he was murdered along with all of his family?

William's voice echoed in my mind, "Each world can have only one master, a title that is passed down through lineage in death or by declaration."

Perhaps this king had been even more terrifying than the empress in Bayartai? But if the murderer had been doing the people a favour by ridding them of a tyrant why would he have burned down the village too? Why would anyone want to kill the master of a land along with all of its people?

Whoever they were, they had somehow managed to overpower a master. Realisation washed over me. I stood up a little straighter, relaxing my shoulders.

Masters were not invincible.

Surely that meant that I could find a way to defend myself against William if he tried to use his power on me again. Surely. But how?

I walked the remaining few paces up to the king and, in one swift motion, pulled the black knife from his eye and ripped the fur cape from his back. Without hesitation, I wrapped the cape around myself and walked out of the castle, ignoring the shiver that ran up my back as I made my way through the ghost town. I ignored, too, the numbing iciness of my feet and the tinge of regret at not stealing a pair of shoes.

I reached the fork where the river rounded the mountain and dashed down the embankment. I drank greedily, the cold tightening my teeth, smarting at my throat.

"Wake the eyes, wake the body." Dad's wisdom echoed through my mind. "Come now, sweetheart," he'd say. He'd be standing in the dark by my bedroom door on an early Saturday morning. "Time to get going, we've got a big day ahead."

So would begin my trudge to the bathroom basin and a cool spray of running water upon my morning eyes. The market would begin in just under an hour and the car hadn't been packed with all the pot plants yet. The freshness of the water and the urgency of the matter forced me to spring into action. Not once were we ever late.

I filled my stomach with the water and continued to trudge through the snow. My body began shivering. I drew the cape in tighter around myself and pressed on along the river, distracting myself by breathing in the landscape. The mountain towered to my right, its ridges zigzagging with lethal stone precipices, naked against the snowy backdrop. I rounded the mountain and snow and broken trees from the avalanche littered the base of the mountain. Beyond that, old pine trees clustered to form the forest I had first travelled through the night before. Mist still clung to the trees, moving slowly through the forest. Nothing else moved, not even the wind blew to rustle the tree branches. I edged closer and entered the forest once more. The light dimmed with the shadow of the trees and the blanket of mist.

Would the Pterodactyls be sitting up amongst the branches once more? My heart did a double-beat. A little bird flew past, a blur of orange. I lost my footing and fell into a tree. Pain beat through me as my shoulder connected with the trunk. I gritted myself against the pain and looked up just in time to watch the bird flit through the forest and disappear behind a tree. Its song echoed back at me. It had looked like the robin from the farm.

Mum used to sing a song about a robin. Dad would whistle along. It had been a long time since I'd heard it.

I tried not to think about the Pterodactyls ahead or the throbbing pain in my shoulder. Instead, I sang.

"Robin flies high,
Touches the sky.
Yet comes back to sing a song of jubilation.
Take my hand,
Leave this land,
Then come back to share your exploration."

My voice sounded shaky and my feet stung with every step. I focused on the memory of my mother's serene face. She would sing as she gardened, while Dad whistled through the kitchen window. Her face would be screwed up in concentration, pulling weeds from beneath the pavers with a vengeance, yet her voice came out smooth and angelic. Dad hadn't whistled since Mum died.

"No one knows
Where the Robin goes,
As winter comes to say hallo.
Then comes spring,
Hear it sing,
As it returns on the morrow."

The mist was dissipating from amongst the trees but the land did not become brighter. What was the time? Was night falling again so soon? I shuddered at the thought of another night in this eerie, quiet forest.

"It sings merrily,
Oh, so merrily,
As the sun shines upon it."

The thought of the baking heat of our old home in summer teased me. I ached to walk up those steps and into that creaky house again. Despite the peeling paint, the old gas stovetop, and the overgrown garden out back.

"It flies swiftly,
Oh, so swiftly
For its time has come."

Dad sitting on the couch in the living room, waiting for me to get home. Maybe that wouldn't be so bad? Maybe it'd be nice to see him again?

"Yes, no one knows
Where Robin goes,
All except for little Robin.
For only it knows
When to go,
And the time to come home."

My teeth chattered, shivering taking control of my body. How long did it take someone to die from the cold, or to get frostbite? I chanced a glance at my feet, not daring to look too closely, shaking the snow from them. They seemed to be the right colour, though numbness had set in.

I hoped I was heading in the right direction.

The smell of vanilla floating out of the kitchen window and up into my bedroom above, drifted into memory.

"One drop," Dad would say. "Just one drop on a hot stove to make it smell like I've been in here all day." He'd wink, then reach into the freezer to grab a store-bought fruit pie.

When I was little, as he prepared dinner, he'd avidly tell me all about the origins of the ingredients going into the meal. He'd pause only to look at me seriously.

"Evelyn, be quiet a moment—the news is on!"

The drone of the TV would fill our silence, then he'd

crack a goofy grin and bellow with laughter, as if it had been me doing all the talking. I'd giggle along and it would end with him tickling me, Mum entering right on time to cover us with dirt from the garden. Then I started high school and my father just wanted to talk about my life all the time. He dared not touch me anymore.

I continued my song with a broken tune, sucking in air between each syllable.

"It sings mer-ril-lee,
Oh, so mer-ril-leee,
As the sun shines upon it."

It was definitely becoming darker. I could no longer see deep into the forest ahead. The terrible bird-like squawk of the Pterodactyls echoed through the forest behind me. I caught my scream in my mouth and ducked down to the ground, covering my head. The snow at my feet was softly packed, delicate and pure. I waited to be plucked up and used as a plaything by the Pterodactyls. Though the squawking resounded again and again, it did not move closer. I must have already passed through the edge of the forest where they nested at night.

I sucked in a deep breath and got to my feet. I reminded myself I could do this. Dying in these forests was not an option. I would confront William and be on my way home before midnight.

My determination grew as I slogged through the snow. I ignored my feet that felt like they were on fire, the stinging cuts on my legs, the constant ache in my shoulder and the grumble of my stomach. I fixed my eyes on home: on the high ceilings, the butter shelf in the fridge filled with chocolate, and the towering figure of my father in the hallway waiting to question me on where I'd been.

He had such a presence, my dad—he filled the whole hallway. He gave the best hugs, not that I'd been given one of those in a long time. I missed the way his arms enveloped me, how it felt like nothing would ever harm me so long as I stayed in his arms. But I hadn't stayed in his arms. I'd run away. And now, look at the mess I was in. If only I'd stayed in his arms.

It would be okay, though. I would make things right. All I needed to do was find my way home to him. Tonight. I just needed to leave William first, to walk away.

Light appeared ahead. Between the trees, I could see the faintest sunset of green. My heart leapt in my chest— the cold was almost over. I would be gone from Purlieu and back home in balmy, sticky, uncomfortable summer. A grin spread across my face and my teeth stopped chattering for a moment.

I hiked up my dress around me and picked up my pace, dodging around trees to keep my eyes on the sunset, dreaming about dipping my feet in a warm bath. The last trees of the forest were now behind me as I stood on the edge of the river embankment. Running away from William had been a mistake. If only I'd had the guts to face him at the ball, I wouldn't be shivering uncontrollably, contemplating how to cross the river without getting wet.

Poking above the little hills on the other side, I could see the treetop of the cottage. I gritted my teeth. It was too late to wonder how things could be different. I couldn't change it. All I could do was gather up every ounce of courage I had left, and face William now.

I wandered along the embankment, looking through the dimming green light for a place to cross. I found a section where the water moved more slowly. Boulders lay scattered across it, the water lapped around them. I made my way carefully from boulder to boulder until I stood in the middle of the river. The next rock was a little off to the right and only large enough for one foot. I stepped out and placed my foot on top. The water lapped up and over the rock, smarting with a deadly cold smack. My body overbalanced and the cape flew from my back to be carried downstream. The image of the ice man's arm floating down the river flashed through my mind. I took a deep breath and ignored the wind whistling across my bare arms, sending a new fit of shivers across my body. I took a quick step to the next boulder but the momentum made me slip, the cold water enveloping me, sending a paralysing shock up through my body. A yowling scream escaped my mouth, stifled as my face entered the water. My feet hit the ground and I pushed against it, despite my stiffening limbs. I broke the surface of the water, gasping for air, and splashed through the water to the other embankment. My eyes were plastered wide open in shock.

I scrambled out of the water, yelping and gasping. I'd lost the black dagger. My heart beat uncomfortably in my chest. I whimpered. I needed to keep moving, I was too close to give up now.

I breached the top of the embankment. The wind barraged me, turning the droplets that covered my body into ice. The ice cracked and fell as I forced myself to continue towards the cottage.

In the green glow left of the dying sun, stationed on the hill like sentries, were three ice maidens. The sight jolted my heart and I stopped in my tracks.

Would they come for me? I edged closer. They didn't move, and I noted that their shape was still fashioned to look like they wore ball gowns. Their bodies were facing neither the river nor the cottage, looking off into the forest with empty faces. Their profiles looked queer without noses pointing out.

Reaching the crest of the little hill I stared at them as I passed, bracing for an arm to reach out and grab me at any moment. But they didn't. Still, I couldn't shake the feeling that they were watching my back as I continued on towards the cottage. I shuddered. It was an eerie reminder of the disastrous ball William had thrown me. How he had blatantly controlled me.

The cottage came into full view on the plain of the clearing. William was off to the left, ferrying the animals from the yard and into the barns. My stomach constricted.

Nerves overcame me but I continued onto the plain. How would William react when he saw me? Would he willingly let me grab my things and go?

Through the whistle of the wind the snow crunched behind me. I whipped around and braced for the ice maidens to be upon me, but they hadn't moved. I saw instead the grey backs of a pack of wolves appearing at the top of the hill by the ice maidens. Their eyes were fixed upon me. Where had they come from?

I cried out, my scream carried away on the wind. They bounded into action across the icy plain, moving quickly over the snow in my direction. My heart pounded and breath escaped me as I turned and ran towards the cottage. I knew they would be too fast, that they would catch me and tear me apart before I got ten metres away.

It was over. All that I had been through in the mountains and with William, everything back home since dealing with mum's death would all have been for nothing. I would be with her soon.

As I stumbled through the snow, I waited for the impact, waited for pain to rip through me as they sank their teeth into me, scratched up my skin with their claws and tossed me about as a plaything before eating me alive.

A sob escaped me. I could hear William's muffled yell and, behind me, a loud thump, the sound of cracking glass and whimpering. The wolves growled but I sensed they had stopped chasing me. I chanced a glance behind, and stopped in my tracks.

A thick wall of ice had appeared directly behind me. It was covered in crack lines and a smear of blood. Lying on the ground on the other side of the ice were three of the five wolves, limp, dead. The remaining two were crouched low, growling. One barked before they turned and ran back the way they'd come.

The smear of blood was at head height. I had been but a moment from impact.

I collapsed on the ground, breathing too fast. Their

teeth had been so close. William had created the ice wall. He had saved me. He had the power to erect walls in mere seconds.

I quivered. What had I gotten myself into?

William was running towards me. He surrounded me with his arms and pressed his lips against my temple.

"Are you okay?

He pulled back from me and inspected my body, pulling my hair back from my face. He wiped the tears that streaked my cheeks.

"Did they hurt you? Are you in pain? You are freezing," he said, stroking my hair. "Where did you go, and what happened to your dress?" He rubbed his hands up and down my arms to warm me.

"I'm fine," I said.

He continued to rub my arms.

"William, stop it." I brushed him away and stood up, folding my arms. "You had no right to use your power on me," I said.

"What are you talking about?" He stood also and motioned to the wolves and the ice wall. His forehead crinkled.

"I used it on them, not on you. I saved you."

"You lost my trust when you used it on me at the ball."

His mouth gaped open. He looked sorry.

"I can't be with you anymore. I'm leaving you, William."

His eyes darkened, the compassion leaving them entirely. He stomped his foot on the ground. "No," he said. His voice was shaky, filled with distress. I steadied my breath and tried to remain calm and in control, ignoring the fear that was bubbling just below the surface of my own voice.

I walked past him towards the cottage. He stomped his foot again.

"You are made to stay with me in Purlieu."

"No," I said. I turned back to him and pointed at the

cottage.

"You're going to watch me go upstairs and get my things. You're going to let me leave, like a real man would."

His upper lip curled. His eyes turned to slits. He spat at me.

"You are not going anywhere." He puffed his chest out and clenched his fists. His mouth turned into a dirty smile. "You are mine, and if you will not choose to stay of your own accord, then I will make you obey."

My stomach flipped over. "No." I turned to run.

11

THE MUSCLES IN my legs screamed in protest. It felt like tendons were being wrenched away from bone. I wanted to move but my legs stayed entirely in place, sitting casually on a tree stump in the animal yard with a cow in front of my face. My arms moved in a methodical, rhythmic fashion, up and down, up and down. I shot her milk into the bucket at my feet, robotically following William's command as he towered over me.

A benign smile was plastered across my face.

I hated him. I hated him. I HATED HIM.

My feet were now warm, the wounds on my legs healing over. Food filled my stomach, but I was his prisoner.

"Perfect, Evelyn. Perfect," he said.

Run. Run. RUN!

My legs ached from resistance. If I hadn't lost that black dagger, if I could move freely, I would drive that blade into his chest and sprint for the Hidden Grove.

I missed the bucket. William's face dropped. He grunted.

"No. You do it like this." He knelt down and wrapped his hand tightly around my hands, pulling on the teat. Milk shot into the centre of the bucket.

"We do this because one should never do anything with the mind that could first be done with the hands," he said.

The fox gave a high-pitched bark from the fence of the animal yard. William's grip on my hand loosened. He stood and poked his head over the cow, his face becoming stonier.

"Stay put."

He walked around the side of the cow towards the gate. His feet crunched away on the snow.

Now was my chance. I tried to get up but I couldn't. It was like my body was glued to the tree stump. I tried to wriggle, to flail my arms about, but my arms were set, hand still wrapped around the teats.

"YOU!" William yelled. "What are you doing here?"

The deep eloquence of Mr Cuthbert's voice spoke back. "Master William, it is Wednesday. I always visit on Wednesday," Mr Cuthbert said.

"Wednesday? It is only Sunday." Chain clinked. "How can it be Wednesday already?" William asked.

My hand loosened on the cow's teat. I uncurled my fingers one by one and sat back. Fogginess lifted from my mind, blown away by the wind of William's distraction. I could look about freely, albeit stiffly.

If I yelled out to Mr Cuthbert, would he respond? Would he save me from William's control?

"This is all your fault. You put ideas into her head," William said, "and she was almost killed in Bayartai."

I tried to stand, pushing up against the weight of a tonne of rocks. My body resisted, roaring in pain.

"The thoughts were already in her head. If anything, I tried to quell them," Mr Cuthbert said. "It is likely your fault for stifling her."

"How dare you speak to me that way!" William said. "Surround him!"

The ice sculptures moved from their sentry positions

around the clearing, flanking William. "Leave, and do not return. I have no need to trade with you any longer."

"But, Master William —"

"I have Evelyn now. I do not need you."

A blur of orange caught my eye as the robin flew past and landed on the fence of the animal yard. It twittered the tune I had taught it in the forest.

I pushed up harder against the weight on my shoulders until I was standing. Over the hide of the cow, I saw Mr Cuthbert's eyes flickered with a wounded look. He straightened his coat and pulled his shoulders back.

"I should continue to see to your needs," he said.

I'd heard those words before. But from where?

"No. It is time for you to leave."

I remembered now—the letter from the old woman of Celoso. *Honour it by continuing to see to the child's needs.* The letter was meant for Mr Cuthbert.

My mouth dropped open. Mr Cuthbert's gaze flickered to me momentarily. Shock crossed his eyes before he returned his gaze to William, as though he'd never seen me.

William was the child.

A stab of pain hit my gut as understanding dawned on me. Mr Cuthbert had been playing me all along. I wracked my brain, trying to recall the words of the letter from the old lady. Something about being free of a bond. I thought Mr Cuthbert had been looking out for me, like an uncle, but he'd only been fulfilling his bond with the old lady—to trade with William for his needs. I was one of William's needs.

He had brought me back to Purlieu from Bayartai on purpose. He had saved me from the natives, not because he cared for me but because of his obligation to the old lady and to William. I was nothing but a pawn to him, something to be traded for yet more gold.

Mr Cuthbert turned and held his chin high, walking towards the Hidden Grove.

"Be sure he leaves," William said. The ice sculptures followed Mr Cuthbert. William watched closely.

If I ran directly to the Hidden Grove, I'd have to pass William and Mr Cuthbert and the ice sculptures. William would catch me and put me under tighter surveillance. If I went back between the barns, however, I could double around through the forest, concealed.

I tried to turn my body. I tried to run for the forest behind the barns, but it was too late. I'd missed my opportunity. I buckled under the weight of those rocks and flopped down onto the tree stump, resuming my position.

My mouth filled with ashes. The repulsive worm had carried me on his very shoulder. My skin crawled at the thought of him touching me. Anger bubbled within me, sending heat rushing up my neck.

I pushed against the weight of those rocks once more and past my muscles that screamed. I dodged around the cow and headed straight for the Hidden Grove. William's face whipped around as I passed. "What? How?" William said. "STOP!"

Shock ran through my body and my muscles turned to lead. I collided with air, yet it felt like hitting a brick wall. William grabbed me under my arm and dragged me to the cottage, leaving a trail of snow in my wake. He shoved me into the cottage. I fell to the ground, knocking my knees on the wood floor of the parlour and tumbling into the rug.

He pointed his finger at me. "How dare you even entertain the idea of leaving me? You are mine." His eyes were clouded over. A vein pulsed in his neck. "There are consequences."

He pulled a set of keys from his pocket and slammed the door behind him. The keys jingled, muffled from outside. The lock clicked.

I had to finish the sweeping before William returned from cleaning the barns. I moved compulsively, not missing an inch of the floor, piling up the dust, dirt and crumbs by the door.

It had to be perfect.

I could use the broom handle to jimmy the cottage door open, wrenching it back like a lever. Then I would run faster than I'd ever run before and be free, but I had to finish the sweeping first—every inch of the parlour floor.

The broom brought up the edge of the rug, folding it over onto itself. I bent over to put it back. There was a gap in the wood. I pulled the rug back further. The gap continued into the shape of a square, cut out with an inlaid brass knocker and hinges. It was a trapdoor.

My fingers itched. I wanted to open it, but I had to finish the sweeping.

I replaced the rug, running my hands along the surface until it was smooth, and continued to push the dust around the room into the little pile by the door.

What was beyond the trapdoor? What could William be hiding?

There was a stubborn spot of mud at the foot of the stairs. It would need to be scrubbed. I swept the little pile of dust into a pan and marched upstairs to the larder to dispose of it and get a bucket and mop. As I went back down to the parlour, I had to be extra careful not to slop hot water everywhere, otherwise it would be the next thing William would have me clean.

I piled the furniture to the side of the room, rolled up the rug, and washed the floor with wide strokes, spending a good five minutes scrubbing at the foot of the stairs. The spot came free and a weight lifted from my shoulders. I replaced the rug.

The floor was clean. I'd finished the task William had given me. What the heck was wrong with me?

I threw back the edge of the rug and grabbed the brass knocker. It could just be a storage cupboard. I pulled up the trapdoor to rest on its hinges. A staircase led down into darkness.

I took the lit oil lantern from beside the front door and travelled down the steps, holding the wall for security, leaving behind the dirty water bucket and the furniture piled to the sides of the room. If it weren't for the lantern I carried, I would have been in utter darkness. Instead, a small puddle of orange light surrounded me, illuminating the dirt steps.

I travelled deeper, deeper, feeling as though the next step would be the last yet imagining it might lead me to oblivion. I gripped the wall tighter. The temperature dropped, the air around me musty and smelling of dirt. It was so thick I could taste it in my mouth. I pressed my lips together and tried to slow my breathing.

I stepped down again. My foot jarred on the ground. I'd reached the bottom of the stairs and stood in an equally narrow corridor, surrounded on all sides with damp, cold earth. Tree roots popped out here and there, dangling like tentacles. It reminded me of the cold darkness of the cave.

A shudder ran through me. What might be hiding in this darkness? What did William keep down here? My fingers trembled. My heart pounded against my chest, faster with each step I took deeper into the tunnel. I picked up the pace.

I reached a dead end, a dirt wall hitting my face. Breath escaped me. I turned around on all sides, pressing my hands against the wall, my heart thumping. A dead end? But why?

I needed to get out, but it seemed I'd have to go back the way I'd come.

It had all been for nothing. There were no secrets, no special hiding places, no mysteries to be unearthed. I was a fool for trying, and if William found out where I was, he'd surely lock me down here in the darkness.

My heart skipped a beat. Sweat gathered on my dirty palms despite the cold. Something was touching my neck.

I jumped back and jarred my shoulder on the dead end. The old bruise reawakened with a dull ache. I threw my arm in the air, holding the lantern up high, looking about. My gaze landed on a tree root dangling directly down from the roof of the tunnel. I held my chest and gathered my breath.

Heat crept up my neck as the stupidity of my fear hit me. It was just a tree root.

I took one last look at it before pushing off the wall to head back to the cottage. But there was something strange about that root. I took another look, reaching up to feel it. It wasn't one root but many tiny ones plaited together. I held the lantern up high and inspected where it popped through the roof of the tunnel. There was no dirt there, only a rectangle of wood with the plait coming from one edge.

I tugged on the plait and the rectangle budged. It swung down towards me, opening out into a short, wooded staircase. My heart continued to thump.

The stairs led up to another space so dark that it rendered my lantern useless. I stepped up, gripping at the walls once more for support. The staircase led into a large open area. Another lantern was hooked on the wall above the staircase. I lit it and the light spread a little further into the room.

The room was presented as a library, with two floor-to-ceiling walls lined in timber bookcases, filled to bursting with books sitting tidily side by side. The only inconsistency was an assortment of cardboard-cased records and a gap for a gramophone. Beside me was a green velvet lounge and reading lamp, and on the other side of the staircase a wardrobe towered.

I stepped into the room and the pool of light followed me, illuminating a large futon in the centre. It was piled high with an excess of pillows. A neat stack of books lay beside it.

I had wondered where William slept at night.

The end wall of the bedroom was covered entirely by a heavy curtain that matched the reading lounge. A desk with inset drawers was pushed up against it. Maybe he kept a spare key to the cottage inside?

I crossed the room and pulled open the top drawer on the left, but found only a lone piece of paper. It was the eloquent note I'd seen in Mr Cuthbert's cabin. I read over the itemised list once more.

- *Master of a land*
- *Sustainable living*
- *Modern lodgings*
- *Provide basic needs*

Did it belong to Mr Cuthbert or to William? Either way, it still made no sense.

The next drawer held old ledgers. I tried the top drawer on the right. It was littered with a set of charcoal sticks, a couple of tools, and his art journal. The last drawer had a wooden box inside. I lifted it out and placed it on the desk, moving aside a delicate viola to make room.

The box was lined with velvet and had nine smaller boxes inside that were shaped just like the one William had placed my mother's necklace in. I realised I'd forgotten all about her necklace.

I grabbed the first box. A little lock of red hair lay on several pieces of foolscap paper that were stuffed inside. My stomach flipped. I gently set the lock of hair aside and opened the first piece of paper. A short note with rounded handwriting and love hearts dotting each i filled the centre of the page. There were three letters. I arranged them by date for two years prior.

Thank you for your kind words. I feel so flattered by them. You are quite the charming gentleman. I like your hair too—it reminds me of a time gone by. B

No one has ever said such kind things to me before. I'm sure I am looking at a different person in the mirror than what you see. Why are you so nice to me? Beatrice

I can't stop thinking of you. In answer to your question, yes, I will join you. My pa won't know I'm gone. I will meet you where we met last time, tomorrow at midnight. Beatrice xo

I hadn't been the first. A mixture of hot jealousy and fear rushed through me. What had happened to poor Beatrice?

I put the papers and lock of hair back in the box and pulled out the next. My hand shook, afraid for what I might find. A torn swatch of tartan cloth and a lone silver earring lay across the bottom of the box. I put it away and started on the next box. Inside was a half-used stick of charcoal and a black hair scrunchie.

How many girls had William lured here, or perhaps, failed to lure here? Bile threatened my mouth.

I opened three more boxes with small, nondescript treasures inside before finding the box with my mother's locket. The metal was cold to the touch as it rested against my chest once more, hiding beneath my clothes.

William had been trying to lure a girl to Purlieu long before I came along. How desperate must he be? I almost felt sorry for him that he had to trick girls and control them in order to make them stay, but mostly I felt sick.

I pulled back the curtain behind the desk, desperate for some air, wanting to get as far away from William and his dirty things as possible. I hoped to find a window, but instead I found another curtain. I pulled the second curtain back and a cold shiver ran over me. The temperature had suddenly dropped and there was snow at my feet. I pulled the third curtain back and wind ripped through me.

It wasn't a window, but the mouth of a cave overlooking the river and mountains and forest. My jaw dropped open. I sucked in a deep breath and let the cold air wash over my skin, sending chills across my body. I was free.

I made to step out of the cave but a tapping sound came from behind me. My body tensed up and my eyes widened. Had William caught up with me?

12

I TURNED AROUND but there was no one in the cave and the sound wasn't coming from the tunnel below. It was muffled and continued to tap-tap-tap.

I followed the sound to one of the bookcases. It vibrated with each beat. A whimper resonated from beyond.

I stepped back, my heart pounding. I wasn't the only girl.

"Hello?" I said.

The tap-tap-tap stopped. Stale silence clung to the air. A soft feeble voice broke the silence.

"Evelyn?"

My heart sank and tears pricked my eyes. I knew that voice. It sounded so wrong without that girlish effervescence, devoid of that ridiculous laugh, always ready and waiting.

"Tiffany!"

Between muted sobs her voice broke. "Help. Me," she said.

"Are you behind the bookcase?"

"Yes."

Pushing and pulling it from every angle, I grappled with

the bookcase, but it wouldn't budge. Books cascaded off the shelves as I slammed them onto the ground behind me until none were left standing. I shook the case, crying out in frustration.

Tiffany continued to sob from beyond. What was she even doing here? I panicked for her, my heart heavy and desperate. I had to get her out but I'd been gone from the cottage for too long. William would be returning soon. There was no way I was leaving without her.

I picked up the viola bow and wedged it between the wall and the bookcase, levering it. The bow snapped in half, leaving a portion of it stuck in the gap. I pried my fingers either side of it and pulled until I felt my fingernails might snap too. The bookcase remained tall and strong.

I ran my hands along every surface and tugged and pushed at the shelves. I kicked at the base of the bookcase and slumped to the ground. It was hopeless. I wasn't strong enough.

There on the ground beside me, where my shoe had swiped, the carpet had pulled back from the wall. I picked at it and pulled it back further. A metal sheet covered the dirt ground of the cave.

The bookcase was bolted down with a metal bracket!

I jumped to my feet and went for the tools in the desk drawer, finding a screwdriver. I moved quickly, turning the screw out of the bracket. I pulled on the bookcase, which gave a little in the bottom corner now. I wrenched back the carpet on the other side, found another bracket and unscrewed that one too. Next I dragged the desk over so that I could reach the top of the bookcase. There on the ceiling in the middle was the last bracket, hidden behind a jutting piece of rock. I quickly unscrewed the last screw and pushed the desk out of the way. With one easy heave, the bookcase crashed down on top of the desk, cracking and splitting in several places. The thump reverberated throughout the cave. Dust flew up around me.

On the back of the bookcase were bloody scratch

marks and dents. I turned back to where it had previously been standing. The gap in the wall was only large enough to fit her body and a small bucket. She was lying against the wall, mascara streaking her face, her body gaunt and pale. She held her hands up to shield her eyes, light streaming into the crevice.

She pulled her hands away and our eyes met. She collapsed in my arms and I held her tight. Her body trembled.

"I'm so sorry. I'm so, so sorry," I said.

She sobbed. I pulled her in tighter.

"What happened? How did you get here?"

It took her a while to settle down. She sucked in a deep breath and sat up a little straighter. "I followed," she said. "Cameron said I should." She choked on her words, voice dry and raspy. "I saw you climb the tree, and when you didn't come down, well, the next day I climbed up too."

"You've been here this whole time?"

"It's been a few days now, I think. It was dark in here, hard to tell."

My heart sank deeper with her every word.

"It was night, and snowing, when I arrived," she said. "You are real, aren't you?" She pushed me away and studied my face.

"I've never seen snow before, Evelyn. How could it be summer and snowing? I don't understand. I kept thinking I was stuck in this long, horrific nightmare, but no matter how wide I opened my eyes, I could never wake up."

"It's real," I said. 'I'm real.' I clenched my jaw. I wished it weren't so.

"He thought I was you," she said. "He threw me in here straight away when he realised I wasn't. Did he lock you away too?" she asked.

In so many words, yes. "You were right about William," I said. "I'm sorry I didn't believe you."

"I'm sorry I didn't push harder to meet him. None of this would have happened if I'd just sussed him out for you."

"No, it's not your fault. You've been an amazing friend. It's me—I've been so selfish. I'm sorry."

She pulled me back into a hug.

"We need to go," I said. I pulled her to her feet. She continued to tremble. I grabbed two of William's coats from the wardrobe and led her to the cave mouth. The sun left a hazy green glow across the countryside.

"Why is it green?" Tiffany asked.

"The same reason it's snowing."

I laced my fingers through hers. She squeezed at my weak hand that was no longer weak. She didn't seem to notice how the scars had healed over, but then again, she'd never really had a problem with the scars, unlike everyone else.

"Please don't freak out," I said, "but we're not on Earth anymore."

She was quiet for a long moment. "I think deep down I knew all along. I just didn't want to admit it," she said.

"Well, we'll be back home soon enough. Come on, let's get out of here."

I tugged her hand and we slunk around the right side of the cave towards the forest, hiding behind the tree line.

"Did he ever touch you, Tiffany?" I shuddered at the thought.

"Not like that."

I nodded. "So he just shut you up this whole time?"

"He brought food occasionally. And he changed the bucket. But yeah."

"I wonder why."

"I don't know. Maybe I'm not his type. "

We moved further back into the forest and tiptoed from tree to tree, following the line of the clearing until we passed behind the barns where it curved around to the right.

I poked my head from behind one of the trees to see if William was still ushering the animals into their barns for the night. It was silent, eerily so. My hand became clammy.

We continued to follow the tree line past the orchard and then deeper in towards the Hidden Grove. The tree arch came into sight, when a twig snapped behind us. I froze. My heart sank.

"Quick," I said. We shifted into a run, Tiffany struggling to keep up. I yanked at her, desperately coercing her to move faster.

"Evelyn, stop!" William called.

My body continued to run, unaffected by his command. We crossed the threshold of the tree arch and the Hidden Grove appeared before us, the snow replaced by manicured grass. Tiffany yelped, faltering. I tugged her onwards.

His footsteps pounded behind us, sprinting to catch up. "EVELYN! STOP!"

We turned up the third row and passed tree after tree in a blur of bark and leaves. I looked about wildly for Old Man's Beard. How would we ever find the way home?

"Evelyn, I command you to stop!"

He was gaining on us. There, ahead on the left, was a mass of the moss hanging from the bows of a tree.

"That one!" I said. I pushed Tiffany ahead of me towards the tree and forced her up it. She whimpered and continued to shake. "Hurry!"

"Evelyn!" William called.

How was I so unaffected by his commands? We climbed the tree, feet slipping and sliding on the moist branches as the snow shed from our shoes. I pushed Tiffany up ahead of me, her feet struggling to stay steady on the branches. The tree swayed with our hurried climb, William rushing up behind us.

My breathing became erratic. At any moment, I could fall. We reached the top of the trunk and I linked hands with her again, stepping towards the portal.

"You! Stop!" William called. Tiffany froze. "Come down," William called. Tiffany turned around, pulling me with her.

"No!" I screamed, tugging on her, but she resisted my pull. She stepped back towards the edge of the trunk. William was just a few branches below now.

I chopped at the back of her knees and she collapsed. I threw my bodyweight into the centre of the tree and we both fell into the light. I existed everywhere and nowhere all at once, the light surrounding us entirely. A tightness ran down my arm and across my hand.

Tiffany got to her feet again.

"No!" I said. I tugged at her.

"Let's go," she said.

My mouth dropped open. William's power over her had dissolved into nothing. I scrambled to my feet and we carried on through the portal, the sharp light vanishing, and down the tree.

William was nowhere to be seen, but it wasn't going to stop us from hurrying on. Our feet landed on the soft grass of the Hidden Grove and we rushed for the tree arch. I tried to focus on the rhythm of my puffing breath rather than the stitch in my side.

I collapsed through the arch and was met by a faceful of sand, Tiffany by my side on the ground. We were on a beach overlooking a golden ocean with white cliffs in the distance and a large corrugated iron warehouse sitting precariously on the dunes.

"We climbed the wrong tree," I said.

Tiffany whimpered.

"Come on." I spat the sand from my mouth and pulled her up with me. We passed back through the arch and up the third row.

Had William lied when he had showed me which tree would lead to Earth? I felt sick. Had he lied to me from the outset?

My breath escaped me. There he was in the distance, flitting between the trees. He stopped dead and stared at me for a moment.

"Evelyn!" he yelled.

I turned to the nearest tree. It was covered in moss and damp bark.

"Tiffany, up here. Hurry!"

We climbed the tree. It shook precariously under our weight, just as the others had, but I had no idea where it might lead. I clung to the hope that we might jump so far ahead in time that William would never catch us.

"You! Stop!" William yelled. He was calling to Tiffany but his powers had no effect. This was not his kingdom. His bodyweight shook the tree even more violently as he took to the branches, just as we reached the top. We left him behind as we passed through the portal, hand in hand once more.

I had no illusions that we'd climbed the right tree this time, interested only in buying us time. No sooner had we crossed through the portal than William appeared behind us, lurching forward.

Tiffany screamed. My heart pounded. We scampered down the tree, William directly above us. The time differences had worked against us instead of for us.

He grabbed a fistful of my hair and yanked me back. I cried out, wrapping my hands around his wrist. He yelled and let go of my hair, shaking me loose. I slid down a few branches to reach Tiffany. My legs connected with the branch, sending a dull, throbbing ache up and down. I grappled for the tree trunk to collect my balance and noticed that the scarring had returned to my weak hand. It was twisted, taut and calloused once more, like the power had been lifted from it when we'd left Purlieu.

No wonder William had freaked out when I touched him. Something deep within me had known he hated my scarred hand.

"Keep going!" Tiffany said.

I shook my head and continued down the tree. I followed her as closely as I could, William not far behind. We hit the ground and Tiffany sprinted for the tree arch.

She was right to run, because we had no time to try for another world. Maybe someone in this one could help us.

As we rounded the last row of trees, the arch ahead, rain bucketed down beyond it. The cold torrent of water smarted my skin as we crossed the threshold into the new world. I stepped in a puddle of water and slid across the ground, sinking a little as I went. The rain was so thick I could hardly see Tiffany ahead of me, skidding and tripping through the mud. The ooze sucked at my shoes as I pulled. It slurped and popped as I came unstuck and fell forward, slamming face first into the mud.

William roared, wrapping his hands around my ankles. I twisted around. He was knee deep in mud and stuck. I slipped and struggled from his grasp, scrambling across the ground until I was free.

"There's no one here," Tiffany said. She was by my side, pulling on my elbow.

William continued to struggle in the mud behind me. Tiffany helped me up.

"We have to go back," I said. Tiffany nodded grimly and we splashed around William, back to the Hidden Grove.

William roared again as we passed through the tree arch. Our feet hit hard ground on the other side and I sucked in a deep breath, free of the torrential rain. The tree nearest the arch was old and haggard. I reached for it, its branches falling to dust at my touch. I reached again for the next branch higher up and it creaked under my weight.

"I will kill her if you don't return to Purlieu with me," William said.

I wheeled around. William was standing beneath the tree arch, chest heaving, the torrential rain behind him. His eyes were slitted, mouth curled up into a snarl. His arm was wrapped around Tiffany's throat, a pocket knife raised above her head.

"No! Tiffany!"

She began to whimper, her eyes wide, glancing about

for an escape. He pulled her in tighter.

"Don't do it! I'll come with you. I'll come with you," I said.

He smirked.

"But you have to let her go home. You have to promise that she can go home to Earth," I said.

He sighed. "And you will come back to Purlieu with me? Willingly?" he asked.

I nodded. Tiffany continued to whimper.

"I knew keeping her around would come in handy," he said.

He pointed the knife at me and directed me between the rows of trees. We walked for a long time into what felt like the centre of the Hidden Grove, Tiffany still in his hold. A tree, larger than the rest and covered in luscious green moss, lay ahead. Magnetism coursed through my body, making my fingers inch towards it. I wanted to climb it.

"Climb that one," he said.

"How do we know that it's the right tree?" I asked.

"Because she won't come back."

I gritted my teeth. He pushed Tiffany forward into the trunk of the tree and grabbed at my good hand, squeezing so tight that the bones felt like they might snap.

Tiffany turned back, her eyes welling with tears. "I'm sorry," she said.

"No, I'm sorry."

She scampered up the tree, leaving drag marks on the bark as she struggled up. A sob escaped her as she climbed. We watched until her waterlogged bushy hair was no longer visible and the tree stopped shaking.

William tugged me away from the tree to Earth and back through the grove. Would I ever see that tree again? I looked back upon it. Though the tree jutted out of uniformity, towering above the rest, I took in every detail of it to be sure I never confused it with another again, committing to memory those drag marks that Tiffany left behind.

"What do you want with me, William?"

He grunted, tugging me along.

"Tell me."

He sighed. "As I told you, I need to make a family of my own."

He looked at me pointedly, through the anger and rejection that twisted his face.

He still wanted me to be his wife. He still wanted me to bear his child.

Panic rose up my throat and made my heart beat uncomfortably against my chest. I shuddered.

"Can you not see how much I need you, how much I want you, how much I love you?" he said. He lowered his voice and directed it away from me. "I have tried again and again to let them choose for themselves but they left me with no other choice." His face softened ever so slightly as he turned back to me. "And I want you to love me too."

"You can't force someone to love you. Especially if you keep them prisoner."

"But you are not a prisoner. You are coming willingly."

I looked at the strong grip he had on my good hand. "Hardly." But he was right. I was his willing prisoner now, for Tiffany's sake.

My heart sank. Emptiness. I felt utter emptiness. I was a lifeless being, floating about at his will. That would be my life now. There would be no escaping it.

He thrust me against a tree. "Time to go home," he said. His face contorted into an ugly smile, his eyes wild.

I looked up. It was the Purlieu tree with its white lichen and branches worn smooth from regular travel. I gritted my teeth and climbed the damn tree for the umpteenth time. It would probably be the last time I climbed a tree, ever. At least that much I could be happy about.

My heart sank deeper with every step. I gazed down at how far we'd climbed and became dizzy at the sight. As much as the idea terrified me, maybe I would be better off to just fall?

William tugged at me and I continued up the tree. On the other side of the portal and down in Purlieu, William shoved me on my knees. He yanked the chain of my mother's locket from around my neck. The blood vessels in his eyes bulged red as he raised his voice.

"You went through my things!" Spittle flew down onto me. "How dare you?"

He pocketed the locket and grabbed me under the arm, dragging me out of the Hidden Grove. My knees chafed. I scrambled to my feet and tried to keep up with him as he marched me back into the snowy forest, back into the clearing, back into the cottage and all the way up the stairs to the conservatory. He threw me inside and I collided with the steps that led up into the room.

"You will obey," he said. He slammed the door. A lock clicked. His muffled footsteps stamped down the stairs.

I had been so close. The tree to Earth had been right there. I stared at the door, sturdy and permanent, and I cried.

13

THE FLOOR OF the conservatory was splattered with paint from those first days I'd spent in Purlieu. It felt like an age ago now. The scrubbing brush in my hand moved back and forth across the flecks, melting them until the bucket of water by my side was milky green.

I looked up and stared out the window at the white landscape beyond. The robin was perched on a nearby branch in the bows of the cottage.

If I had wings, I could fly out the window. If only I had wings.

I scowled at a particularly stubborn spot on the floor and continued to scrub.

"You are not smiling," William said. He was watching me from the velvet-winged chair. "That is a very unloving thing to do," he said.

"I'm obligated to stay in Purlieu, for Tiffany's sake. I don't have to like it," I said. I stopped scrubbing and gave him an ugly grimace.

"I do not like it. I command you to smile properly," he said.

He stood up, towering over me. My lips curled up and my teeth bared, giving William my best smile. I felt sick inside as the compulsion took me. I couldn't press my lips together. My cheeks started to ache.

"And you have been scrubbing incorrectly. Put more weight behind it and the spots will lift right off instead of bleeding down into the wood."

My jaw finally clenched shut as my body bent over the scrubbing brush and pushed back and forward with a power I didn't know I had. It hurt my hands but I continued to scrub. I looked up at him as I moved back and forward, snarling my lip up at him in disgust.

How could he not see it was wrong to control someone and keep them captive? He raised an eyebrow and walked the few short paces between us. He smirked.

"Kiss me," he said.

I stood up, horror rushing over me. My body moved into his, our lips crushed together. He wrapped his arms around me and kissed back, holding me there in a pose that felt like death.

He wanted me to be the mother of his children. Who was to say that he wouldn't take that by force too? I needed to get out of here before he had the chance.

He pulled away and pushed me back to the floor, his authority thoroughly established.

"I want that done before the morning."

I stood by the door of the conservatory, keeping my breath quiet as his footsteps stomped up the stairs. The lock clicked twice and he opened the door with his foot, hands holding a breakfast tray.

I stepped in behind him and slapped my hand over his mouth, the other around his neck. If he couldn't speak, he couldn't command me to do anything.

The breakfast tray went crashing to the floor, poached eggs and toast crushed by the overturned wooden plates. William turned and threw me on top of the breakfast tray.

"Stay," he said.

I tried to move, but I couldn't, the knees of my pants squished into the eggs. I cowered instead. He was too strong for me.

If I were going to escape, I needed to better understand the limits of his powers. I could eat this elephant, one bite at a time.

His face crumpled in frustration. He let out a huff.

"You ruined it."

Maybe I needed to lull him into a false sense of security? I thought fast.

"I wish it were just like old times," he said.

I made my face appear downcast. "I do miss painting," I said, "with you." I glanced up at him. His mouth had dropped open. Silence hung in the air.

"Perhaps we could," he trailed off. He closed the door behind him and pulled me to my feet. Internally, I cringed at his touch.

He led me into the room and set me down before a canvas. Warily, he stepped away and watched me as I picked up a paintbrush. He did the same.

Could he only place one command at a time? How could I convince him to use his powers so that I could test it without setting him off?

"You have been staring at that blank canvas for some time," he said.

I shook my head and smiled at him. He was halfway through a painting of his own. I was fairly sure I knew what his subject was.

"It's been a while. I wasn't sure what to paint," I said.

"I only paint something if I can bear to stare at it forever," he said.

I mixed paint colours slowly. "The cold is just making it hard to think straight, that's all," I said.

"Oh," William said. "I can fix that." He closed the curtains and lit the lamps.

I continued to mix the paint. A few minutes passed. "I'm still cold," I said.

William sighed. He left the room and returned with a fur coat, wrapping it around my shoulders.

"Thank you."

He returned to his painting.

I moved towards the door.

"Where are you going?"

"I'm hungry."

I motioned towards my intended breakfast, still lying in a mess on the floor. I put my hand on the doorknob and turned.

"Lock!" William called. The door lock clicked twice and my hand jarred.

"Reconstruct." The tray on the floor clattered and flipped right side up. The plates tumbled back onto the tray and the eggs and toast began to wriggle back together. My knees itched. I looked down and saw the eggs that had squished into the knee of my pants vibrating, trying to escape the clutches of the cloth. They flew threw the air like magnets and attached themselves to the plate. The eggs wobbled as though they'd just come out of boiling water.

My jaw dropped.

"Eat," he said.

I knelt down and grabbed up the wooden fork, scooping the egg into my mouth. It was cold. I swallowed, wanting to gag, but went for the toast instead. I hated myself for every mouthful I took but I couldn't stop eating. I needed to finish it. But just because I was eating, it didn't mean that I couldn't do something else at the same time, right?

I picked up the plate and stood up. William was watching me. I started pacing the room as I chewed.

"Stop it. Sit down."

I promptly stopped walking and sat on the spot with crossed legs. I continued to chew.

"Would you stop acting strangely?"

I tried to respond but I needed to keep eating. That

was answer enough to my investigation. The only question that remained was how many commands could he place at once, but I'd pushed his buttons enough for one morning.

Gulping, I swallowed the last mouthful. I smiled apologetically to him and returned to my canvas, satisfied.

"That's much better," I said. "Thank you." I feigned a smile and dunked my brush in green paint to begin painting a garden.

He shook his head and let out a long sigh. He continued to watch me for a moment; I could feel his gaze piercing me. I placed down stroke after stroke until he returned to his work.

The life-sized portrait of my mother took shape before me. She was standing by the rose bush, pruning. I had gazed down on her from my bedroom window as she gardened, my leg swinging from the windowsill, art journal in hand. She had wiped her forehead with the back of her arm and spotted me.

"What are you doing up there, missy? Spying on me, no doubt," she had said.

"Oh no, you've seen me! I'll never be a ninja at this rate."

We shared a laugh and both returned to our work. I had loved to look down upon her as she worked.

It was the second time I had painted her in this position, but this time I chose to include the perspiration forming on her forehead. It was a part of her, after all.

William shuffled over to me and looked over my shoulder. "You really need to get over it," he said.

I turned around, wide-eyed. My mouth dropped open.

"I have gotten over it," he said.

I raised my eyebrows. "What do you mean?"

He scratched at the stubble across his chin. "You know, my parents abandoning me in Purlieu. I have gotten over it. You should forget about her, too."

He nodded at my painting. No matter what he claimed, I knew he wasn't over it. I knew he was still waiting for them to come for him. But if they had any inkling of what he was like, what he was capable of, they would never come for him. Maybe they had known. Maybe that was why they had abandoned him.

I pressed my lips together and chose not to say anything. He shrugged and returned to his own canvas. I focused on the locket around my mother's neck, adding layers of shading to give the appearance of a gold glint.

There were objects that held memories of my mother, but none of the stuff my father had been going through on the night we'd fought really meant anything. Her clothes, her gardening magazines, they were only things. The garden held my true memories of her—where she spent her time and poured out her love. But the garden no longer included her. Home no longer included her. She wasn't coming back. I was ready to accept that.

I would not turn out like William. I refused to.

Maybe Dad was right to get rid of Mum's old stuff. I had been holding on, unable to face her death, thinking she might come back for it all.

I might not like the fact that she wasn't returning, but Dad was right: we needed to move on. Not William's idea of moving on, waiting around in silent hope and putting life on hold, but making real changes.

I wished I could tell Dad that. I wished I could tell him that he was right. I wished that I could apologise.

"I would like to get over it, just like you have," I said. "Maybe if I spoke to Dad about it. You know, if I went home and cleared out all the memories of Mum. Maybe that would help."

He stepped away from his canvas and faced me again. "What good would that do?" He raised his voice. "There are no memories of her here except for the ones you keep creating." He pointed again at my painting. "No, the only way is to forget about it, to forget about your parents," he said. "Parents only hurt you."

He spat the last sentence out like the words were dirty.

"But if I could just visit my dad," I said, "I would come right back."

He rubbed his jaw. "He is probably an old man by now. You may as well give up on it and get used to being here, with me."

My heart quickened. What did he mean? "An old man? But I thought Purlieu and Earth were basically on the same time."

"Are you stupid? How could you not have figured it out? The worlds run on different time because every time the power is used, the time quickens." He shook his head and huffed. "You are impossible," he said. "So much for like old times."

He threw down his brush. It clattered to the ground. He left the conservatory and locked the door behind him.

Dad could be an old man? I crumpled to my knees. I had thought it would be okay. I had thought I'd gotten it wrong about the time differences. Surely it wasn't true.

Mr Cuthbert's pocket watch flashed across my mind and how he had been willing to kill just to get it back. He and William had compared the time the first day I'd met Mr Cuthbert. William had been late to meet him and hadn't realised it. Had William been using the power on me from the start?

My heart sank. It was true. It had to be. So how much time had passed? I'd been in Purlieu for what, maybe three weeks? Had William really used so much of the power that the Earth had zoomed off into the future?

Dad would think that I had abandoned him for good. That I didn't care about him. That I had left him with no intention of returning. I couldn't bear the thought of not being able to apologise.

I held myself tight and rocked back and forth. I needed to stop William from using the power. I needed to give him no reason for it, but could it be too late? Could Dad really be an old man by now? Would I ever make it back home in time to apologise?

I couldn't just sit around waiting for William to let me go. I had to get out myself, so I walked over to one of the windows and threw the curtain open. The sun was now high in the sky. The brass lever was cold in my hand as I put my weight onto it, the windows screeching open a fraction. I lay flat on the ground and let out all the breath inside me, attempting to squeeze beneath the gap. My head was too big. I tried at a different angle. Still too big. Returning to the lever, I lifted my body off the floor to force it down further. It didn't budge. It was as open as it would go.

The wind whipped through the gap in the glass and sent shivers across my skin. Memories of the cold cave returned to me. I closed the windows.

Combing the room, I looking for something to jimmy the door open, but the room was fairly bare. The thick paintbrush was too wide to fit in the door jam. The smallest size fit the gap, but when I pulled like a lever it snapped, clattering to the ground.

I pried at the door with my fingers, kicked at the hinges, rattled at the knob. It was hopeless and I knew it.

I scoured the room. From the velvet chair to the telescope to the oil lamp to the paintings, there was nothing capable of such a job. But perhaps one of the paintings had some metal plating on the backs?

Flicking through the stack of work I'd done since being in Purlieu, I noticed that the canvases weren't even wired at the back. I dumped them on the ground, but the smudged painting of Dad on the day of Mum's funeral caught my eye. I gazed at his eyes. I would never see those sad eyes again. He would die alone and so would I.

His eyes mirrored how I felt now.

Why had he refused to cry? Why had he shut his emotions off when Mum had died? Why had he acted as though she had never existed?

At the funeral, he had stood by my side yet not said a word or shed a tear. When people approached him, he had brushed them off, not hugging them back when they hugged him, offering a limp handshake, giving short answers. How could he be so rude? How could he taint the memory of my mother? How could he make it look as though he didn't really care?

When we'd gone home, the house had been so silent. Eerily silent. He couldn't even look in my direction. So I'd raced to my room and slammed the door. When I eventually came out, he had a smile on his face. A twisted smile. And he had a thousand questions about school and Tiffany and 'when would I be home?' The questions hadn't stopped since.

I started avoiding the house, spending my evenings and weekends at the art gallery or anywhere to get away from him. I hated myself for it about as much as I hated our tense dinners, the growing bags under his eyes, how he would look at me too intently as he probed what I would be doing the next day.

I had wanted to shout at him, to tell him to mind his own business and leave me alone. I had wanted to get as far away as I could. It was why I'd been saving up for my gap year: I was going to travel and paint in any place that didn't remind me of home, in any place that was as far removed from him as possible.

I couldn't get much further away than Purlieu. I smiled wryly. The joke was on me.

Why did he have to smother me? Why couldn't I be honest with him and ask for some space? Why didn't I have the guts to ask him to wrap his arms around me so that I could cry?

Just as he hadn't reached out to me that day in the morgue, I hadn't reached out to him. I hadn't spoken to him. I hadn't hugged him, and I hadn't cried. It had been as much my fault as his. I could see that now. He was afraid of losing me too. That was why he had sent a barrage of questions my way as soon as I entered the house each night. He was hurting just as much as I was, and it had been too easy to place the blame of my pain on him, to see him as the only perpetrator. But I was just as guilty.

I wanted to see him and tell him I was sorry. I wanted to make things right.

I sighed and made to move away from the painting but those eyes caught my attention again. At this angle, they appeared not sad but happy. I missed that version of my dad.

I took the painting and flipped it upside down, replacing it on the stand where the mostly-finished canvas of Mum still sat. I painted around his eyes, over the dry paint, forming a smile, making him happy. Just how I wished him to be.

I painted him standing in the kitchen looking out to the garden, paused in his whistling of the robin song, my mother singing from just beyond.

I remember he had stood there one afternoon as I walked into the kitchen. He was looking out on her with such joy on his face. When he turned to look at me, he gave me that same smile. He loved me as much as he loved her. I guess I had forgotten that. Now he'd lost not only his wife but his daughter too. The two people he cared about most in the world.

I had to get back home. I had to see him.

It would be better to try to escape. Even if he were an old man now, even if we only had a few moments together, it would be better for him to know the truth of my love for him and for us to reconcile than for him to die alone. Even if it meant risking me dying while trying.

I put my brush down. The painting was rough, just enough to cover the one below it. It didn't matter, for my memory of that moment was strong. I didn't need to immortalise it on canvas.

He smiled at me as I paced the room, following the four glass walls. Round and round I went, turning over everything I had learned about William and Purlieu and the power, searching for something that might be a clue of how to escape him. Some Achilles heel, some routine that I could exploit, some piece of information he'd let slip.

If the floor were made of dirt there would have been a high trench marking the ground where I'd run circles for the past five hours. I peered below to the farm where William was filling the animals' troughs for the night. Bodie was by his side, snapping at the goats to submit.

I moved again down the steps to the door and jiggled at the handle. I shouldered the wood panelling. I drew fists and banged on the door, once for every time William had done wrong by me. For the things he had said about Dad. BANG. For luring me to Purlieu. BANG. For telling me the wrong tree home to Earth. BANG. For sending the ice sculptures after me. BANG. For locking me in the cottage. BANG. For threatening Tiffany's life. BANG. For forcing me to kiss him. BANG. I yelled out in frustration and slumped back into the door, chest heaving. My knuckles ached.

I had to get out before he did something worse. Something irreversible.

I looked again from the winged velvet chair to the telescope to the few canvases, brushes and paints, to the unlit lanterns that scattered the room. None of them would help me get through this door.

Was there anything on me that could help? I turned out my pockets and found only my phone. I rubbed at my face, sighing, and pulled at the wild tendrils of my hair, fixing it back into the bobby pins. I fingered the smooth cold surface of the bobby pins. Could I pick a lock?

I turned and knelt, holding my eye to the lock. All I could do was try. I pulled two bobby pins out of my hair, brushing away the strands that now hung loose across my face again. I spread the prongs apart like I'd seen in the movies and set to work, jostling the pins around in the lock.

I'd never taken the time to consider how a lock

worked, and now I couldn't really see clearly what I was doing, if anything. I figured I had to press some kind of a button, if only I could get enough strength behind the bobby pins without bending or snapping them. I continued to jostle the bobby pins around, prodding and poking from different angles.

Was this a waste of time and energy? Would I ever escape?

The green glow of the setting Purlieu sun cast odd shadows over my shoulder and onto the door handle. Blisters began to form on my fingers as I jabbed at the unyielding lock. Heat washed over my cheeks as I stared at the brass plate of the lock that held the handle in place. There was a screw either side. I was an idiot.

I pulled my bobby pins from the lock and stood up to stretch out my tired, aching back. Bending down once more, I aimed a bobby pin at the Phillips head screw in the brass plate. It was old and set in place but at least I could see what I was doing. The bobby pin slipped from the screw and my knuckle slammed into the door. I shook it out and tried again.

A smile spread across my face as the screw began to turn. It moved slowly at first and then with ease until it dropped out onto the ground at my feet. I jumped back in surprise.

I aimed for the second screw and repeated the process until it too lay by my feet. I took a hold of the cold metal of the brass handle with both hands. I put a foot to the door and yanked as hard as I could.

It pulled out and I fell back into the stairs, jarring my tailbone. The door creaked open. I was free.

I let the handle clatter to the ground and shoved the bobby pins in my pocket. I dashed down the stairs without so much as a backward glance, stomping my feet loudly, carelessly. I reached the base of the stairs and headed for the cottage door, when movement caught my eye. I flattened back against the wall, my heart sinking and pounding all at the same time. A tall figure stood against the circular wall of the parlour.

It was Mr Cuthbert. He was suspended in action, removing a painting from the wall—of the bright yellow harvest before the storm. My painting. He wheeled around and faced me, painting in one hand, black dagger in the other.

Had it been he who set alight the village and killed all those people in the castle? He wasn't just a merchant. He was a mercenary.

His face flashed from shock to guilt to nonchalance. He raised an eyebrow.

"What can I say? William's talents just do not compare," he said.

He motioned to my painting in his hands, starting to jimmy the back of it open with his dagger. Several other paintings were already removed from their frames and rolled up, sticking out of the top of the carpetbag by his side.

"You're a scoundrel," I said. I bared my teeth at him. "For stealing my paintings. For setting me up. For killing all the people of Purlieu."

His smile evaporated at the last accusation. He stopped to stroke his beard.

I hated the way he always touched it, pulling at the grey locks. He did it all the time. Actually, not all the time. Realisation washed over me, my dad's voice ringing in my ears.

"It's all in the tells," Dad had said.

Mr Cuthbert always touched his beard when he was about to lie. Come to think of it, so did William. How had I not picked up on that from the beginning? How could I be so naïve?

"Whatever are you referring to? You are still alive. William is still alive."

"You know what I mean—all those people in the village beyond the mountain, including the king. You did it, didn't you?" I said. Tears welled in my eyes at the memory of the grandly dressed skeletons, frozen in time, their lives stolen from them. "Why did you do it?"

He waved a hand in the air. "Just part of the job."

"It's despicable."

He shrugged and tossed his dagger into his carpetbag. He picked up the bag, tucked the harvest painting under his arm, and made to turn for the door.

"Did you know all along that William wanted to impregnate me?"

His jaw clenched. He paused. "I would go find that locket of yours, if I were you," he said.

A long-ago conversation flashed across my mind of the day I'd first met Mr Cuthbert. What had he said? Something about never travelling without his pocket watch and that I should do the same.

He avoided my eyes and made for the door, dashing outside without answering. I couldn't believe I'd ever seen him as a friend, an ally. Was I really so blind to people's true character to have fallen for both William and Mr Cuthbert's deception? I shook my head, willing the tears away, and made for the door which now stood ajar. Yelling came from beyond. I halted.

"Leave, and never return."

"Now Master William, you do not understand. You need to stop using the power. Remember how I taught you about the time dilation. Remember how I told you about New Tahiti? About the withered tree? It was true. It was all true."

I peeked through the gap in the door. Mr Cuthbert was on the ground. The ice sculptures had him pinned down. William was several paces away, towering over him with his back to me. Bodie was by his side, snarling.

"That world ceased to exist because that master was power hungry," Mr Cuthbert said. His face had a sense of urgency about it. He was pleading with William.

"Why should you care about what happens in Purlieu?"

Mr Cuthbert's lips pressed together. He hung his head. "Tell me!"

Mr Cuthbert continued to remain silent. How was he doing it? How was he defying William's commands? How had he managed to kill the original king of Purlieu and all his subjects?

"Tell me!" The fox gave a high-pitched bark.

A glint of light shone from around Mr Cuthbert's neck. His gold pocket watch. He never travelled without it, he'd said, but he hadn't been referring to the pocket watch itself, rather the gold chain that came with it, hadn't he? Was that it? Was there something about wearing gold that stopped the powers from having an effect?

I thought back to the time Mr Cuthbert had chased the child in Bayartai as though his life depended on it. I'd worn the gold locket when Tiffany and I had tried to escape. William had commanded me to come back to Purlieu with him but his commands had no effect on me as we escaped up that tree. And William had always been so adamant that I not wear it.

My breath escaped me. Could I really stop William's power from having an effect? Could I really ignore his commands that made me a prisoner, and escape instead?

I turned to head for the trapdoor down to his room to get my mother's locket back.

"Tell me or you die!" William said. I looked back through the gap in the door. William had conjured up an ice dagger and was holding it above his head, aimed at Mr Cuthbert. He swooped in and held it to Mr Cuthbert's throat.

My eyes drew wide. This could be the only chance I would have to get the locket back and escape. I turned away from the door and made my way towards the trapdoor again. I pulled back the rug and wrapped my hand around the brass handle.

I paused. Despicable as he was, I couldn't just let Mr Cuthbert die. But he was despicable. Maybe he deserved it?

Who was I kidding? No one deserved it.

I gritted my teeth, threw the rug back, and slipped through the gap in the parlour door. Cold wind lashed through my hair as I stepped out into the clearing.

"Stop!" I said.

William stepped back from Mr Cuthbert and turned around to see me. His eyebrows were raised. He drew them down into a frown immediately.

"Stay!" he yelled.

My feet froze to the ground. My heart sank. What had I done? The fox turned on me and continued to snarl. William turned back on Mr Cuthbert.

"Did you let her out?" William asked.

He drove the ice dagger back down to Mr Cuthbert's throat. Droplets of blood formed and ran down his neck.

"No. No. I swear it."

"Don't do it, William." I yelled.

"Why should I?" He didn't take his eyes from Mr Cuthbert. "Why?" he repeated.

I hesitated. He wheeled around and strode the few paces between us, resting the cold dagger on my collarbone. It sent a shiver over my skin. I sucked in a breath. Why hadn't I minded my own business?

"Because he knows how to find your parents," I said. If William reunited with his parents, perhaps he wouldn't need me anymore?

I glanced past him to Mr Cuthbert, whose face was unreadable. William's mouth dropped, the dagger relaxed in his hand. He took a step back and turned on Mr Cuthbert.

"Is it true?"

Mr Cuthbert pulled at his beard. "No," he said. He was lying.

All William had ever wanted was a family. I had to help him see that he had one, that he didn't need me.

"But it makes sense," I said. "By killing the people on the other side of the mountain, you made a world William

212

could be master of, just like the list said. That's why no one else lives in Purlieu."

I could see William turning it over in his mind. The list was in the desk in his cave. He had to see the correlation, surely.

"One can only be a master by lineage in death or by declaration," William said. "Those tyrants over the mountain, they were my family?"

Mr Cuthbert shook his head and smiled to himself.

"No," I said. "I don't think so. There's an old lady who leaves gold for Mr Cuthbert through the wall of Celoso and I think it's as payment for taking care of you."

She had to be a servant or grandmother or something.

If William could only meet his parents, perhaps he would let me go? William flicked from Mr Cuthbert to me and back again. Mr Cuthbert stared blankly back. William pressed the dagger against Mr Cuthbert's throat once more. More blood trickled down his neck, mingled with melting ice. He clenched his jaws tighter.

"She was not always an old lady," Mr Cuthbert said, looking at me pointedly.

The child was hers? But William was twenty and she was grey and wrinkled. How fast was it possible for time to pass between worlds? My stomach dropped as Dad's face flashed across my mind.

"You have to understand," Mr Cuthbert said. "I am a merchant. I do what I must to survive. I merely rid the queen of her illegitimate child."

William slapped Mr Cuthbert. Mr Cuthbert's face lolled. He blinked before focusing on William again.

"You knew who my parents were and you never told me?"

"She made me promise," Mr Cuthbert said.

"It cannot be true. I refuse to believe it. I refuse to believe either of you—you are conspiring against me." He stepped back from Mr Cuthbert and paced back and forth, rubbing his hands over his face. "My parents may have abandoned me in Purlieu as a child but they will return to me. One day. You will see."

Mr Cuthbert shook his head. William was deluded. We both could see it. William rushed at Mr Cuthbert once more and held him by the shoulders. "You dare to defy me?"

Mr Cuthbert's fingers inched up and touched his beard, scratching at it just the same way William did.

"Look, I merely provided her with safe passage to a world where the time passed faster, so she could give birth without her husband finding out. We agreed that I would raise the child from afar in exchange for gold instalments. It is your choice whether you decide to believe it or not."

William staggered back from him, dropping the dagger. "No," he said. He sounded hollow. He fell to his knees. Bodie came to his side and licked his face.

"You sent me off to Earth in search of my parents when all along you already knew where they were! I cannot fathom it. It cannot be true."

Mr Cuthbert shrugged. "She made me promise."

William spat at the ground. "You coward, hiding behind a woman."

"Well where do you think the gold came from to build that fancy pocket watch around your neck, huh?" Mr Cuthbert said.

"No—I will not listen to this. How can I believe a word from your mouth? You have been lying to me my entire life. All those extended stays in the cabin, our trade partnership, your high praises of my work—you did it all just because she was paying you to."

"It was not *all* a lie."

"She's dying," I said.

Mr Cuthbert looked to me, devoid of emotion. "She is already dead," he said.

"What?" William asked.

He jumped to his feet and towered over Mr Cuthbert, holding the ice dagger ready to strike. He was blubbering now, spittle flying in all directions. "My mother—she existed within arm's reach and I only find out now, after she is already dead? How could you?" He slapped Mr Cuthbert again. "Out! Get out!" William yelled. "Leave and never return."

The ice people stepped back from Mr Cuthbert.

"But he can take you to where she lived, to your family," I said.

I needed them to reconcile. I needed Mr Cuthbert to take him away to Celoso. It was my only chance of being released from this bondage.

"I have no family," William said.

The wounded look flashed across Mr Cuthbert's face once more. He gathered his scattered bag and my painting, tucking it under his arm again.

"Leave. Now!"

Mr Cuthbert stood, straightened his coat, put his nose in the air and walked indignantly towards the Hidden Grove.

William growled in impatience. "Bodie, go," he said. The fox set off after Mr Cuthbert, who moved into a run. Bodie quickly caught up and snapped at his heels. Mr Cuthbert skipped away, yelping, holding my painting over his head. They disappeared into the forest.

He was unwilling to sacrifice the painting for his own safety. Could someone truly be so despicable?

William wrapped his hand around my wrist, and squeezed.

"William, it's not too late. You can still go after him. He can tell you all about your mother."

"I have no mother. You are the only woman left in my life." His eyes had clouded over. He pulled me after him towards the cottage, my feet finally coming unstuck.

"No," I said. I dug my heels into the snow. He dragged me along.

"You continue to defy me." He threw me onto the ground of the parlour.

"I'm sorry."

"Up. Up the stairs. Now."

Ignoring my aching palms and the bruising to my knees, my legs forced the rest of my body upright and moved purposely up the stairs. I was an idiot. I should have saved myself. I should have escaped while I had the chance. What was wrong with me? It was like I wanted to stay his prisoner forever.

I reached the top landing and my legs loosened. He pushed me inside. Inspecting the empty door lock, he cast his eye across the room to the brass handle lying on the stairs and the screws on the ground of the landing.

"How did you do it?"

I shook my head, my eyes filling with tears. "I promise I won't do it again," I said.

He ran his hands along my arms, my body, my legs, roughly patting me down for evidence. When he came up dry, he shoved me down, my head banging against the ground.

"I'm sorry," I said.

"Tell me!"

My mouth formed the words before I could catch them. "My bobby pins. I used my bobby pins."

His eyes flitted to the ones still holding my hair. His forehead crinkled and he yanked them out, pulling my hair with them. I shrieked at the pain.

"Are there any more?"

I began to tremble.

"Are there any more?" he yelled. "Tell me!"

"Yes."

"Where?"

"In my pocket."

He forced his hand into my pockets and retrieved the two bent bobby pins. He rammed them into his own pocket, picked up the brass handle and screws, and moved towards the door.

"Fix yourself," he said.

The brass handle flew through the air and clattered into the hole in the door. The screws followed closely behind, screeching back into place. He reached out and turned the handle, opening the door to check the lock on the other side.

He moved to the velvet chair and picked it up, throwing it down the stair well. It thumped and clattered, echoing as it went. He picked up the blank canvases, his painting of me, the painting of Dad, the canvas stand, the paint and brushes, and threw them all after the chair. The glass container smashed. Water slopped everywhere.

All that remained was the telescope that was bolted to the ground, the gas lamp by the door, and the painting of my mother. William made for the painting next.

"No!" I yelled. "Please don't." I crawled across the ground and gripped onto his pant leg. "Please."

William raised an eyebrow and twisted his lips into a malicious smile. He turned back to the painting.

"Animate," he said, "and do not let her leave."

The painting jerked and stood itself upright. My mother's eyes blinked. Her mouth drew up into a creepy smile while her eyes stared vacantly at me. She started to pace back and forth in front of the door to the room, the bottom corners of the painting twisting like feet to move with her.

I shuddered. "No. Make it stop."

William watched the painting pace, his malicious smile remaining.

"I promise I will behave."

He nodded his head. "Yes, you will behave." He turned to me and pulled me to my feet. "Kiss me," he said.

My lips reached out in obedience and pressed into his. I drew back immediately in disgust, hot tears falling down my cheeks.

"My parents are dead to me. It is time I made a family of my own."

He looked intently into my eyes, the malevolence

softening.

"Make love to me, Evelyn."

My stomach dropped, my heartbeat quickened. Panic rose in my throat as my body pressed forwards once more. Connected at the mouth, William pushed me to the ground and was on top of me in an instant, as if to prevent my escape. Though panic-stricken, my body responded to William and his movements. I was the snake, and he the charmer.

He pulled at my clothes, forcing them out of the way until we were skin on skin.

No.

Panic turned to horror as my body took over, relishing in his. But I didn't want to keep going. I tingled from head to foot. My head spun from fast breathing. A war battled within me, and time moved too fast for me to keep up. I felt William's body readying itself.

Stop.

It wasn't enough. I tried to form the word but it never came. My legs wrapped around him against my will, yet I cried internally for help.

I thought about the ice that clung to the branches of the cottage tree and the crisp evening sky. The little robin flew into my mind, jittering about, looking for food. It flew high and swept a wide gaze down upon the earth. It darted about, but still could not find any food, for the ground was covered in a thick layer of snow. Landing on a branch, it shivered with cold, weak from hunger. Its eyes grew heavy.

William cried out in satisfaction, bringing me back to the present. His eyes were bunched up as he recovered, breathing heavily. My head clunked to the floor.

I watched the story in my mind unfold. The robin spotted something in the distance—a hole in a tree where the knot used to be. It plucked up all the strength it could and flew forth. The further it travelled, the heavier its wings became. Snow started to fall. Dodging the falling projectiles, the robin's efforts seemed futile; it would never make it. But alas, hope beyond all hope, it did make it. The robin sailed into the hole and was met with warmth. The inside of the tree was covered in moist, green moss. The winter could be survived after all. The robin chirped a song of relief.

William's breathing returned to normal. He caressed my face, staring intently into my eyes.

I wanted to vomit.

What had once been enchanting to stare into now made my stomach turn. I hated his eyes, and I had been right about one thing—they had been mysterious. Only they had hidden things that I wished I'd never found out.

He smiled, got up, and left. The door banged behind him and the click of the key turned in the lock. The painting of my mother continued to pace. I rolled over and held myself, beginning a painful descent into a cold, uneasy sleep.

14

I WATCHED HER as she paced back and forth in front of the door. The creaking tap, tap as the painting twisted and trod, twisted and trod, had carried through the night and into the early hours of the morning. It was still dark when I woke, aching and parched, covered in a cold sweat, William's hands all over me in the nightmare I'd just jostled from.

She never missed a beat, that vacant smile unfaltering. But it wasn't really my mother, despite the uncanny resemblance from my brushwork. Yet it pained me to see her obey his command, to come alive but be so lifeless.

There in the pacing imitation body of my mother I saw the manipulation and control that had led me to Purlieu, that had locked me in this stronghold of shame and utter desolation. My body would no longer be violated by him. I would no longer be his prisoner.

With each round of her pacing my agitation grew. My chest heaved as I watched. How dare he? I hated him. I hated him so much.

My mouth tasted of ashes.

I jumped to my feet and went after the telescope, removing the main shaft from the legs. I yelled and kicked and screamed at the glass wall and threw my body behind the telescope as I swung it at the wall. It bounced back at me and I fell to the floor.

The Pterodactyls resting in the bows of the tree startled, wings spread wide. They settled and continued to sleep. I got up and went after the glass again but felt arms around me. No, not arms—the top corners of the painting. My mother had wrapped herself around me, constricting the movements of my body.

"No, Mum."

I threw her back from myself and attacked the glass once more. It shattered, leaving a hole large enough for me to climb through. Shards fell like rain, big and small, scattering around me. Before it even settled I made for the hole but my mother was upon me once more.

"She's just a stupid painting!" I yelled at myself. I threw her off me again and ran for the lantern by the door. "You are not my mother. My mum is dead!"

I threw the lantern at the painting and it smashed, the glass and wood and metal and oil crashing to the ground. The painting went up in flames. Her face began to melt and crack and trickle away. The painting thrashed about, unsure what to do. The fire spread from its feet to the floor.

It ran back and forth, trying to throw the flame from its body but the blaze only increased. It thrust itself beneath the gap under the door, slipping away. Flames were left in its wake and the door ignited.

The room began to fill with smoke.

I went for the hole in the glass and crawled through, tearing my pants on the broken glass and scraping my leg. I stifled a yelp. I clung to the branch on the other side of the glass. It was a long way up. I quietly made my way along the branch.

Banging came from behind me, amidst the sound of licking flames. The Pterodactyls were lined up on the branch before me and below me. I gulped. I could do this.

I jumped from the branch and aimed for the Pterodactyl directly below. My legs collided with its velvet soft back. I grabbed at its feathers and held on for dear life. It vaulted off the branch in fright and fell. My stomach lurched. It spread its wings wide. The ground rushed at us but it swooped as we neared, gliding above the snow. It landed, sending snow spraying onto the trunk of the cottage. I jumped from its back before it took flight again, just as a roaring yell came from above. William was looking down upon me through the hole in the glass. I made for the cover of the cottage and opened the door of the parlour to escape any commands he might attempt to make upon me. The Pterodactyl cawed and flapped its wings, returning to the sky behind me.

I skidded into the lounge. The trapdoor was already wide open. I ran into its darkness, grasping at the walls of the staircase as I went. My bare hands scratched against the jagged rocks and roots that jutted out from the wall but I carried on in my blindness.

I could do this. I could escape him. I had to escape.

There was no difference now to any other time I had attempted to leave, except that this time I was equipped with one piece of knowledge I hadn't had previously.

There was light at the end of the tunnel, shining down on the stairs that led into William's bedroom.

"Evelyn!" William's voice echoed through the tunnel. His footsteps rushed down the stairs behind me.

I panicked, rushing at the stairs and up into his room, now impeccably neat. The bookcase had been replaced. I went straight for the desk, passing two neat piles by his bed. One with canvases, paints, and brushes—the very ones he'd thrown down the stairs—the other with my school bag and uniform. I grabbed my bag, leaving my uniform behind, and opened the drawer of the desk containing the box of boxes.

Though my hands jittered with adrenaline, I pulled out my mother's locket and drew it straight around my neck, the gold sending a cold shiver down my back. My hands shook as I tried to clasp it together.

William's footsteps rushed up the stairs behind me. I whipped around. The clasp locked into place.

"Put it down, Evelyn."

He was too late. The gold was around my neck. He couldn't control me.

I paused, half expecting the gold not to work, but when my body didn't obey his command to put the necklace down, I sprang back into action, dodging around the desk and rushing through the curtains.

William was not far behind me. I could feel his presence.

"Evelyn!"

I cringed and sprinted out onto the snow and up towards the cottage once more, eyes only for the forest beyond that concealed the Hidden Grove. His feet crunched on the snow behind me.

The cottage came into view above a small rise. The fire had spread to the entire top level and was now reaching out to the branches. The Pterodactyls had scattered. Flames, as they licked the sky, cast light upon the path I trod. I sprinted forward.

"You are destroying my home!" he yelled. Leaves and bark started to fall from the cottage. "You are ruining my life!" William yelled.

"I deserve a life too!" I yelled back. Angry tears filled my eyes as I tripped up and over the rise.

"I will kill you. I swear it."

I had to escape this time. He'd said it—death was all that remained for me in Purlieu. If I didn't escape, it would be the end of me, but I refused to be some forgotten teenage girl who'd disappeared into a forest one day and never returned.

I made it below the bows of the cottage, my eyes on the forest beyond. With my mother's gold locket protecting me, William couldn't control me. All I had to do was outrun him.

"Stop her!"

The ice sculptures that scattered the yard as statues came to life. From every angle, they came at me until I was surrounded. I scrambled to a stop, narrowly avoiding crashing into them. They formed a circle, allowing a gap only for William to enter. He conjured another ice dagger.

This was it. This was the end of me. I had gotten so close.

"You ruined my life," I yelled.

"It did not have to be this way, Evelyn. If only you had obeyed."

"I have a mind of my own, you know." Hot tears streamed once more as I yelled.

Ash and branches began to fall into the clearing. The cottage was ablaze, a torch that lit the night sky.

"The stupid part is that I liked you. I actually loved you," I cried. "Why couldn't you just love me as I was? You made me feel as though I could never live up to your standards. If you had treated me like most decent human beings would, I probably would have stayed of my own free will."

William scoffed.

My cheeks flushed at the heat coming from above. My skin smarted, my hair littered with ash. How long would the tree hold before crashing down upon us?

The ice sculptures blank faces were becoming glossy as the heat began to melt their bodies.

"You always run away from your problems, Evelyn."

"I wasn't running. I was leaving you, William. There's a difference. And this time? This time I was running *to* something." My dad's face flashed across my mind.

"You are cruel and hateful. You can take my mother's locket and make me do what you want but you will never control my mind. You can never make me love you."

A long, thick branch fell with a thud and crunching of branches. It wiped out a third of the ice sculptures. From the ground, they melted beneath the flames that the branch bore. Their arms reached up and their bodies jerked, silently trying to evade the heat. My stomach flipped at the sight.

A smaller branch fell between William and I. Picking it up, I waved the flame about. No one would ever tell me what to do again.

I turned around and thrust the branch at one of the ice maidens. It remained still, awaiting its next command. The bough that had once held the weight of three Pterodactyls thudded behind the ice sculptures. I took my chance, ditched the branch in my hand, and ran at the bough, jumping through the flames. My entire body felt like it was on fire, but it was over before the pain even reached me. I landed on the other side, tripping through the snow until my feet caught up.

"Stop her!" William yelled.

I turned around as I ran and the ice sculptures were after me, clambering over the bough. They melted as they attempted to plough through.

"No!" William yelled.

I faced the forest and sped past the farm and the orchard, my eyes set on the tree line.

"Bodie! Bodie, get her!"

Memories of Mr Cuthbert being chased by the fox ran through my mind. The fox gave a high-pitched bark from the farm and started towards me. I entered the forest and jumped over tree roots, ducking low-hanging branches. I could feel Bodie gaining on me as his paws scratched at the snow.

There was the group of man-sized mushrooms and the tree arch. I was so close.

Bodie's jaw sank into my pant leg. I tripped forward. He snarled and pulled. I shook my leg desperately. A whimper escaped my mouth. I shook and shook and shook and the fox flew into the nearest tree. He whined as he connected with the tree trunk.

I scrambled to my feet and continued into the grassy comfort of the Hidden Grove. My heart skipped a beat. I ran on past row after row after row before ducking between two trees. The way to Earth was somewhere in the middle of the grove.

Bodie howled. The scratch of his paws continued behind me. Yet there was the enormous tree marked with those beautiful drag marks Tiffany had left behind.

Home. I could almost smell the eucalyptus. I could almost feel the warmth of Dad's arms around me. I could almost hear whistling coming from the kitchen.

Bodie's jaw locked onto me again. I went flying forward and my chin hit the ground. His teeth pierced the skin of my ankle. I cried out. He wouldn't let go. I crawled towards the tree, the fox still attached to my ankle, reaching for the lowermost branch.

He growled and thrashed his head as my limp leg hung from the branch, his jaw latched on, body swaying. I ignored the pain that seared up and down my leg and climbed up onto the branch. Tears formed in my eyes. I clenched my teeth and swung my leg at the tree trunk. Bodie's body hit the tree. He whimpered and let go, dropping to the ground. He lay still for a moment. I watched with bated breath. He rolled over and started barking at me, jumping at the tree.

There was movement in the grove. William. I had to keep climbing.

Blood seeped down my leg and into my shoe. I put weight on it and it collapsed under the burden. I pulled myself up by my arms, my damaged leg hanging below.

The tree shook in my hands. William had caught up and was scaling fast from below.

I had to keep going. I had to reach the top.

I clenched my teeth. Placing my damaged leg onto the branch, I put my weight on it again, forcing it to remain strong as I pushed up to the next branch. My breath whooshed out. I clenched my teeth again, put my weight on it, and pushed up, letting my breath whoosh out. I moved into a rhythm.

William's hand wrapped around my wounded ankle. He pulled. I lost my footing. I grabbed about and latched onto a branch. My fingers slipped. I screamed.

We free fell, bashing into branches. Leaves rushed past my face.

No. I wasn't going back there.

I scrambled to wrap my arms around something. The fingers on my weak hand gripped onto a branch. Pain ripped up my arm to my shoulder as I jolted to a stop and it took the weight of my body. But my weak hand, it felt nothing. It stayed firm. Losing the nerves in it had to come in handy at some point.

I pulled myself up and enveloped the branch with my arms and legs, scrunching my eyes together as breaking branches, rustling leaves and William's scream filled my ears. There was a deep thud. And silence.

Did he survive the fall? Would he come after me again? I swung up onto the branch and peered below.

I wasn't far from the ground. His body was twisted in an unnatural position, one leg at odds with the other. He was still. I held my breath.

A moan emerged. William stirred.

"Evelyn."

I trembled and rose to my feet on the bough. He sat up and gazed up at me with those hateful eyes.

"My leg," he said. He reached out and held it, groaning. His pants turned dark, slowly soaking with blood. He would be okay.

"Evelyn, help me."

I stared back at him a long moment. "No," I said. Not a part of me wavered in my resolve.

"Evelyn, I'm bleeding to death here."

"It's a broken leg, William. You'll survive, but only if you want to."

I would not allow him to keep me captive any longer. I

turned and looked up the trunk of the tree, reaching my arm to the branch above.

"No!" William said.

I swung myself up onto the branch and continued my rhythm: clenched teeth, push up, whoosh.

"Evelyn, come back!"

Clenched teeth, push up, whoosh.

"I command you to return." He roared in frustration, his voice echoing through the Hidden Grove. "You will obey me!"

I stopped and looked down upon him. He was on his feet, leaning into the tree for support.

"I will not bow to your will, William."

His mouth bobbed open. I was free.

I smirked at the irony of his name and continued up the tree. Clenched teeth, push up, whoosh. His voice became distant, as his threats grew hollower.

The top of the tree was in sight. I'd now reached higher than any of the surrounding trees. I could see the mountains to the right, the cottage directly behind now entirely ablaze. It looked like a tower of hell. Nothing would survive that hell. Only me.

William had lost his grip on me. My body felt light, my mind unshackled. His voice was distant and inconsequential as he continued to roar and shake the tree.

I pushed myself up onto that final branch, not looking back, and stepped to the centre of the trunk. Lightning, frozen in a moment, flashed around me. I was everywhere and nowhere all at once, like I was hovering on the purlieu of my own life.

As my body continued forward across the other side of the trunk, the light disappeared as soon as it had come, and eucalyptus met my nose.

I breathed it in deeply. My heart smiled.

I swung down the tree, branch after branch, racing as much to grow the gap between William and I as to reach my destination.

Home. I was going home.

My dad's face filled my mind, along with those broad shoulders that took up the entire hallway. All I wanted was to throw myself into his arms.

I reached the lowermost branch and gritted my teeth once more as my feet landed on the grass. Pain seared up my leg. I limped along through the Hidden Grove until the pain was so constant that it didn't matter if I put weight on it or not. I moved into a sprint and rounded the last of the trees before heading for the tree arch.

Was that really the laugh of a kookaburra? Could it truly be real? Or was it William laughing at me because I was about to run straight back into Purlieu? It was too dark through the tree arch to tell.

I closed my eyes and leapt through. Twigs snapped under my feet as I landed. Thick humidity clung in the air, the smell of eucalyptus strong in my nose. I was home.

Moonlight seeped through the canopy above, dotting the path through the bushland. I moved into a run once more, weaving between trees, dodging low-hanging branches, skipping over protruding roots.

I didn't hear William's footsteps behind me, nor him calling out, but I felt him near. He was under my skin. At every turn, I expected his face would appear; that his voice would suddenly fill my ears; that when I reached the path to the art gallery, he would be there with folded arms, waiting for me.

My footsteps crunched on fallen leaves, my breath heavy. I dug my heels in and sped up, guided by the soft light cast up the well-worn trail. A possum scampered across a branch in front of me. I squealed and jumped back behind a tree. My breath heaved. My hands were shaking. My lips had tingled, growing numb. I poked my head from out behind the tree.

The bushland was silent. There was a glow up ahead. My heart skipped a beat. The possum scampered again, urging me forward. Every lunge I took brought me closer to the light and further away from William. Free. I was almost totally, remarkably, gloriously free.

I closed my eyes and welcomed the moonlight as it caught on my face, the gaps in the canopy growing. I opened them again. I was so close.

The figure of a man appeared at the end of the trail, his silhouette tall and strong as the moonlight glowed from behind him.

My heart pounded. I was moving too fast.

We collided.

I SCREAMED AS I scrambled to my feet. It was the middle of the night and my car was parked at school. How could I quickly escape William?

But it wasn't William.

"Evelyn?" Cameron's dark eyes peered at me. His woody hair was lost in the backdrop of trees, like he was one with the bushland.

I batted him away. "Get away from me."

"Evelyn, you're a mess."

I pushed him back and looked for the exit but he was blocking the end of the trail onto the path.

"Are you okay?"

I was hyperventilating. He placed a hand on my shoulder and gripped it. My skin crawled at his touch. I shuddered away from him and tried to make sense of his presence.

"Cameron, what are you doing here?" How much time had passed on Earth? His mouth bobbed open. We stared at one another as my breathing settled.

Footsteps crunched on the path behind him. I jumped. Tiffany's haggard face emerged.

"Evelyn?"

She pushed past Cameron, who stumbled into the low-lying brush, and wrapped her arms around me in a tight embrace. Her body shook. I squeezed her back.

"I'm so sorry. I'm so, so sorry," she said. She was crying.

"I was going to go back to get you. We all were."

Darius' face appeared behind Cameron. He was wearing his school uniform. They all were. It didn't make any sense.

"It's okay. Let's talk about it later. We have to get out of here," I said. "Did someone drive?"

Tiffany and Darius looked at Cameron. He nodded once. I took Tiffany by the hand and pulled her after me, moving into a run once more.

"Hey—wait!" Cameron called.

We travelled down the path towards the art gallery until the blazing poinciana trees came into view. They were still flowering. Fallen blooms littered the ground at my feet. Had no time passed at all?

We turned left at the end of the wind tunnel, and towards the underground car park. I had an insatiable urge to get behind the wheel and drive far, far away.

Cameron clicked the car open. I grabbed the keys from him.

"I'm driving," I said.

"Evelyn!" Tiffany said. Her eyes were wide with shock.

"What?"

She searched for the right words, as she looked me up and down.

"You should rest," Cameron said.

"It would be safer if Cameron drove right now," Tiffany said.

I looked down upon my torn pant leg and my shoe soaked in blood. My arms were covered in black ash. My chest tightened. I didn't want someone else to drive. They stared at me, wary of what I might do.

I shrugged and gave up the keys. We piled in, Tiffany

and I in the back. Cameron slouched into his chair and set the car into gear. We drove up from the car park to the main road.

Once we reached the highway, I rested my head back and let out a long breath. My mind was clear. I felt lighter, like I might float up and bump my head on the roof of the car.

I was free. I was actually free.

"I called Darius as soon as I got across," Tiffany said. "We were coming up with a plan. We were going to go get you, I promise, but then you just appeared."

Cameron eyed me through the rear-view mirror as though he wanted to say something but thought better of it.

"What day is it?" I asked. Tiffany cringed and looked out the window.

"Friday. It's been four days," she said. A tear trickled down her face.

"You were both reported as missing persons," Darius said.

"Four days. Just four days? How could so little time have passed? Except time had moved in the opposite direction than William had said.

Purlieu, and the power William wielded over me, seemed utterly unbelievable now that I was sitting in a car, driving through the suburbs of a very populated, technologically advanced Earth.

"We're missing persons?" I asked.

"That's what happens when you disappear from a school excursion into the bushes and don't come out again," Darius said.

People actually cared about me enough to notice I was gone, to be concerned that I was missing? I had been such a fool for leaving.

The streetlights carved a path for us through the darkness as we passed low-set Queenslanders placed between bushland. I wound the window down and let the wind rush across my face. The cicadas hummed along with the engine. I never wanted to leave again.

Darius reached back and gripped Tiffany's hand tightly. So that was a thing now.

We reached Tiffany's house first. I got out and gave her a long hug.

"Are you going to be okay?" she asked. I nodded. "Okay. Let's talk tomorrow," she said. I nodded again.

"I love you."

"I love you too," I said.

"I'm sorry."

"I'm sorry too."

We gripped each other one more time. Darius was waiting for her. He made to walk towards the house.

"Where are you going?" she asked.

"I'm not leaving you," he said. Darius had come for her when she needed him. Perhaps he did actually like her after all.

She smiled. They took each other's hand and approached the front of her house. The light was off inside. I waited until they were enveloped by the darkness of her house before getting into the passenger seat. Cameron was quiet. He drove down the road, perpetuating the silence. I bet he hated that he was lumped with taking me home, that he couldn't hide behind Darius.

My house wasn't far from Tiffany's. Cameron knew the way from when we used to be friends, but he turned coward when he ditched Tiffany and I after my hand had been mangled on the flying fox. I had every right to be angry with him for it, but I'd never shown it.

He pulled up at the kerb outside my house. It was hidden in the shadows of night, all except for the little beacon of light coming from the front room, illuminating the front porch.

Tears welled in my eyes. I hadn't thought I would ever see it again.

"Please don't tell anyone I was there tonight," Cameron

said. "That I brought you home."

My mouth dropped open. I turned to face him. He avoided my eyes, the streetlight catching on the scattered freckles across the bridge of his nose. He didn't want to ruin his reputation by being associated with me. My mouth turned down in disgust, but I wouldn't run from his insult this time.

"If you're so ashamed to be seen with me, then I guess you'll be doing your own school work from now on," I said. I gave him my most scornful look, turned, and left the car with my head held high. He may have gotten me home but I owed him nothing.

His car disappeared around the corner as I sat on the front porch.

I had escaped. I was safe. I was home. Everything was going to be okay.

I took a deep breath and entered the house. The floor creaked and the hum of the fluoro light echoed from the living room to my left. There was Dad, sleeping amidst the mess of Mum's belongings. He was just like I remembered, with no more wrinkles than I'd left him with. He wasn't an old man. I let out a sigh of relief.

I'd been gone four days. What if he didn't forgive me? Or what if he'd been glad to be rid of me? I had to try. I had to tell him how sorry I was.

I crossed the threshold into the living room. It had been a long time since I'd done that. He looked really tired. Like he hadn't slept since I left.

I jostled his shoulder. "Dad?"

He roused and looked up at me, eyes squinting, confused. "Evelyn?" His eyes shot open. He got to his feet in a hurry and took me by the shoulders.

He hadn't touched me since before Mum had died.

"I'm sorry, Dad. I'm so sorry for yelling and for the things I said and for running away and for thinking you didn't really care about me and that it would be better if you had died instead of Mum. And I know it's not your fault. She loved the garden and she loved her job and it's not your fault she went to work that day. She would have died anyway. I'm so sorry."

The coroner had said the car accident—instantaneous death—was a mercy. The disease would have killed her anyway. Slowly, painfully. I was crying now.

"I'm glad she died the way she did, even if we didn't get to say goodbye." I sucked back the tears so that I could continue. "You were stifling me, but I understand now. I know you just wanted to protect me. I know you were doing the best you could. I know you love me."

I had run out of things to say but I knew there was more I'd forgotten.

He was silent. He wrapped his arms around me and shook. He descended into weeping like he was letting out over a year's worth of grief. I hugged him back and sobbed too.

He drew back and looked me square in the eyes, face wet and shining. "Will you forgive me?" he asked.

"For what?"

"For not being there for you in the way you needed, since your mum passed away."

I looked down at the piles of her things that surrounded us, to the stack of gardening magazines and paperwork and her nurse's scrubs. They reminded me of her warm gold locket, resting upon the skin of my chest.

I looked back up to him. "I forgive you."

I undid the clasp of the locket and dangled it for him to take. His jaw dropped. He took the locket and traced his finger across the oval surface. A tear ran down his face.

"I thought I'd lost it."

I hobbled into the entry hall and up the stairs, then stopped dead. Dad had started to whistle the robin song. I listened for a moment before joining in, singing loudly enough that he could hear.

"Yes no one knows
Where Robin goes,
All except for little Robin.
For only it knows
When to go,
And the time to come home."

I shed my clothes and kicked them aside on the cool bathroom tiles. In the mirror, I surveyed the damage. My skin was mingled with ash and sweat and blood and tears. Cameron was right—I did look like a mess.

Dad's voice floated upstairs. "No Sam, call off the search. She came home. Yeah, she's safe now," he said.

He was quiet a moment. He must have called work about the missing persons case. "I know how it works, Sam, but she's not coming in."

Silence again. My stomach constricted at the thought of being probed about what had happened. What could I possibly tell them?

"No, I refuse to comment on it," he said. "It's not important."

Silence again.

"No, we won't talk about it on Monday. Pull the missing persons and forget it ever happened." He was still trying to protect me. I let out a breath I didn't realise I'd been holding. My shoulders relaxed back.

I stepped into the shower and leant against the wall as the cool water ran down my back. The ash and remains of blood mingled with water and disappeared down the drain. The image of the roaring fire consuming the cottage seared across my eyes. The conservatory was gone, utterly enveloped by flame.

If only I could say the same for what William had done to me, but I would never get back what he'd taken.

I slumped down on the ground and burst into tears, weeping for all that had happened since the night I ran away from home. I shook in fits, my body tense.

If only I hadn't run. If only I'd talked it out with Dad. If only I'd listened to Tiffany and not taken her for granted. If only I'd picked up on the warning signs and not made excuses for William's behaviour.

But now, I was ruined.

I grabbed at my loofah and scrubbed at the skin on my arms, my shoulders, my neck, my breasts. I scrubbed my stomach and my feet, my legs, my thighs. I loaded my loofah with soap and started again, my skin rubbing red raw. Still I felt him clinging to me. I felt his hands on my body. I felt his lips crushing mine as he commanded me to kiss him. I felt the tear and the bruising as he thrust himself inside me.

Sucking in a breath, I stifled my sobbing. I left the shower and threw some old clothes on, ignoring my hair as it clung to my face. I poured the contents of my backpack out on the floor and started sorting through it. Tossing my car keys, phone charger, hair straightener and toiletries onto my bed, I moved on to my art journal. I flicked through it, the charcoal thumbprint William had left upon it from the first day we'd met glared out at me.

From the very beginning it had been a carefully tested and refined attempt to get me to Purlieu.

I threw the journal in the metal bin by my door. It flipped open and the eyes that I had sketched of William on our first date glared back at me. Bile threatened at my mouth. I grabbed the clothes I'd brought with me to Purlieu and stuffed them in the bin, concealing those hateful eyes.

I went for the notes from William, in the small chest on my dresser, and the dried-up flowers in a vase under the windowsill. I stuffed them into the bin and tucked it under my arm. Grabbing my phone and a box of matches, I headed downstairs.

The glow of dawn threw orange light onto the mess of a garden that hadn't been touched since Mum had died. I stopped to look at it, reaching out and fingering the leaves, breathing in the dirt and fragrance of wild flowers. I pulled the brazier from out of the overgrowth, snapping vines that had wrapped around it, and angled a couple of logs into the base. I lit some kindling and threw it onto the logs. As the flame licked at the logs, trying to spread, I turned on my phone.

The home screen flashed on with a picture of William and I. Accessing settings, I deleted the photo, replacing it with a picture of Mum and Dad from a Saturday morning market over a year ago. I went into the gallery and deleted all the photos of William and of Purlieu. I swiped onto the picture of the queen of Celoso and hesitated. My phone started to vibrate, a flood of messages and missed calls coming in from Dad and Tiffany and a few people from school.

I opened one of Tiffany's messages. She was apologising for yelling at me and asking where I'd gone, saying that she didn't like the look of William. My phone turned off. I'd run out of battery.

Tiffany really was a good friend. I needed to make sure I treated her better.

I shoved my phone in my pocket and returned my attention to the brazier. The logs had caught now. The heat reached my skin, reminding me of the fire in Purlieu. A shiver ran up my back. I took a deep breath.

I threw the notes William had written to me into the brazier, followed by the dried-up flowers. I fed my clothes in one at a time and took a step back at the smell of burning cotton and melting polyester. I tore my art journal in half and placed it purposely into the heart of the flames.

The memories of William burned and flaked and melted. Ashes fell through the grate onto the ground. I watched my art journal with one of William's charcoal thumbprints slowly be taken by the flames.

I had run away *with* him when I should have run *from* him, and the mark that he had left on me could not be so easily removed.

A hot breeze blew, summer not willing to give way to autumn, and the wind picked up the ash. It flew up above the brazier and into the arms of the trees, like the robin.

With Tiffany and Dad by my side, I could get through this. Like the robin, I would be okay.

Stay tuned for the next book in the series:

THE HIDDEN GROVE SERIES: BOOK 2

Michaela Daphne

In an ominous underground citadel of
the Hidden Grove, Evelyn's father is taken captive.
Can she free him before they're both executed?

Coming soon.

Make your own jewellery and resin homewares with

Mill Lane Studio

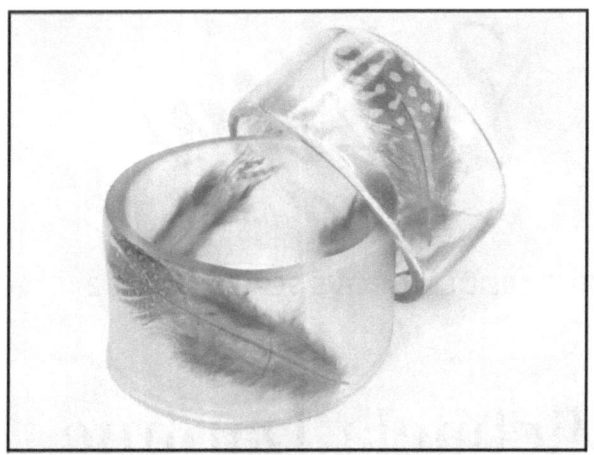

www.milllanestudio.com

ABOUT THE AUTHOR

Michaela Daphne has been dreaming up tales for as long
as she can remember, staying up until the wee hours of the
morning with pictures running through her mind.
Purlieu is her first book and is inspired by personal
experiences of her own life.

She lives in Brisbane, Australia with her husband.

Follow Michaela Daphne on Instagram
@michaeladaphnewriter

or visit her website at www.michaeladaphne.com.